CROW SONG

ANTHONY M. STRONG

Also by Anthony M. Strong

The John Decker Thriller Series

What Vengeance Comes

Cold Sanctuary

Crimson Deep

Grendel's Labyrinth

Whitechapel Rising

Black Tide

Ghost Canyon - April 2021

John Decker Series Prequel

Soul Catcher

The Remnants Series

The Remnants of Yesterday

Standalone Books

The Haunting of Willow House

Crow Song

West Street Publishing

Cover art and interior design by Bad Dog Media, LLC.

ISBN: 978-1-942207-13-9

For Paul, who read some of the earliest stories in this book. It's been a while since you left, my friend, but the memories remain.

CROW SONG

Foreword

Welcome, readers, to Crow Song, a collection of chilling tales compiled from almost thirty years of writing. The oldest story in this book is The Cellar, written back when I was in my early twenties.

The Frequent Visitor, another early tale, was inspired by a supposedly true story relayed to me by a relative. I changed the circumstances and many details, including the ending, but the germ of an idea this tale grew from concerned an allegedly haunted house in Birmingham, England. The resulting yarn though, is fiction, and bears little resemblance to the inspiration.

Other early tales were rewritten and expanded, including The Last Bus, and Secrets.

And lastly, the name. Crow Song. The tales within this book contain a lot of death. It wouldn't be a true work of horror fiction otherwise. Which brings me to crows. These jet black avians, and their *cousin*, the raven, have been associated in many cultures with death and the afterlife for centuries. There is the medieval Welsh text, The Mabinogion, which refers to the raven as a harbinger of death within it's eleven tales. Other legends state that crows can actually sense the approach of death. When crows gather together, it is ominously called a murder of crows. In Greek mythology crows and ravens were considered symbols of bad luck. Crows are carrion eaters, they feast on the dead, and they should have plenty of food in the pages of this book.

So pull up a chair, light a fire on a cold winter's night, and read a chilling tale or two. And if you see a crow at your window, don't worry, it's probably not there for you…

Evil Eye

JACK FLETCHER WAS NOT a happy man. Not happy at all. Two minutes and a toilet break, that was all it took. He was on the way back to his desk when the telephone rang. And there was Jerry, good old over ambitious Jerry, bounding from his cubical in the direction of Jack's phone, answering it, taking the order. Jack's big order that he'd been working on for a month, not to mention his commission. Had he been a man to handle difficult situations with a measure of fortitude Jack might have shrugged the incident off and moved on, but he was not.

That's why, later that evening, he found himself perched on a barstool in the Laughing Barrel, a dive bar ten minutes' walk from the one room apartment he'd taken not because he liked it, but because it was cheap. Sales were an up and down business, and recently things were leaning decidedly down.

He starred, sullen, into his Scotch as if the amber liquid might contain some deeper truth, instead of just melting ice and a black plastic stir stick. He downed the drink in one, relishing the burn as it worked its way to his stomach, and then pushed the empty glass across the bar. One drink would not cut it, not tonight.

The bartender was nowhere to be found, as usual. He glanced around the bar, his eyes resting on the chalkboard propped near the door. Darts on Tuesday, Quiz night every Wednesday, and a band called *Slow Death* at 9pm on Saturday. He wondered why he came here. He hated music, quiz night was lame, and as for darts… He sure would have liked something sharp to throw at Jerry though. That would be sweet.

"Same again?" The incredible disappearing bartender had emerged from wherever he'd been hiding.

"Sure. Why not. Make it a double this time."

"You alright?" The bartender pulled a bottle from the well and filled Jack's glass. "You look like you lost a dollar and found a penny."

"Ain't that the truth?" Jack ran a finger around the rim of his glass. "Except I didn't find the penny."

"Tough day huh?"

"The worst. Got screwed out of my biggest sale this year, twenty thousand units, and all because I needed to pee. Goddam Jerry."

"Jerry?"

"Just some shithead at the office. Can you believe I worked on that deal for weeks only to have him answer the phone and take the goddamned order? A thousand bucks of commission, gone."

"Well, better luck next time."

"Yeah. Next time. Luck won't pay the bills though that's for sure." Jack could feel the anger rising again. A tight knot that started in his stomach and worked its way up until it clumped in his throat. He swigged the whisky. It didn't help, not yet. Maybe a few more and it would.

"So get even with the son of a bitch." The bartender fixed him with a deadpan stare. "Give him a taste of his own medicine."

"Sounds grand. Any ideas?"

"Yeah, I do as a matter of fact. Guy came in here just last

night and showed me this killer app. Seems like it'd be just what the doctor ordered."

"An App." Jack finished his drink and watched the bartender refill it for the third time. "You mean one of those phone things."

"Sure. There's an app for everything these days."

"Even revenge?"

"Even that. Give me your phone."

"I'm really not in the mood for games."

"It's not a game. You'll like it. Come on, the phone."

"It's free, right?" Jack pulled his phone out and handed it to the bartender.

"Of course." The bartender fixed his attention on the cell phone. "There." He handed the device back.

Jack looked at the phone, at the new icon that had fixed itself to his home screen, a glowing red circle with a bright blue eye in the middle. "What now?"

"Start her up."

"Okay then." Jack pressed the icon. The screen flickered for a second. Four words appeared on a flame red background, *Evil Eye, The App*. The letters faded and a text box popped up. Underneath, in small type, *'Enter a phone number.'* A green submit button pulsed, daring him to continue.

"Well go on then. Put it in." The bartender leaned forward, watching, waiting.

Jack switched to his contacts and found the number. He typed it into the box, his finger hovering over the submit button.

"Are you going to press it or what?" The bartender urged.

"What will it do?"

"It'll drive him crazy, that's what. Completely screw up his phone. Fake text messages, phony calls with no one on the other end, he won't get a lick of work done. You'll love it. It's hysterical."

"Here goes nothing." Jack pressed the button. The text

box disappeared. A new message popped up. *'Congratulations. You've given the evil eye.'*

JACK AWOKE to a brass band parading inside his skull. He groaned and rolled over, wishing he'd stayed at home instead of going to the bar. The alarm clock announced that it was 8.36am. Great, he was late for work.

His mouth felt like the inside of a carpet showroom. He tried to remember how many shots of whisky he'd downed. The last thing he remembered was sending some stupid app to Jerry, who, no doubt would be stealing more of his sales right now.

He swung his legs from the bed, stumbled to the bathroom and found a bottle of Advil. He downed two pills and put his mouth under the faucet, gulping down the cold water, before pulling on yesterday's shirt and pants and heading to the car.

By the time he arrived at work the parade in his head started to quiet down. The drive across town had been hell. Traffic was backed up thanks to an unseasonal rainstorm, and then he'd been forced to park two blocks away and walk through the downpour. Worse, his umbrella seemed to have wedged itself under the seat and refused to budge. He didn't have time to mess with it. When he reached the office he was wet and humorless. He slipped behind his desk and logged on to the computer, hoping his tardy arrival had not been spotted.

"Late night?"

"Huh?" Jack looked up to find Jerry grinning down at him. He hadn't seen it before, but Jerry's round face, ginger hair, and freckled, pale skin made him look like a naughty schoolboy.

"You look like crap, and you're forty minutes late."

"Thanks for noticing." What he really wanted to say was *screw you and the horse you rode in on*, but he didn't.

"Don't worry. I've got your back old buddy." Jerry winked at him, a grin plastered on his smug face.

God, I hate you, thought Jack. "Thanks."

"Oh, by the way, I took the Jackson Hardware order a few minutes ago. You weren't here. Hope you don't mind."

"It's fine." Why would he care, after all, it was only money.

"Like I said, I got your back."

And my commission, Jack mused. "What would I do without you?"

"I know, right? Hang on." He rummaged in his pocket and pulled out his phone. "Damn. Not again."

"Problem?"

"Some idiot's been texting me all morning. Same thing over and over."

"Really?"

"Three words, *ARE YOU SORRY?*" Jerry scowled. "Don't people have anything better to do with their lives?"

"So text them back."

"I did. I told them it was a wrong number. Didn't help. It's getting a little annoying to tell the truth."

"I bet." Jack grinned.

"It's not funny."

"No, it's not, you're right."

"They've been calling too, ever since last night. Woke me up four times before I put the damn thing on silent. When I got up this morning there were sixteen messages. Sixteen."

"Did you listen to them?"

"Same thing, some weird voice asking if I'm sorry. Guy sounded drunk or high or something. Still, to dial the wrong number that many times…" Jerry's phone sprang to life. The screen lit up even though it was still set on silent. "See. There they are again. Over and over."

"So answer it."

"I did already. Again with the 'am I sorry' crap, then they hang up." He hit ignore. "I even tried returning the call, but the number's disconnected. Not in service. How can that be?"

"Beats me." Jack could barely contain his mirth. The app was working like a charm. He'd have to buy the bartender a drink.

"Anyway. I can't stand here chatting all day."

"Big sale?"

"Maybe. Got a meeting downtown. Should be a good one if I can land it."

"Well I'd better not keep you," Jack said.

"Right." Jerry turned to leave, then glanced back. "Oh, by the way, I told accounting to credit you with commission for that order yesterday. Seemed only fair since you worked on it for so long. Like I said, I got your back."

Jack opened his mouth but no words came out. Shit, now he felt like a total ass. Maybe he should tell Jerry about the app, own up to the prank. But Jerry was already striding across the room toward the front door, pulling his coat on as he went. Through the plate glass windows lining the front of the building Jack could see the street. Pedestrians sauntered along the sidewalk, Cars and trucks raced by on their way to destinations unknown. Jerry reached the door and pulled it open.

Jack looked down at his computer screen. It was too late to do anything now. He'd wait until Jerry got back and tell him everything. He wondered if he could cancel the app, shut it off. At least he could save the poor guy any more aggravation.

When he glanced up again Jerry was on the sidewalk. He was about to cross the street, but then he hesitated. He pulled his phone out, lifted it to his ear, and stepped from the curb.

The bus didn't have time to stop. The thud could be heard even through the windows and over the hubbub of office noise. Jerry flew into the air, his coat billowing. He seemed to hang there for a second as the bus screeched to a halt, and then he cut a graceful arc into the traffic moving in the other direction. The second thud was dull, like a hammer hitting a bag of broken sticks.

Jack leapt to his feet and raced to the door, oblivious to the screams of the receptionist. He ran out into the street to the spot where Jerry had taken flight.

To his left and right he heard hushed voices.

"He didn't even look." Said a young woman, her face a picture of shock.

"It was the phone, he was shouting something at the phone." An older man in a dark suit lectured his wife. "See, I told you cell phones are a distraction."

Jack took a step into the road. He rounded the bus and there was Jerry, good old over ambitious Jerry, lying on his back next to a green SUV. His arms and legs were flailed as if he was making snow angels on the concrete. A pool of blood circled his head.

Jack bent over and fought the urge to throw up. His phone buzzed. He pulled it from his pocket. The screen flashed on, bright with a backlit glow. The Evil Eye icon pulsed red. Two words flashed across it. App Complete.

Mirror Mirror

DAY 1

THE MIRROR SAT out by the curb, leaning against a Green plastic trashcan, just waiting for someone to come by and snatch it up.

Jamie Beaumont might have driven right by it, might not even have seen it, except that just as he turned the corner onto Dawson Avenue, as the car started along the street, the sun glinted off the silvered, smooth surface, and threw a shaft of light directly into his eyes.

He slowed and pulled over, easing the car to the curb. This would be his third find today. God bless summertime in Boston. School would be out soon, and the students were either finding new digs, graduating and moving on, or going home for the summer. That meant all the stuff they couldn't be bothered to move or sell was out in the street, a treasure trove of freebies for those not fortunate enough to have wealthy parents that could bankroll a college degree.

Jamie hopped from the car and inspected his new find. Sometimes things looked good when you saw them, but then, when you got up close, they were nothing more than junk. Not this time though. The mirror was old. That much was evident. In fact, it was ancient. The frame was ornate, delicate. Carved bunches of grapes crept up the sides, the vines and leaves intertwined and twisting around to the top until they met in the middle at a thin, strange-looking face carved with bulging eyes and a gaping, downturned mouth. The whole thing was covered in gold leaf, worn in places to reveal an undercoat of red primer. Dirt had collected in the spaces between the carvings, turning the cracks and crevices black. The mirror itself had seen better days. While most of the surface was still bright and reflective, the edges were tarnished, with copper-colored flecks creeping in toward the center. In one spot near the base, the silvering had worn away, and the surface was dark and dull, a black void that seemed to suck up the light. Still, beggars could not be choosers, as his grandmother always said, and besides, the age and imperfections gave the mirror some character. Not only that, Jamie liked it.

He gripped it by the sides and lifted it up, surprised at how heavy it was, and struggled back to the car, leaning it against the wheel arch while he opened up the back, grateful that he had a station wagon. Soon the mirror was sitting comfortably between a weathered oak nightstand and two mismatched dining room chairs.

When he got back to his apartment, he parked up at the rear of the building, grateful that there was actually space. He took the mirror, the heaviest of the items he'd scored, and entered the building, grunting as he heaved it up the two flights of stairs to the third floor, cursing the fact that the elevator was out of order yet again. He'd told the landlord at least three times over the last few weeks, but it still had not been fixed, which was typical.

By the time he reached his apartment and pushed the key in the lock, he was sweating and breathless. He paused for a moment to regain his composure and then wrestled the mirror across the threshold, leaning it against the hallway wall with a sigh of relief. He was about to make his way back down to the car to grab his other finds, lug them up the stairs while he still had some motivation left, when his cell phone rang. He pulled it out of his pocket and punched the green button to answer.

"Hey."

"Hey, you."

He recognized the voice of Cassie Roberts, his girlfriend of two years, instantly. "What's up?"

"Nothing much. Thought you might want to get a pizza and watch a movie tonight."

"Sure. My place or yours?"

"Gee, I don't know." She giggled. "You have the bigger bed, so what do you think?"

"I thought you wanted to watch a movie and eat pizza."

"I never said that was all I wanted."

"Really?" He grinned.

"Unless you'd rather I go home after we eat."

"You can stay," He said, then, just to joke around, added, "it's not like I have anything better to do."

"Ouch. Harsh." She feigned annoyance. "Just for that, I get to choose the first piece of pizza."

"You know all the pieces are the same, right?" He made his way to the living room and flopped down on the old couch his parents had donated when they bought a new one. "It doesn't matter which one you eat."

"It so does," she scolded him. "There's a science to picking the perfect slice. It has to be just right. Not too crisp, not too doughy, and with the right ratio of sauce to cheese."

"You're weird." He glanced through the door, toward the mirror. "I found something cool today, something that will look great in the apartment."

"What?"

"Come on over, and I'll show you. I could do with some help deciding where to put it."

"Tell me now," Cassie pleaded, impatient. "You know I hate waiting."

"Later."

"Fine." She sounded miffed. "Seven o'clock work?"

"Sure does."

"Great. I'll see you then."

The line went dead.

Jamie looked down at the phone for a moment, at the picture of Cassie on the screen next to the number, then got to his feet and pushed the phone back into his pocket.

———

"SO THIS IS IT?" Cassie looked at the mirror, standing five feet tall against the wall, a mix of disdain and disappointment on her face. "This is your big surprise? I thought you said you'd found something cool."

"I did. Look at it. It's awesome." Jamie leaned against the wall, a slice of pizza in his hand. He took a bite and swallowed before speaking again. "You don't like it?"

"I hate it." She wrinkled her nose. "It's junk."

"It was free. What do you expect? Besides, I thought you liked the shabby chic look."

"I like shabby chic alright." She took a bite of her own pizza. "But this is just plain old shabby."

"Well, I like it. It has character."

"It has dumpster written all over it more like," She snorted.

"Want to help me place it?"

"Not really." She ran a finger across the glass. "It's all tarnished. Looks dirty too."

"It needs a little love, I'll give you that."

"And that face gives me the creeps." She pointed at the carving on the top of the frame. "It looks almost demonic."

"It's old. People liked that ornate stuff back then."

"Back when?"

"I don't know. It looks like an antique though. It's probably an heirloom. I'm surprised anyone would throw this away."

"I'm not."

"I wonder if it's worth anything?"

"I'll give you ten bucks if you let me put it back out on the sidewalk." Cassie laughed.

"Funny." Jamie shot her a look. "Just help me move it, okay?"

"Whatever, it's your apartment." She finished off the slice of pizza. "So where do you want to put it?"

"I don't know." Jamie looked around. "The bedroom maybe?"

"Great. I have to look at that thing every time I spend the night? No thanks."

"Come on. You did say it was my apartment. I don't tell you where to put stuff at your place."

"That's because I have taste. Style."

"Are you going to help me or not?" Jamie took a side of the mirror.

"I suppose." Cassie helped him lift, and together they maneuvered the mirror into the bedroom.

"We can just lean it here." Jamie led them to the middle of the room, positioning the mirror against the wall across from the bed.

"That's bad luck you know."

"Bullshit."

"It is not. Look it up on the Internet," Cassie replied. "It's some kind of Feng Shui thing."

"Well Feng Shui or not, I like it where it is."

"Your call." Cassie sat down on the bed. She toyed with the top button of her blouse. "So now that we've moved your junky old mirror, how about we do something a little more fun?"

JAMIE AWOKE SUDDENLY.

The room was dark and cold.

He lay there for a moment listening to Cassie on the other side of the bed, her breathing shallow, her chest rising and falling as she slept. Occasionally she mumbled something unintelligible in between light snores.

He looked up at the ceiling, and then glanced around, wondering what had awoken him. He was not a deep sleeper, but the apartment was generally pretty quiet, with the bedroom at the rear. The few traffic noises that did interlope from the street outside were so familiar that he barely noticed them anymore.

This was different though.

Something had pulled him from his dreams. He held his breath, listening, but all was still and silent. He listened for a few moments more and then, hearing nothing out of the ordinary, settled back down. He closed his eyes, rolled over to go back to sleep, snaking an arm around Cassie's waist and nestling up against her. He felt his mind loosen, felt sleep creeping in to claim his conscious thoughts…

The scratching sound pulled him back from the brink.

He twisted, sat up straight, the sheets falling away. That was not his imagination. This time he knew what had roused him.

He looked around, barely able to see anything in the gloom.

It came again, a scratching, scurrying sound, like hard nails skittering across the bare floorboards.

Jamie swung his legs from the bed. Was there a rat somewhere in the apartment? He had never seen one in the seven months he'd lived here, but that didn't mean they weren't around. It was an old building, and the place was not exactly the Ritz. The landlord, actually slumlord would be a more fitting description, hardly kept the building in tiptop condition. Typical for Boston student housing. Charged too much and cared for too little.

He tiptoed to the edge of the bed, not wanting to wake Cassie, and found his jeans, pulling them on. If there was a rat, he did not want to be in the buff when he met it. Rats could bite.

He stepped to the bedroom door and opened it, wincing when the hinges squeaked, then padded into the hallway, listening for the sound.

Nothing.

Whatever had caused the scratching noise had fallen irritatingly silent again. Jamie scanned the darkness, looking for any sign of movement, and then went into the living room.

Everything was just as it should be.

Jamie lingered for a moment longer, his eyes roaming the room, and then turned back to the bedroom, stopping in the kitchen on his way back to see if the pizza had been put away. The pizza box was safely tucked up on the top shelf of the fridge. He slipped through the door of the bedroom and closed it as gently as he could, and turned toward the bed.

As he crossed the room, he sensed movement, a blur of deeper black against the darkness. It was not much, but enough to catch his attention. He stopped and looked, his eyes darting from the bed to the nightstand, the floor, and then, finally, the mirror. At that very moment, he could have sworn he saw a shape in the glass, a reflection of something, of someone. He turned, expecting to find that Cassie had awoken and was sitting up in bed, but she was still lying on her side, her legs pulled up, the comforter draped over her. She was just as he had left her.

So what had he seen?

There was no sign of movement now. Jamie glanced back to the mirror, but if there was anything there, it was gone. All he saw was the reflection of the room, and nothing was out of place.

He undressed, then moved to the bed and pulled back the covers, sliding under them and resting his head on the pillow. He lay there for a while, on edge and listening, just in case the scratching sound came again, but it didn't. Soon his eyelids became heavy, and he drifted off to sleep.

DAY 2

Cassie was already gone when Jamie awoke the next morning. There was a note sitting on the pillow. He picked it up and read it, smiling at her scratchy handwriting.

EARLY CLASS TODAY.
  Call me later.
  Love Cass.

CASSIE MIGHT HAVE MORNING CLASSES, but his lectures didn't start until lunchtime. He nestled back down under the covers and stayed there for a while, enjoying the feel of the blankets against his skin. Jamie closed his eyes. When he opened them again the alarm clock on the nightstand told him that an hour had passed. He must have fallen back to sleep.

Still, he was in no rush to get up. He glanced toward the window and the glorious New England day outside. His eyes roamed the room and finally settled on the mirror propped against the wall. He studied it, the intricate carvings, the sculpted face sitting atop the frame. It really was a beautiful piece.

His eyes dropped to the glass. He could see himself lying in bed, the covers ruffled. A bright beam of sunlight sliced through the window blinds and splashed a dappled pattern on the wall behind him. It danced and shimmered as trees in the street outside moved in the breeze. He sat up, his eyes fixed on the mirror. The room looked different in reverse, like he was looking at a stranger's bedroom, only it was familiar at the same time.

A bird was singing outside, the rhythmic chirp drawing his attention toward the window for a moment. He listened for a few seconds, and then looked back toward the mirror.

Something was different now.

The room on the other side of the glass looked darker, as if storm clouds had moved in, blocking the sun. The bright pattern cast across the back wall of the room, behind the bed, was gone. Now the wall was an even tone of diffused light. The sudden change startled him. He glanced backward and up, expecting to see the same even tones, but the wall was still bathed in golden sunlight.

Jamie turned back to the mirror.

The dapple pattern of sunshine was back. The reflected room looked just like the real room once again. He scratched his head, confused, a frown furrowing his brow. He swung his legs from the bed and walked to the window, lifting one of the plastic blind slats and peering out. He studied the landscape for a moment, the street outside. Everything was bright and cheery, and the sky was a deep, seamless blue. If a cloud had passed by, it was gone now. He shrugged and turned back into the room, his mind turning to other things. For one, he was hungry, starving in fact.

As if to agree with this assessment, his stomach rumbled. He stepped around the bed and found some clean clothes. There was an excellent Bagel shop a few blocks away, and if he hurried, he could still get there before they sold out of all the good stuff.

THE COLLEGE CAMPUS was bathed in late afternoon sunlight intertwined with long fingerlike shadows by the time Jamie got out of class. Parking was always an issue on the university grounds, at least around the lecture halls, so he'd left his car parked up at the rear of the apartment building, which meant he would have to either take the subway several blocks or walk home. Since it was such a nice evening, he decided to take the long way and use leg power.

As he walked, his mind turned to Cassie. She would be out of class by now for sure. He pulled the phone from his pocket, his finger hovering over her number. Should he call her? He didn't want to disturb her if she was busy, but on the other hand, he wanted to hear her voice. After a moment's hesitation, he pressed the call button and waited for her to answer.

"Hey, you." Cassie sounded pleased to hear from him. Good, he hadn't caught her at a bad time.

"Hi. What are you up to?"

"Nothing much. In the library hitting the books. You?"

"Just got out of class." He stopped at a crosswalk, waiting for the green light. "Last night was fun. You want to come over again?"

"Nah," She said. "Lots to do. How about tomorrow night?"

"Okay." He was disappointed. The crossing sign turned green, and he stepped into the road. "If you're sure."

"I'm not." She sounded uncertain. "But I have a double Literature class tomorrow, and even though an evening with you is infinitely better than an evening with Dostoyevsky, I should probably give him some of my time."

"Crime and Punishment?"

"Yep."

"Good luck with that." Jamie turned a corner. He could see his apartment building now.

"Thanks."

"Look, I'm almost home." He hurried along the sidewalk.

"I'm going to make something to eat and then try and get some studying in. Talk to you later?"

"Sure."

"Love you."

"Love you more." The line went dead.

He looked at the phone for a moment, then pushed it back into his pocket, before mounting the front steps and waving his key card, waiting for the door to buzz so he could enter.

He took the stairs two at a time and was only slightly out of breath when he emerged in the hallway leading to his apartment. He was about to unlock his door when he heard someone speak.

"You need to keep it down in there."

"I'm sorry?" Jamie turned to find his neighbor's door open. The man filled the frame. He wore a sleeveless white tee, which exposed two arms covered in faded tattoos. There was a scowl plastered on his unshaven face.

"I said keep the damn noise down."

"Sorry John." Jamie was confused. "I'm not sure what noise you mean though, I've been in class all afternoon."

"Well, you need to tell your friends to keep it down then. It sounded like you were dragging the furniture around or some damn thing, all sorts of bumps and bangs all afternoon. I work nights you know. I don't appreciate being woken up like that."

"It must be someone else," Jamie said. "As I said, I wasn't here, and there's nobody else in the apartment."

"I know what I heard." John glared at Jamie. "Next time I'll be over banging on your door. Better yet, I'll just call the Super. There are rules about excess noise you know."

Jamie shrugged. "I don't know what you want me to say, John."

"How about an apology." John turned and disappeared back into his apartment, slamming the door so hard that the wall shook.

Jamie watched the empty space his neighbor had occupied

moments before, confused, and then turned back to his own door and inserted the key. When he entered the apartment, nothing was out of place, and there was no sign anyone had been there.

FOR THE SECOND night in a row, Jamie awoke with a start. The room was swathed in blackness, with only the dim glow of a streetlamp casting a sliver of yellow across the wall. He reached out, his hand searching for Cassie until he remembered that she wasn't there. Tonight she was tucked up in her own bed four blocks away.

He was alone.

Only he didn't feel like he was by himself. He could not explain it, but he had the sense that there was someone else in the room, that he was being watched.

The hairs on the back of his neck stood up. A tingle of apprehension nagged at his gut.

He listened, his ears straining to pick out any unusual sounds.

A dog barked somewhere in the distance, and a moment later a police car, or maybe a fire truck, joined in, the plaintive rise and fall of the siren a distant intrusion that soon faded to nothing. On the street outside he heard a car door slam, and a flurry of excited voices, someone returning from a club perhaps. All of these sounds were normal, the backdrop of city life that went mostly unnoticed. But not the scratching noise he heard next.

It was close.

He was sure it was in the room with him, coming from the other side of the room, near the end of the bed. He held his breath.

It came again, louder this time.

He slid out from under the covers, grabbed his pants and

pulled them on. He reached for the lamp sitting on the night-stand, his fingers barely touching the cord. Something made him stop, hesitate to bathe the room in light. Did he really want to see whatever was in there with him, observing him, hiding in the darkness?

It occurred to him that he was being foolish. If he turned the lamp on, there would be nobody in the room. It was his overactive imagination working against him. He was creeping himself out, that was all.

He pulled down on the cord.

The room lit up with soft white light, but only for a second.

There was a sharp pop, and the room was plunged back into darkness.

"Crap." Jamie stared in disbelief at the lamp. Really? The bulb had chosen that moment to blow? That seemed a little too convenient.

The scratching, clawing sound was loud this time.

He fought back a shudder.

His heart thudded in his chest.

Whatever was in here with him was not his imagination. He moved to the end of the bed, to where he thought the noise came from and peered down.

Nothing.

He stood still and listened.

Again all he heard were the normal sounds of the city outside. That didn't mean there wasn't something in here though. He crossed the room, reached out and flipped the main light switch.

The overhead light came on, the room springing into view. As it did, Jamie caught a flash of movement near the mirror. A black shape that flitted across the room in the brief moment between dark and light, something that seemed to disappear into the glass, to meld with it. It was fast, visible for no more than a split second, but he was sure of what he had seen.

He stared at the mirror. Everything appeared normal now. Still, a churning feeling of fear overcame him. Jamie crossed to the bed, plucked up his pillow, and pulled the comforter off.

He didn't want to sleep in that room, not tonight.

He padded down the hallway into the living room and threw the pillow and bed linens on the couch. He would sleep out here tonight, and deal with whatever was going on in the bedroom tomorrow.

DAY 3

Jamie awoke to a throbbing back and a painful neck. The couch was hardly the place to get a good night's sleep, and even though he'd only spent half the night on it, that was enough to convince him he didn't want to spend another.

He staggered to his feet, went to the bathroom and brushed his teeth, then put on a pot of coffee and went to get dressed.

He didn't have class today. He had intended to spend the day studying, but instead, he found himself at the desk in the bedroom, sitting in front of his laptop.

He glanced around the room, nervous, but there was nothing to see, so he turned his attention back to the computer. He brought up his web browser and typed two words into the search bar.

HAUNTED objects

THE CURSOR BLINKED, and then a bunch of results popped up. When Jamie looked at the page count, he saw that there were over three hundred pages of results.

"This is going to take all day." He muttered to himself, sipping the hot coffee.

Even so, Jamie scrolled through the results, clicking on any that looked promising. The first chronicled a supposedly haunted brush that made the owner's hair fall out if they used it - Hardly relevant, and more than a little dubious.

The next link he clicked told the tale of a haunted doll that apparently ran around at night terrorizing all those who lived with it. On one occasion it was even seen looming over a bed with a steak knife from the kitchen clutched in its porcelain hand. This was no more believable than the last account and didn't get him any closer to finding out about his own object.

Another account, however, was a little more interesting. It seemed that a pair of brothers in London had purchased an old mirror from a flea market and brought it home, hanging it in their hallway. From that moment on they had no peace. Vague figures moved around their house at night, they heard strange noises and footsteps when nobody was there, even voices. The Phantoms would whisper things, including their names, which terrified the pair. Eventually, things came to a head when one of the brothers tried to kill the other, and then claimed a spirit that lived in the mirror possessed him. When the pair investigated the origin of the mirror, they discovered it had hung for many years in a local mortuary, and before that it was rumored to have belonged to a man who killed his entire family and then disappeared.

Jamie read the story a second time, and then studied the photograph that accompanied it, a picture of two guys posing next to the troublesome object. While it didn't resemble his mirror – it was smaller with a less ornate frame – it gave him a chill to look at, so he clicked the tab to close the browser window.

The one thing that struck him the most about the mirror in the article was its background. Jamie had no idea if the mirror really had been in a murder house, or if it ever actually hung in a morgue, but now his interest was piqued. He wanted to know more about the mirror leaning against the wall behind him. There was only one way to do that. He would have to go back to where he found it.

He jumped up, closed the laptop, and found a clean set of clothes, selecting a shirt and jeans, and grabbed a belt and socks. He dumped these on the bed. Then he headed to the bathroom to freshen up.

After his shower, he returned to the bedroom and dressed. When he looked for the belt he'd placed on the bed only moments before, it was gone.

He searched around, wondering if it had fallen to the floor, but there was no sign of it. He returned to the bathroom, thinking that he'd put it down somewhere in there, but he hadn't. On his way back to the bedroom, he took a quick look around the living room, even though he knew it wouldn't be there. How could it? He hadn't even gone into the living room in the last hour. Empty-handed and frustrated, he returned to the bedroom, found another belt, slipped it through the loops of his jeans and buckled it. He could worry about the missing one later. There were more important things to do.

As he passed the mirror on his way to the front door, he could not help glancing toward it and wondering if something was lurking there, watching him, biding its time. Soon, hopefully, he would know.

———————

THE BUILDING WAS a large brownstone that stood back from the road. Jamie found a parking space a block away and walked back. He now stood outside the imposing structure, looking up at it. This was where he'd found the mirror. It was at the curb, right here. Of course, that didn't mean it necessarily came from this building, but it was a fair bet.

He took the steps leading up to the front door two at a

time. When he reached the top, the door was locked, but there was a buzzer in the wall, with four buttons, each one marked with a different name. Apparently, the place had been turned into rentals.

He didn't know which apartment the mirror might have come from so he would have to try all four. He pressed the first button, the ground floor rental. A moment later a voice answered.

"Hello?"

"Hi. I was wondering if you could help me. I'm looking for the previous owner of an old mirror. I found it a few days ago on the sidewalk outside your building."

"What?" The voice sounded confused.

"There was a mirror out here, next to the trash. Was it yours?"

"I have no idea what you're talking about, and I don't have any money to give you."

"No. I'm not looking for money. I'm not trying to sell you anything." Jamie said. "I'm attempting to find the owner of an old mirror I found."

"Get lost. If you press my button again, I'm calling the police." The buzzer went dead.

Jamie stared at the speaker for a moment, shocked by the rudeness of the person behind the button marked 1A – DAWSON.

He hesitated for a second before depressing the next buzzer up, not wishing to get yelled at again.

It didn't matter.

This time there was no answer, but that was to be expected considering that it was the middle of the day.

He moved to the next buzzer and pressed again. A female voice answered. She sounded infinitely more pleasant than the previous respondent.

"Hi. Can I help you?"

"I hope so." Jamie repeated his story about the mirror. A

few seconds later there was a loud click, and the front door swung inward.

"Come on up," the voice said. "Third floor."

Jamie stepped inside and made his way to the stairs, climbing up to the third floor and soon found himself outside apartment 3A. He was about to knock when the door opened to reveal a woman of perhaps twenty-five.

"Hello." She pulled a strand of long dark hair from across her face, her deep blue eyes studying him momentarily before she spoke again. "Come in."

"Thank you." Jamie moved out of the hallway.

"My name is Jennifer by the way."

"Jamie."

"Excuse the mess, I've just moved down from Vermont. Grad school." Jennifer left the front door ajar and motioned for him to follow her into the living room. "It certainly is a different world down here."

"It certainly is," Jamie replied. "I spent a year in Vermont when I was a kid. I seem to remember it was nothing but farms and hippies."

"Pretty much." A smile crossed Jennifer's lips. "You were asking about a mirror?"

"Yes. I came across it out by the curb." Jamie took a moment to take in the airy surroundings, the elegant room filled with sunlight from the west-facing windows. Several moving boxes marked living room in black marker were open on the floor, the contents spilled out across the hardwood. "It's old, with carvings on the frame."

"I remember it." She said. "It was here when I moved in, along with a bunch of other stuff. I hauled it all out last week."

"So it didn't belong to you?"

"Heaven's no." She shuddered. "That ugly thing? It gave me the creeps to tell you the truth."

"So who did it belong to?"

"The previous tenant I guess." Jennifer rubbed her hand on her jeans. "She was a student. The landlord said she just up and left with three months left on her lease and a month of rent due. Left everything here too, even clothes and a working cell phone charging on the nightstand."

"Really?"

"He tried to contact her apparently, but couldn't track her down, so he sold what he could to recoup his losses. The stuff that was left when I moved in was mostly junk."

"That's odd, that she would leave like that." Jamie wondered why anyone would abandon their furniture, their belongings.

"It happens sometimes I suppose. People get behind on the rent and move out in the middle of the night. It is weird that she didn't take her stuff with her though."

"So that's it?"

"Pretty much. The landlord didn't go into much detail, never told me her name or anything. You could probably get more information from him. I think he has an office in Cambridge somewhere. I can give you his name if you want?"

"No need." Jamie couldn't see the point in pursuing it any further. The owner of the mirror was long gone and if the landlord couldn't track her down for rent owed, what chance did he have? He thanked Jennifer and turned toward the door, about to leave, then turned back. "One more thing."

"Yes?"

"Did you notice anything strange happening when you had the mirror?"

"Strange?" Jennifer looked puzzled. "No, not really, although I put it out in the street pretty much the day I moved in, why?"

"No reason." Jamie smiled. "Thanks for your time."

JAMIE DROVE BACK ACROSS TOWN, no wiser than he was before. Things had only gotten weird after he'd brought the mirror into the apartment. He'd spent months living there with no odd noises, no dark shadows or unexplained events, until two nights ago. He found it hard to believe that the mirror was responsible, but he also knew what he'd seen, and the dark shape had definitely disappeared through the glass. If he had managed to find the previous owner, he might have been able to figure out what was going on, but as it was, he still had a lot of unanswered questions. He turned into the alleyway running along the side of his building and parked up. He was about to climb out of the car when the phone rang.

It was Cassie.

"Hey." She was cheerful as ever.

"Hi."

"What are you doing?"

"Nothing much." He mounted the steps and entered the building. The phone cut out for a second, but then he heard her speak again.

"Want to do something tonight?"

"I don't know." What he wanted to do was see if something came out of the mirror again. He wasn't going to tell her that though, so instead, he lied. "I have a lot of work to do."

"Oh." Cassie seemed taken aback. "If you're sure."

He was about to say that he was, that he should really study all night when an idea struck him. "Actually, I would like you to come over."

"Really? Great," she said. "I can stop and pick up take out on the way."

"Sounds good."

"Chinese okay with you?"

"I'm easy." He was almost at his apartment now. "Make sure to get extra spring rolls if you're bringing Chinese."

"Will do."

"And bring your camera."

"What?" Cassie sounded confused.

"I want to borrow it for a day or so. You don't mind, do you?"

"No. Of course not."

"Fantastic. I'll see you later." He was about to hang up when a thought occurred to him. "It does take video, right?"

"Yes, why?"

"No reason."

"Really? No reason." Cassie sounded suspicious. "I'm not doing that if that's what you are thinking."

"Doing what?" He was confused now.

"I'm not letting you video us. No way."

"Oh." Enlightenment dawned. "Nothing like that, I promise. It's for a project I'm working on."

"Well alright then." She laughed. "I'll see you this evening, around seven?"

"Fine."

"Great. Ciao." The phone went dead.

Jamie inserted the key into the lock and pushed the door open. When he did so, he found a slip of paper pushed underneath. He bent down, picked it up, unfolded it, and read the words scrawled on the page.

I TOLD you yesterday to keep the noise down.
One more day of this and I'm calling the cops on you.

HE COULD GUESS who left him the note, but what he could not figure out was why. There was no noise in his apartment, of that he was sure. He hadn't even been there for most of the day, so there was no way his apartment was the offender. But strangely, this was the second day in a row that John had complained about noise. In the end, Jamie crumpled the note and threw it to the ground, watching it land beside his neighbor's door. The man was an ass anyway. Screw it. He had other things on his mind.

He turned and went back into the apartment, grabbing a bottle of water from the kitchen on the way into the bedroom. When he got there, he stopped in his tracks and stared at the bed. There, sitting on top of the bed, plain as day, was his belt, the same belt he had searched the entire apartment for only hours earlier.

CASSIE ARRIVED at seven on the dot. She carried her DSLR in one hand, and a white plastic bag, tied at the top in the other. She handed him the camera. "I have no idea what you want this for."

"An experiment, that's all."

"So tell me."

"Maybe later." He took the camera and walked toward the bedroom. "Why don't you get the food ready?"

"Sure."

He entered the bedroom and went straight to the desk, where he set the camera down. He leaned over and peered through the viewfinder, adjusting it until it was positioned correctly, then set the dial to video. When he was satisfied that he had as much of the mirror in the frame as possible, he stepped back to admire his handiwork. Now all he needed to do was wait until darkness fell and press the record button. There should be enough space on the memory card to capture several hours of video. Now he would see if there was anything odd about the mirror. Maybe he would even catch the source of the weird scratching sounds.

From the other room, Cassie's voice drifted in. "Food's ready."

"I'll be right there." He crossed the room, turning back

just before he reached the door, taking one last look at the camera, and then hurried down the corridor, toward his Chinese food.

Day 4

For the first time in several days, Jamie got a full night of sleep. Unlike the night before, he didn't sleep on the couch, since Cassie was over. She had asked him why his pillow and comforter were in the living room, but he lied and said he was studying and felt cold. She threw him a strange look but said nothing more about it.

She also didn't mention the camera perched on the desk, even when he went over to it and pressed the record button. Either she didn't notice, or she figured that as long as it was pointing away from the bed, it didn't matter.

When he awoke, Cassie's arm was draped over his chest. He lifted it and repositioned himself, nestling into her back. As he did so, a stab of pain flared in his chest.

He rolled over and sat up.

Cassie stirred. "What's going on?"

"I don't know." He let the covers fall away to reveal his bare chest. When he did, he saw the row of large red welts running across his ribcage.

"Jesus." Cassie sat up. "When did that happen?"

"I don't know." Jamie touched the scratches. They burned.

"They weren't there last night."

"I know."

"You must have scratched yourself in your sleep." She reached out, her fingers hovering over the red marks, but she didn't touch them, didn't want to hurt him. "Have you ever done anything like that before?"

"Not as far as I know." He glanced toward the camera on the desk. The red record light was off, which meant it had either run out of space, or the battery was dead. He had a feeling that if he played the recording back, he would see what had scratched him.

"I'll get you some antiseptic ointment." Cassie slid from the bed and reached for a tee shirt, pulling it on, but not before he glimpsed her naked body in the morning sunlight.

"You look hot." For a moment he forgot about the scratches, about the camera. He reached out and pulled at the bottom of the tee, enjoying the sight of her round ass.

"Stop that." She swatted his hand away. "Didn't you get enough last night?"

"Nope." He lay back down, a grin on his face.

"Well, we don't have time anyway. Classes, remember?"

"We could skip class."

"Not likely." She went to the bathroom and was soon back with a tube of ointment. She sat on the bed and took the top off the tube. "This is going to sting," she said as she touched the ointment to the scratches.

"Ouch." Jamie pulled away. "That does sting."

"Don't be such a baby." Cassie rubbed the antiseptic across the scratches. "I really have no idea how you could have done this to yourself."

"Beats me." Jamie suffered through Cassie's nursing. He had a pretty good idea of how he might have come by the scratches. His mind turned once more to the camera, what it might have recorded. He wished he didn't have class, but if he skipped out on his lectures, Cassie would be mad. He would just have to wait until later to check the footage.

BY THE TIME he got home, Jamie was itching to see what was recorded on the memory card. He made a beeline for the desk as soon as he got in the door and settled down in front of his laptop.

He reached over and grabbed the camera, opening the

door to the small compartment that held the memory card slot and plucked the card out. He inserted it into his laptop. There was one video file on the memory card, which he played.

The screen changed to show his bedroom, the mirror center frame. The light was on, and he could hear a conversation in the background, picked up by the camera's microphone.

Cassie was talking.

He remembered the conversation. They were getting ready for bed. He noticed the reflection in the mirror and saw Cassie appear. She flopped down on the bed, her pose provocative. Apparently, he'd inadvertently recorded their fun and games, even though he promised her he would not. He watched for a while, knowing Cassie would be mad if she found out, but unable to help himself. He hovered the mouse over the time bar and pulled it forward, moving past the good stuff. While it was fun to watch, that was not the purpose of the recording.

It was dark now. The bedroom lights turned off.

The room was still.

He could make out two lumps in the bed, one of which he recognized as Cassie, the other was himself. It was quiet now, with the only sounds being the occasional car horn or motor outside, and their own gentle snoring.

He skipped ahead a little more, searching the recording for anything out of the ordinary, but there was nothing. He looked down at the time bar. There were over five hours of video still to play. This was going to take a while.

Jamie settled in, his eyes fixed on the screen. After about an hour he started to think the whole thing was a waste of time. There was nothing on the video. Worse, he was eating up hours he could be using to study. But he kept going anyway. Something had scratched him in the night, left deep gouges across his chest, and he knew it wasn't self-inflicted. Still, after another hour his eyes became heavy, and he found himself falling into a trancelike fugue, the monotony of the playback sleep-inducing. It was only when his phone rang that he snapped back awake.

He picked up the phone and answered. It was Cassie. She wanted to know what he was doing. He lied and told her he was studying, and it was okay if she didn't come over. After hanging up, his eyes skipped down to the time bar. Another forty-five minutes had elapsed. Had he really zoned out for that long? He was about to rewind the footage when he caught sight of something moving across the screen.

He sat up, his eyes glued to the monitor, and watched.

The shape seemed to just appear, as if out of nowhere, and glide across the room right in front of the lens. When it moved out of the camera's field of view, Jamie thought he might have lost it, but then he saw it appear in the reflection of the mirror, a vaguely man-shaped shadow, standing by the bed, hovering there, watching them sleep.

Watching him.

A shudder of cold fear coursed through Jamie. He leaned close, trying to get a better view. He realized he was holding his breath, and let the air out, long and slow.

After about a minute the shape moved again, leaning in close to the bed. Jamie watched, fascinated and terrified at the same time. This must be how he got the scratches. Any moment now he would have video proof, he would see the shape actually causing the long angry welts.

He sat still, not even daring to blink, afraid of missing the moment. Then, just when he thought he would see something happen, the recording stuttered, the image disappeared, and then the screen filled with static.

"What the hell?" Jamie exclaimed aloud. "Really?"

This was unbelievable.

He sat and stared at the electronic snowflakes. He waited, hoping the recording would resume, but it didn't.

He let the mouse pointer hover over the time bar and

dragged it to the right, fast-forwarding through the static, afraid that there would be nothing but white snow all the way to the end of the recording, but then, ten minutes, further along, the bedroom appeared on screen again. Now though, he saw no sign of the black shape. Whatever had been there was long gone.

He watched to the end anyway, hoping against hope that something else would show up, that he would see anything out of the ordinary, but all he saw were the reflected outlines of Cassie and himself sleeping, and the dark, quiet bedroom.

Eventually, he closed the laptop and rose. He stretched, stiff from sitting at the desk for hours, and glanced toward the clock on the nightstand next to the bed. It was almost midnight. He'd spent longer than he intended viewing the recording. For a moment he harbored the thought of copying the video file and then returning the card to the camera and recording again. Maybe he could capture something else. Then he remembered the static, how the video cut out right before the interesting part. All he had recorded were some easily dismissed shadows that looked vaguely like a man, but that was hardly conclusive proof of a ghost. If he'd caught it harming him that would be different, but he hadn't, and there was no guarantee that the recording would not cut out again tonight. Besides, he had a better idea, and all he needed to do was drag in the high backed chair from the living room, and he would be all set.

JAMIE SAT in the chair in front of the mirror, his eyes glued to the dull reflection. The clock on his nightstand said it was 3 A.M., but so far he'd found it easy to stay awake, thanks in part to the strong pot of coffee he'd been consuming for hours. Now his eyes were drooping, and he was finding it more difficult to keep sharp, especially given the tedious nature of his task.

So far nothing strange had occurred, there were no scratching sounds, no dark shapes, and no sign that the mirror was anything more than what it looked like, a large chunk of tarnished glass and old wood.

But that didn't mean things would stay that way. The strange events of the past few days had proven that whatever was lurking in his apartment had an odd knack of appearing when you least expected it. Which was why he must stay awake and wait, even if that meant sitting up all night. The problem was, his body had other ideas, and he soon lost the battle to keep his eyes open.

The next thing he knew, all hell broke loose.

He jolted back to reality as a series of crashes resounded through the apartment. He'd only closed his eyes for a few moments, probably not even a minute, but it seemed that was enough time for his unwanted guest to make an appearance. But this time the sounds were not in the bedroom. They were further along the hall.

He jumped up, half convinced that he as being robbed, but another part of him knew he was not.

He hurried from the bedroom into the living room, but everything was in its place there. Whatever had caused the crashes was not here.

That left the kitchen.

He crossed the hallway and stopped in his tracks, surprised and scared by the sight that awaited him.

The floor was covered with shattered jars, spilled cereal boxes, and canned goods. The kitchen cabinets were wide open. What food had not been thrown to the ground was perched precariously at the edge of the shelves. Some of it looked like it might topple at any moment.

He picked his way through the mess, accidentally stepping in a jar of spilled peanut butter, which clung to his shoes, and closed the cupboard doors. There was no point in risking more mess.

That done he turned his attention back to the task at hand. He stormed down the hallway back into the bedroom, sudden anger replacing the fear that he should have been feeling. He could feel the adrenaline pumping through his body.

"Come out." He stood in the middle of the room and shouted the words, knowing his neighbor might be next door and hear him, call the cops, but not caring. "Show yourself."

Nothing moved. Nothing stirred.

"Are you afraid of me?" he bellowed. "Because I'm not afraid of you. Not anymore."

He stood in front of the mirror, defiant.

"What are you, a coward?"

For a moment nothing happened, but then he caught a glimpse of something behind him, a shape moving in the reflection, dark and brooding.

He swiveled around, half expecting nothing to be there, but something was there. The figure detached itself from the shadows in the corner of the room, seemed to elongate and stretch, taking on a human form although no features could be seen.

Jamie took a step backward, his bravado waning.

The figure hovered for a moment, floating above the floor, and then shot forward.

Jamie screeched and flung his hands up in a defensive gesture just as the shape reached him, hit him. He felt tightness in his chest, a crushing restriction that made it hard to breathe, and at the same time, a deep overpowering sadness, mixed with something else.

Hate.

He stumbled, feeling his legs go out from under him, and sank to the floor, reaching toward the bed for support.

The shadow passed through him and then it was gone, right back into the mirror.

Jamie gasped.

What the hell was that? He'd never experienced anything like it in his entire life.

He was grateful for one thing though. The odd emotions he'd glimpsed when the shadow passed through him were retreating now, and as they did, he regained some form of composure. He struggled to his feet, feeling weak and scared. His sane mind was telling him that what he'd just witnessed was not possible, but he knew what he had seen and felt. He knew something else too, with absolute certainty. There was something wrong with the mirror, something very wrong. Something evil was living inside of it, using it to get to him, and he didn't want it in his apartment one moment longer.

He knew what he needed to do.

Jamie approached the mirror and gripped it tight, lifted it from the floor. It was heavy, and he found it hard to move, in fact, it seemed much more cumbersome than when he'd brought it up the stairs four days ago. Jamie struggled to drag it to the front door, and then maneuvered it to the top of the stairs. The elevator was still out of order, of course, so he spent almost half an hour getting down to the ground floor, and across the lobby.

He reached the main doors, pulling back the latch after making sure he had his key card to get back in, and then pulled the mirror out to the street.

There was a lamppost right outside the building. This seemed like as good a place as any to unload the mirror, so he propped it against the metal post, relieved to let go of the thing, and turned back toward the building. He waved his key card over the reader, heard the front door click open, and stepped across the threshold into the lobby. As he did so, he turned back toward the street, caught a glimpse of the mirror leaning against the post, bathed in cool yellow light from the sodium vapor streetlamp.

He breathed a sigh of relief.

The damned thing would be gone soon. Stuff like that didn't linger long in the city. A passerby would stop, load it into their car, and take it home to their own apartment.

He turned to the stairs and began to climb, weary and a little disturbed, but happy to have gotten rid of the mirror. Now all he needed to do was clean up the mess in the kitchen and finally get some sleep.

Day 5

Jamie opened his eyes.

Sunlight streamed into the room.

He lay there, his mind replaying the strange events of the last few days. It all seemed so odd, so unbelievable, but yet he knew what he had witnessed. The inexplicable destruction in his kitchen, the loud noises when he wasn't home that angered his neighbor, the shadowy figure flitting through the apartment at all hours, these were all things he could not explain away. And then there was the video, which left little doubt regarding the source of the strange events, the bloody gouges on his chest, and the dark apparition.

That was over now though. The mirror was gone. It was either out by the road, or already in the back of another poor soul's car. And that was fine with Jamie. Let it be someone else's problem. He was just glad he didn't have to look at it anymore.

He sat up, stretched, yawned.

His stomach growled, reminding him that he was hungry. He swung his legs off the bed and stood up, intending to put some coffee on and grab a bite to eat before heading out to class. But then his eyes fell on a shape at the end of the bed. They grew wide with disbelief.

The mirror was right there, leaning against the wall as if he'd never moved it.

"What the hell?" Jamie said aloud, the words hanging in the air. "That's not possible."

Only it had to be possible because he knew what he was looking at. His mind raced, going over the events of the previous evening. He remembered dragging the mirror down the stairs, heaving it outside and putting it by the curb. It was heavy, like moving a lead weight, and his arms still ached from the exertion.

Yet here it was, sitting there, mocking him.

He jumped up, found his clothes and pulled them on, grabbed his jacket, then hurried from the apartment without looking back at the hulking piece of wood and glass.

Was he losing his mind? He'd heard of students working too hard, cracking under pressure, going nuts, acting weird, but he'd never put much stock in it. Now though, faced with the reality that either he was going mad, or that the mirror was somehow stalking him, he was forced to rethink that position.

He reached his car, unlocked the door and slid behind the wheel. Cassie would know what to do. She always did.

He pulled onto the street, into the heavy Boston traffic, and drove across town to the university. As he went, he snatched up his phone and dialed her number.

"You're up early." She sounded bright, cheerful.

"Are you free right now?" He couldn't remember if she had lectures today, and if she did, what time they were.

"I have a few minutes." She must have detected the stress in his voice. "You sound strange. Are you alright?"

"Not really." When he thought about the mirror, the scratching sounds, the black shape, his stomach churned. "I don't want to talk about it over the phone though."

"Okay." There was a moment of silence. "Meet me at the coffee shop on campus, next to the library."

"I can be there in five." He was already entering the college grounds. He passed by the auditorium, the admissions building, took a left and navigated the broad central avenue running between frat houses and dormitories. Up ahead he saw the building that housed the school library, a gothic looking stone structure, the oldest building on campus. Next to it nestled a row of newer structures, a taco restaurant, the school bookstore, its windows adorned with sweatshirts and mugs bearing the university logo, and a bar that was popular with the student body. The final building in the row was the coffee shop.

He pulled his old Toyota into a parking space next to Cassie's beaten up Jeep and climbed out, picking through the scattered students that milled on the sidewalk. When he entered the coffee shop, he saw Cassie immediately. She was sitting in the corner, in a booth far from the counter, with two paper cups topped with plastic lids in front of her. When he approached, she looked up.

"I already ordered you a coffee."

"Thanks." He slid into the booth.

"You look like shit."

"Good to see you too." He feigned a smile, but it lacked any humor.

"So tell me, what's all this about?" She leaned in.

"I'm losing it, Cass." He wanted to launch into the whole story, tell her everything, but it was so odd, he was afraid that she would think him crazy.

"Come on, spill." She took his hand, squeezing it.

"I'm seeing things." He took a deep breath. "Hearing stuff that's not really there."

"Like what?"

"Scratching sounds." He paused, the ridiculousness of what he was about to say weighing on him. Would she believe him? Would she get up and walk out? "I keep seeing this black shape, like a person, only there's never anyone there. I think it comes from the mirror. I think that's what scratched me the other night."

"That's not possible Jamie." Her eyes were wide. She searched his face, finally meeting his gaze.

"I know that. I see it though. It was there the night you stayed over, the night I got scratched, and again last night. I think it's haunting me, Cass. It wants something."

"What do you think it wants?" Her voice was low, her tone even.

"I don't know. Me?"

"Jamie, have you been taking anything? Any meds?"

"Like what?"

"Like pills. There's no need to be embarrassed if you are. Lots of students take stuff for stress, especially with finals coming up."

"No." He pulled his hand away. "You don't believe me."

"I think you believe it." She shook her head. "But ghosts coming out of mirrors? Listen to yourself."

"I know what it sounds like."

"Do you?"

"Yes."

"I think you should see a doctor." She leaned forward. "Maybe you do need something for stress."

"It's not stress." His voice faltered. "At least, I don't think it is. Maybe I'm just going mad."

"Why would you think that?"

"I tried to get rid of the mirror last night. I put it out by the curb. It came back, Cass." He drew a deep breath, steadied his nerves. "The damn thing was there, in the bedroom, this morning, like it had never been moved."

"Are you sure you weren't dreaming?"

"No. It wasn't a dream." He shook his head. "It was real Cass."

"It can't have been." She shifted her position, held his gaze. "It had to be a dream, a really vivid dream. What else could it be? Objects don't move on their own. Mirrors don't have legs."

"It wasn't a dream," he said through gritted teeth.

"It makes sense though. You've been under a lot of stress, fixating on the mirror. Of course, you are going to dream about it. The reason why the mirror is still in your bedroom is that you never moved it. You just think you did."

"I'm telling you, Cass, there's something wrong with the mirror."

"And I'm telling you it's all in your head."

"Fine." Jamie felt a wave of deep, red anger rising. He clenched his fists, unclenched them again. "This was a mistake."

"What was?"

"Talking to you. Telling you about the mirror." He could see Cassie's face change, see the hurt in it, but he didn't care. "If you loved me you'd believe me."

"That's so not fair." A tear pushed its way from the corner of her eye and meandered down her cheek. "I do love you."

"Like hell you do." The sudden rage came out of nowhere. He slid out of the booth, pulled a five dollar bill from his back pocket, threw it on the table. "That's for the coffee."

"I don't need your money." She sniffed and wiped the tear away.

"Keep it." He turned and stormed out of the coffee shop, slamming the door as he went. Several people turned in his direction, startled by the sudden noise, but he ignored them. He pulled his keys out of his pocket, climbed into his car and threw it into reverse, barely bothering to look before backing up.

He floored the accelerator and peeled off, pointing the car in the direction of the apartment. The mirror had to go, for good this time, and he knew just how to do it. But first, he needed to stop and pick something up at the hardware store.

JAMIE PUSHED the apartment door open and stepped inside, the brown paper bag from the hardware store clutched in his hand. He moved down the hallway to the bedroom and reached into the bag, pulling out a wood handled hammer. The instrument felt heavy in his hand. For the first time in days, he felt in control.

He went to the mirror, stood in front of it, and gazed into the glassy surface, and beyond it, into the reflected room. Now, with the hammer in his hand, he felt safe, invincible.

He studied his own image, his face. God, he looked awful. No wonder Cassie was worried about him. He would have to apologize to her later. He'd treated her like crap at the coffee shop, made her cry.

That was not like him.

It was the mirror. Jamie knew that now. It was exerting some sort of hold over him. It was like a poison, weaving its way into his life and turning it sour.

Well, screw that.

In a few minutes, the mirror would be nothing but shattered glass and a splintered frame.

He raised the hammer, swung it downward in a tight arc. It hit the glass with a sharp thud. A spider web of cracks shot out, radiating over the mirror's surface. He pulled the hammer back and struck again. This time a large chunk of the mirror broke away and fell, silver shards glinting as they exploded across the hardwood floor.

A cold rage gripped him, consumed him.

He let the hammer fall time and again, even after there was no glass left in the frame, at which point he turned upon the frame itself, reducing it to a pile of kindling. By the time he stopped, he was out of breath and sweating, standing amid the shattered remnants of the old mirror. Now all that remained was to get a garbage bag and clean up.

A sense of relief flooded over Jamie. It was like a dark veil had been lifted. He dropped the hammer to the ground and went to the kitchen, where he grabbed a glass from the cupboard and filled it with water. He drank deeply, the liquid cold and refreshing, then bent and found the box of trash bags under the sink. He pulled the dustpan and broom from the hall closet, and armed with all the tools necessary to clean up the mess he'd just made, he was ready to banish the mirror to the trash in the basement of the building. He made his way back to the bedroom.

When he got there, he stopped in the doorway, alarmed.

The broom and trash bags fell from his hands.

The mirror was there, leaning against the wall, without a scratch on it.

"No, no, no." Jamie ran into the room, his eyes searching for the hammer, finding it on the bed, as if he'd just put the hammer down and left again without even using it.

"I destroyed you." He turned to the mirror, his voice rising in pitch, the anger back in full force. "I broke you to pieces."

Only he hadn't. That much was obvious.

He stood there, staring into the mirror, trying to figure out why he remembered breaking it apart, smashing it to nothing more than shards of broken glass. It had only been a few minutes ago.

He grabbed the hammer. This time he would make sure it stayed in pieces. He would not leave the room until it was safely in the trash bags and on its way down the garbage chute.

He raised the hammer high above his head, was about to bring it crashing down on the mirror yet again, when he felt the tool twist in his hand, slip from his grip as if an unseen hand had yanked it away.

The hammer flew across the room and hit the wall near the bed with a dull thud. It stayed there for a moment, wedged into the hole it had created in the drywall, and then came free, landing on the pillow in a shower of plaster dust and debris.

Jamie stood stock still, his heart pounding, his mind racing.

He had two choices.

Either he retrieved the hammer and made another attempt to destroy the mirror, something that seemed impossible given what just happened, or he could flee the apartment. It took him all of about two seconds to pick the latter.

JAMIE WAS out on the street, running for his car, by the time he calmed down enough to think clearly. He wasn't sure what just happened, but he knew one thing, the mirror was not going to let him destroy it. There was something dark, something evil, living inside that tarnished glass, passing through it into the real world, and it didn't want Jamie to close the doorway.

He stopped and bent over, catching his breath.

Now that he was outside he felt safe, but he needed somewhere to go, somewhere to formulate a strategy. Clearly just attacking the mirror, or removing it from his apartment, was not going to work. He considered tracking Cassie down. Maybe he could stay at her place for a few nights while he figured out what to do. Except that they had just been in a huge fight, and he had been horrible to her, said things he didn't mean. He also didn't want to disturb her during lectures. That was the least of it though. He was sure she would forgive him for the argument. She loved him, and she knew that he loved her in return. And that was the real problem.

He loved her.

He didn't want to drag her into this. The mirror was dangerous, and he didn't want her anywhere near it, or him, until he figured out what to do.

So where could he go?

He was supposed to have classes today, but the thought of sitting through lectures made him feel ill. Besides, he would not be able to concentrate. And then it hit him - the school library. It was quiet and would be mostly empty at this time of day. It would give him the space he needed to plot his next move.

He opened the car door, slid into the driver's seat, and started the engine, reversing out of the parking space and pointing the vehicle in the direction of the university campus for the second time.

Traffic was light now. With rush hour over the roads were much easier to navigate. He was soon pulling up in front of the library.

He climbed from the car and mounted the library steps. He was pleased to see that the building was almost deserted. He walked through the lobby, his feet ringing on the marble floor, and reached the heavy double doors into the main room, ignoring the mousy librarian who looked up, surprised, when he entered.

Rows of tall shelves filled the space, each one packed with books of every size and description, all neatly categorized by subject. The air was musty and stale. In years past this space would have been the center of life on campus, the repository of all knowledge, but now it served more as a place to sit and browse the web, or to find a haven of peace and quiet to study, than to actually read the volumes that sat idly in the stacks. To the left and right, he passed rows of group study rooms, most of which were empty. Only one contained a small bevy of students hunched over, deep in conversation, their chairs pulled up in a circle. They ignored him as he passed by.

He reached the back of the main room and took a set of winding stairs to the second floor, coming out onto a balcony that overlooked the room below. Here low tables and uphol-stered chairs were arranged in a semi-haphazard manner, a place to relax and work away from the claustrophobia of the main floor.

The balcony was empty.

Good.

He slid down into one of the soft chairs and closed his eyes. He felt a throbbing pain in his head, the start of a tension headache, but he paid no attention to it.

Jamie's mind was in turmoil. He could see no clear solution. He couldn't just dispose of the mirror, that much was clear. He had tried twice already to no avail. Even reducing the thing to kindling didn't work. The mirror didn't want to go, it was as simple as that. So what did the mirror, or rather whatever dark force lurked within it, want?

He thought he knew the answer to that one. It wanted him. It had attached itself to him the moment he stopped and picked it up. He remembered the flash of light that dazzled him, drew his gaze, as he drove past the mirror on the sidewalk. Was it possible that it had already decided to haunt Jamie that far back? Was that randomly thrown shaft of sunlight just a coincidence, or had it called out to him?

His sane, rational side didn't want to believe such a thing. He was, in fact, still struggling to comprehend any of this. It didn't make any logical sense. Ghosts didn't exist. Demons, hauntings, poltergeists and such were nothing more than the product of overactive imaginations. Only he knew now that they weren't. There was evil in the world, and it was sitting in his apartment at that very moment, mocking him, waiting for him to return.

Only he had no intention of returning. Not until he had a plan, a way to defeat it. After all, it was just wood and glass, regardless of what lived inside of it. It was manmade so it could be destroyed – he just had no idea how.

Maybe he needed to tackle the root cause of the problem. If he could dislodge the entity that was using the mirror, he might be able to dispose of it once and for all. It sounded crazy, but what he needed was an exorcist. That might be the only way to defeat this thing. Only he had no idea where to find one. It wasn't as if they advertised online or left their business cards in the coffee shop. Maybe he should speak to someone with a little more experience in the spiritual side of things. There was a chapel on campus, one of those interfaith things that served everyone, regardless of belief. It might not get him anywhere, but it was worth a shot.

He stood up, intending to make his way over to the chapel, his mood improving slightly at the thought of getting some real help when his phone buzzed.

He looked down at it, at the screen.

It was a text message from Cassie.

He read it with a growing feeling of horror.

WAITING AT YOUR APARTMENT. Where are you?

HE FELT a chill of dread run through him. Cassie was in the one place he wanted to keep her far away from. Who knew what the mirror would do to her?

He typed a quick message.

GET OUT NOW. I'll meet you at the coffee shop.

HE WAITED, praying that it went through, that she saw it. The phone chirped and a new message popped up.

NO. I will wait for you here.

DAMN. Jamie hated how stubborn she could be. He dialed her number and put the phone to his ear. It rang twice and went to voicemail. He tried one more time, but again it went straight to voicemail. Why wasn't she picking up?

He sprang to his feet and hurried toward the stairs, taking them two at a time. Halfway down his foot missed a step and he almost fell, but he shot a steadying arm out at the last moment and saved a nasty tumble.

He sprinted through the main floor, drawing the ire of the librarian who glared at him as he passed, and was at his car in no time. He jumped in and drove just a little too fast across town, making it back to his apartment in record time. He was breathless by the time he reached the third floor. When he got to his unit, the door was ajar, a thin crack of light spilling into the hallway. It seemed odd that Cassie would leave the door open. A sudden premonition hit him. What if the mirror had done something to Cassie, hurt her already? Worse, was she dead?

He pushed the door open and stepped inside, a lump in his throat.

The apartment felt empty, quiet. Jamie saw no sign of her.

"Hello?" He called out. "Cass, you here?"

There was no answer.

He checked the living room, then the kitchen, and finally found himself in the bedroom. Cassie was nowhere to be seen. Why would she send him a text message saying she was waiting here, and then leave? That didn't make any sense. On the other hand, it would explain the door. Maybe she fled and forgot to close it?

But then she would have called him, wouldn't she?

He turned to go back into the hallway, to look for Cassie, but then, just as he reached the front door, it slammed shut with such a force that he jumped backward with a cry of alarm.

He reached out and grabbed the handle, turned it.

The door refused to open.

"Come on." He turned the handle again, panic rising inside of him like a dark wave. "Open."

Still, the door remained stubbornly closed.

He kicked it, the force sending a stab of pain up his leg. Despite this, he kicked again, his foot connecting with the door just below the handle. All he achieved was another jolt of pain. He was about to have another go at the door when his phone sprang to life. He reached for it, looked down at the screen, at the new text message.

WELCOME HOME, Jamie.

THIS WAS NOT FROM CASSIE, he was sure. It might look like it was from her, but he knew it wasn't.

He walked back to the bedroom.

The hammer was still on the bed, just where it had been when he left earlier. He hurried past the mirror to the other side of the room, skirted the bed, and leaned over to retrieve the hammer.

He picked it up and moved back toward the hallway. He might not be able to destroy the mirror, but he could smash through the door, locked or not. He reached the end of the bed, giving the mirror a wide berth.

The bedroom door swung silently inward and clicked shut.

"Shit." That was not good.

He paused for a moment, unsure of what to do. There was no way he would be able to break through two doors, at least not fast enough to save himself from whatever was in his apartment. The window was another thing though. It couldn't stop him from breaking out a couple of panes of glass and crawling onto the ledge. He might even be able to make it to the fire escape and climb down to the street.

He passed the mirror once more, hammer at the ready. As

he did so, Jamie turned, looked into the glass even though he knew he should not.

And that was when he saw it. There, in the reflection, was a dark shape. It seemed to hover behind him, drawing closer. He knew he should turn and run, knew that whatever was there, lurking in the glass, was only in the reflection and not in the real room he now occupied. If he turned toward the actual bedroom, it would be empty. Except he could not draw his gaze away from the black shape, could not stop looking, even when it seemed to pass right through his reflection and push out from the mirror, so close now that he could smell the reeking stench of death it emanated.

He also knew that he should scream, but he couldn't. It reached out toward him, dark fingers clutching at his shoulders, gripping him, pulling him toward it. He raised the hammer, in one last vain attempt to defend himself, but he never got that far…

———

CASSIE USED the spare key Jamie had given her to let herself into the apartment. She was worried about him. He'd been acting weird lately, not like himself at all, and he was usually so down to earth. It had taken her the best part of the day to decide to come here despite the two missed calls. Even if she hadn't been in class, she probably would have ignored them. He had been so angry at the coffee shop, that she was not sure she wanted to see him, at least for a while. His outburst had scared her, and she wanted time to come to terms with her feelings, decide how to handle things. Eventually, she could not ignore the fact that she loved him. She could also not shake the feeling that something was wrong, and so she decided to check on him, make sure he was alright, and then tell him that she wanted to take some time apart to figure things out. Maybe that would knock some sense into him.

She thought back. All of this craziness started when Jamie found that damn mirror. For some reason, it had become the object of all his stress. She determined to make him get rid of it. They would load it into her car and take it to a thrift store. If what he said was right, and she didn't believe for a moment that it was, then let the thing try and find its way back from a store halfway across town.

In the meantime, she needed to find him.

She walked down the hall and checked the living room, then went through to the kitchen, but there was no sign of him. Next, she entered the bedroom, her eyes instantly drawn to the full-length mirror, the root cause of Jamie's stress, leaning against the wall, opposite the bed. It was ugly, that was for sure, but it was just a plain old mirror. Nothing more.

She drew closer, stepped toward it, her eyes lingering on the frame for a moment before flicking to the glass, and the reflection of the bed, the nightstand, and Jamie's jacket lying draped over the comforter.

She turned toward the room, expecting to find Jamie slouched on the bed, angry, or hunched over his desk under the window, just like he always was, but the room was empty.

Her eyes settled on the bed, on the comforter. She had a feeling something was off, but it took her a moment to realize what.

The jacket.

It was missing.

She looked around, confused. Jamie was nowhere in sight. She was alone, so who had taken the jacket?

Her eyes found the mirror again, and as she glanced past it, she saw the reflection of the bed for a second time. There was no jacket on the bed in the mirror now. Maybe she only thought she saw it, a trick of the light or something. What other explanation could there be?

She stood there for a moment, unsure what to do, and then reached into her bag and pulled out her phone. She tapped at the screen, found Jamie's number, and lifted the phone to her ear, waiting.

It started to ring.

It rang not just in her ear, but also in the room. She could hear the annoying jangly ring tone that she had begged him to change on more than one occasion. She listened, redialing when it went to voicemail and tried to follow the direction of the ring. She searched the desk Jamie used for studying, then rifled through the bed covers, thinking the phone might be caught up in the sheets. She got down on her knees and peered under the bed, lifting the skirt back and using the screen from her own phone to illuminate the dark space. All she found was a single sock with dust bunnies clinging to it like attacking alien parasites. That only left the nightstand, and she could see there was no phone there.

So where was it?

She redialed a third time and backtracked toward the door, passing the mirror as she went. The ring was loudest here.

She stopped and listened. It sounded like the phone was somewhere on this side of the room. She gripped the mirror and leaned it forward, careful not to drop it, then peered behind. Nothing. Still, it was louder here than anywhere else in the room. On a whim she leaned in and placed her ear to the mirror glass, and then jumped back, startled.

She stared at the mirror for a moment, and then pressed her ear against the glass again.

Was she going crazy? The ringing appeared to be coming from the mirror itself, or rather, from beyond it. It was like the phone was somehow in the room on the other side of the reflection.

But that was impossible.

She must be hearing things. It must be something to do with the acoustics in the bedroom, the way the sound bounced off the walls, tricking her ears. Only somehow, deep down, she knew it was not, knew Jamie had been right about the mirror all along.

She stumbled back, alarmed, and stood there, unsure what to do next.

The phone quit ringing, and she heard Jamie's voice.

"I can't come to the phone right now. Leave a message."

There was a long beep and then silence.

Her eyes wandered back toward the mirror – the ugly, grimy, terrifying mirror. When they did, she saw something that made her blood run cold, because she knew that just like the jacket, like the ringing phone, what she was seeing would not be in the room with her, but only in the reflection.

There, almost obscured by the tarnish that spread from the sides of the mirror like a copper-colored haze, she could barely make out the corner of the room beyond the desk. And in that dark corner, there was Jamie, huddled on the floor, arms crossed and legs drawn up to his chest.

She stood frozen, transfixed, knowing that the corner behind her was empty. Jamie moved, raising his head, and then he spoke, mouthing a silent warning.

Run.

Cassie opened her mouth and screamed…

The Return

HOW LONG HAS IT BEEN, Ben thought, surveying the narrow path leading from the parking lot into the woods. Ten, twelve years?

He did some mental arithmetic and came up with a figure. It was more like fifteen years. God, it didn't seem like that much time had passed. Standing here, in this place, it was like he was a ten-year-old child all over again. He felt that same tingle of anticipation, that same excitement. He almost expected his father to come around the car at any moment, a pack slung over one shoulder, the old two-man tent that not even gale force winds or golf ball sized hail could bring down, slung over the other. A lump formed in his throat when he thought about that, a lump he quickly swallowed, taking a few deep breaths to push the emotion back into its little mental box, locking it away. His therapist might not approve, but at this moment, if Ben was going to hike up to the old campground and relive that last camping trip, he needed to keep a clear head.

He glanced toward the ranger station, a log-built structure that looked like it had been there since settler days, but in reality was only a few years older than Ben himself. As a child this building had fascinated him, and he often imagined himself holing up for the bleak, long winter there, his rifle in hand to protect against a native attack or bears. The roman numerals on a plaque above the door dispelled that pioneer daydream, at least after his father explained that they stood for the year 1986. After that, he never looked at the cabin the same way again.

"Got it." Sally Hale, Ben's girlfriend, emerged from the building clutching a slip of paper. "One camping permit for Eagle Lake."

"Great." Ben watched her cross the gravel parking lot, her feet crunching stones as she walked. "We're all set."

"Can you believe they charged fifty bucks for this thing?" Sally drew level and pecked his cheek before talking again. "Fifty dollars just to rent a square of dirt for a couple of nights. Hardly seems fair."

"Used to be six bucks back in the day." Ben mused, hitching the pack higher on his back.

"Not anymore." Sally picked up her own pack and put it on, pulling the straps tight over her shoulders. "Are we going then?"

"Sure." Ben took one last glance around, making sure they had everything, before stepping toward the trail.

* * *

It was cool and shady under the canopy of trees, a welcome relief from the harsh afternoon heat. Ben took the lead, guiding them toward the lake at a fast clip, eager to reach the campground.

"Hey, wait up," Sally called out, breathless. "It's not a race, you know."

"Sorry." Ben slowed, allowing her to draw level. "I'm just eager to get there, that's all."

"I know babe." Sally reached out and took his hand, squeezing it. "We have plenty of time though. Let's just enjoy the walk, shall we?"

"You're right," Ben said. For a moment the ghost of Ben's father was there, his voice echoing in Ben's head, saying those same words, as he had done so many times when Ben was a kid.

"How many times did you come here with your dad?" Sally asked.

"Every year until I was ten. It was a tradition. Just him, me and nature." Ben smiled at the memory. "He loved it up here. He said it reminded him of why he was alive. He taught me how to build a fire, how to track animals, all sorts of things."

"It must have been nice."

"It was." Ben nodded, his mind drifting to that last trip, the last time he'd walked this trail with his father. It was earlier than usual by a full two months, which meant he should have still been in school, but instead, they drove the two hours from their home in Boston, heading north on 95, and then leaving the highway behind and meandering down back roads. Ben could still remember the trek to the camping area, how slow his father had been, how long it had taken them. At the time he didn't think much of it, at least not until a month later when he was sitting beside a hospital bed watching the old man take his last gasping breaths. The signs of sickness had been there for a long time, but at ten years old you just don't notice that kind of thing.

"Hey." Sally's voice broke into his stupor. "Penny for your thoughts?"

"What?" The memories retreated into the dark corners of his mind.

"You spaced out there for a second." Sally looked concerned.

"Sorry."

"Are you handling this okay?" Sally raised an eyebrow. "We can turn back if you're not up to this."

"I'm doing great."

"Are you sure?"

"I am. Why wouldn't I be?"

"You keep everything inside, that's all, store it all up." Sally pulled a bottle of water from her pack and twisted the top off, gulped down half of the contents, and then offered the rest to Ben. "I worry about you."

"There's no need." He took the water and drained the last of it. "I really am fine. I think coming up here again, finally dispelling the ghosts of the past, it's a good thing."

"It is," Sally agreed. "A really good thing. And I'm glad I'm here to share it with you."

"Me too," Ben said, feeling his mood lighten a little. "Me too."

They walked on in silence for a while, following the trail as it turned toward the lake and dropped down through a narrow valley. Eventually they came to a jagged bluff, a spine of rock thrust up from the ground as if some ancient earthquake had heaved it from the earth. They climbed to the top and stopped for a moment, stunned by the beauty of the vista that presented itself. Below them, the lake spread out across the landscape, a shimmering blue oasis within a carpet of green.

"It's breathtaking," said Sally, her eyes wide with awe.

"Eagle Lake." Ben mumbled the words under his breath, as if saying them out loud might shatter the picture of pristine perfection.

"The campground can't be far." Sally took a step toward the path. "Look, the rail goes all the way to the water."

"Come on." Ben was eager to put the trip behind them. "It's not far away."

"Lead the way." Sally followed Ben down toward the shoreline.

As they drew closer, the dirt gave way to fine grit, almost like sand. When they reached a split in the path, one side running toward the north end of the lake, the other veering out around the south end, Ben paused.

"What's wrong?" Sally came to a halt behind him.

"Just getting my bearings." Ben looked both ways. "It's been a while and looks different than I remember."

"I think I have a map of the trails if that helps. The ranger gave it to me before we left." Sally reached back into her pack and produced a folded map.

"Let me see that." Ben opened the map and studied it. He pointed at a tent icon along the northern trail. "This isn't where the camping area should be."

"What do you mean?" Sally raised an eyebrow. "They have it printed right there."

"I know, but it's wrong." Ben shook his head. "This isn't where we camped."

"Maybe you're not remembering right."

"Our campground had a view of Camelback Mountain directly across the lake." Ben traced a finger toward the peaks that dotted the far side of the lake. He lingered over one peak in particular, the one shaped like two camel humps. "If the camping area is to the right, the mountain would be all the way off to the left, past the lake and beyond the tree line. See?" He jabbed at the map with a finger.

"Not really," Sally said.

"Trust me. This is not where we stayed." He folded the map. "We need to go left."

"We're only permitted to camp in the designated area. Remember what the ranger said?"

"There must be another camp."

"There isn't." Sally pointed right, down the track that led to the camping area. "You saw the map. We have to take this path."

"No." Ben was adamant. He could remember the mountain, how it looked from the shore. He was sure the camping area he'd stayed at all those years was to the left. "It's not correct."

"So maybe they moved the camping area to the other side of the lake."

"Then we need to find the old campground." Ben had made his mind up. "We have to take the left-hand trail."

"Ben, don't be stubborn," Sally pleaded. "The ranger said—"

"I heard you the first time. We have to camp in the designated area. But seriously, who's going to know?"

"I really think we should follow the ranger's advice."

"Why?" Ben threw his arms up. "It's all just woods. Who cares where we camp?"

"There must be a reason," Sally countered. "They wouldn't go to all the trouble of relocating the camping area for nothing."

"It's probably just some bureaucratic crap. You know the thing. Some environmentalist says there's a nest of who knows what rare bird, so the place ends up off limits."

"I don't know."

"Come on." Ben took Sally's hand and led her toward the left fork. "It will be fine. I promise."

"Alright. I give up." Sally let him lead her along. "But don't blame me if we end up covered in poison ivy or something."

"Not a chance." Ben was walking faster now. The further along the trail they went, the more familiar things looked. It was more overgrown than before, but that was to be expected if the campground had moved to the other end of the lake.

It wasn't until they came to a chain-link fence, with a small metal sign hanging from it, that Sally spoke up again.

"See?" She pointed at the sign. "Look at what the sign says. Keep out. No hiking beyond this point."

"So what?" Ben grabbed hold of the fence, intending to climb over.

"Really? You really want to do this?"

"Yes." Ben looked down toward the ground. "I really do."

"Why?" Sally said. "Why are you so adamant about finding the same camp? Look, I get it, I really do. Your father brought you here on one last trip before he died. I understand that, but we don't know what prompted them to shut this area."

"You don't understand." Ben shuffled his feet.

"So tell me." Sally wiped a bead of sweat from her forehead. "Make me understand."

"It's not just about camping in the same spot," Ben said. "That's part of it, I mean, we shared so many memories up here. But there's more. When we came here on that last trip we buried something."

"What?"

"A box." A memory of his father holding the box out, letting Ben drop it into the hole, and then the two of them covering it over with the loose soil, patting down the earth until it was all level again, flashed through Ben's mind. He'd thought about that box so many times over the years, thought about coming up here to get it, and now he was. He wasn't letting any stupid fence get in his way. "We put things in it, personal things."

"Like a time capsule?"

"Right." Ben glanced along the trail, past the fence. "It's still up there, buried next to a rock that looks kind of like an elephant."

"Really? An Elephant?" Sally burst out laughing.

"Well, that's what it looked like to me when I was a kid, anyway." Ben couldn't help but grin. There was every possibility that the rock would look nothing like an elephant when they got there, that his childhood imagination had just seen that in it. "So I need to go to the old camp."

"Alright." Sally's voice softened. "We'll look, and if it's okay, we'll camp there so you can find your box."

"Thank you."

"Just promise we won't stay if it doesn't look safe."

"Why wouldn't it be safe?" Ben climbed over the fence and held his hand out to steady Sally as she climbed over.

"I don't know," Sally said. "But just promise me, ok?"

"Ok. If it looks funky up there, we'll leave," Ben said.

They started off again, with Ben taking the lead. The trail was clogged now, thick bushes growing out over the pathway, choking it. Weeds snagged their shoes as they walked, and twice Ben stopped to pull branches out of the way, holding them back while Sally passed. A little further along they were forced to climb over the rotten trunk of a fallen birch tree that straddled the path, its long dead upper branches lost somewhere amid the brush on the other side of the trail.

After ten minutes of hard walking, Ben held a hand up and stopped. "I think this is it." He pointed to a gap between the trees that opened up to the lake where a small clearing near the water was visible.

"Are you sure?" Sally leaned over, catching her breath. "It doesn't look like it was ever a camping area."

"I'm sure." Ben pointed toward a rusting piece of square metal attached to a steel pole. "Look, there's the old BBQ grill."

Sally pushed past Ben and made her way toward the lake. She approached the grill and reached out, touching it. Rust flaked away in chunks. She wrinkled her nose and wiped her hands on her jeans, leaving behind small red streaks of oxidization dislodged from her fingers. "Well, we won't be cooking on this tonight, that's for sure."

"This place has seen better days." Ben stood in the center of the clearing and looked around, taking everything in. On one side, near the tree line, was a small, squat building with the word *Toilet* still visible on the door despite a thick layer of grime. A notice board at the entrance leaned at a drunken angle, threatening to topple at any moment, a few bleached tatters of paper held on by rusted thumb tacks, the remains of posters and park rules, still attached. He kicked a discarded coke can, the red lettering faded to a dull orange by the sun. "It doesn't look like anyone has been up here in years."

"So maybe we shouldn't be here either," Sally said. "You know, we could just dig up that box and then walk back to the official campsite to put the tent up."

"What?" Ben looked crestfallen. "We're here now. Besides, we'll get a bit more privacy out here, if you know what I mean. There are no other campers around."

"Oh, I think I know what you mean." Sally blushed despite herself. "Boys. Do you ever think of anything else?"

"I think about pizza sometimes," Ben quipped, snaking his arms around Sally and kissing the side of her neck. "It doesn't hold a candle to you though."

"Hey mister, we have work to do." She pushed him away. "Later, alright?"

"Promise?"

"If you're a good boy." She fluttered her eyelids. "First, let's get the tent set up since you're bent on staying here."

"Fine." Ben faked a pout and wriggled out of his pack, placing it on the ground and unclipping the green bag that contained the tent.

"Besides, we need to find your box. Isn't that why we're up here?"

"Alright," Ben laughed. "You win. First the tent, then the box, then you."

"See, saving the best for last." Sally helped Ben slide the tent out and unfold it. Together they spread it on the ground, making sure it wasn't sitting on any debris or rocks, and then drove the pegs into the ground with a rubber mallet. Before long they were pushing the poles in, bringing the whole thing upright, until their makeshift shelter was complete.

After that, Sally pulled two chocolate bars from her pack and handed one to Ben, keeping the other for herself. She kneeled on the ground in front of the newly erected tent and tore the wrapper, biting into the bar with gusto. "This is so not what I should eat," she said between mouthfuls.

"You love chocolate." Ben flopped down, stretching his legs and leaning back on one elbow. He unwrapped his own bar and ate, making quick work of the snack.

"I know. My diet doesn't though." Sally was licking her fingers where the bar had melted. She glanced around. "So where's the elephant?"

"What?" Ben looked perplexed for a moment and then grinned. He scanned the clearing, his eyes alighting on several large boulders near the water. "I'm not sure."

"You don't know which rock it is?" Sally asked. "That's going to make finding your box difficult."

"No, I do." Ben jumped to his feet. "It's been a long time, that's all."

"I guess it doesn't look as much like an elephant as you remember."

"Hey, I was ten." Ben strolled toward the rocks. He stopped next to a large boulder with a mottled surface. "I think this might be the one."

"You sure?" Sally squinted, shielding her eyes against the sun, which had slipped low on the horizon. "Because it just looks like a plain old rock from where I'm sitting."

"It's this one, for sure." Ben pointed. "Look, see that ridge there, running down the right side, it looks a bit like a trunk, and that hollow could be the eye."

"Boy, you sure had a vivid imagination as a child." Sally scooted over to the rock. "So what now?"

"Now we dig, I guess." Ben strode over to his pack and unzipped it. He pulled out a gardener's trowel.

"You brought that up here just to dig for the box?"

"Yup," Ben beamed. "Well, and to bury our poop. We're in the wilds now."

"Aw. My little boy scout." Sally laughed. She pointed at

the low building near the tree line. "There's a toilet over there though, genius."

"That thing?" Ben grimaced. "It's got to be nasty as hell in there. I bet it hasn't been cleaned in, like, forever. No way I'm using that."

"Suit yourself," Sally retorted. "But this ass likes a toilet seat. There's no way I'm crapping in the dirt."

"Don't blame me if you catch something." Ben turned the trowel over in his hand and walked back to the rock. "Or worse, a snake bites your butt."

"That will not happen," Sally said. "Where did you bury the box?"

"That's a good question." Ben scratched his head. "If memory serves, it was on the side nearest to the lake."

He squatted down and examined the ground, then pushed the trowel deep into the earth.

"Can I help?" Sally hovered behind Ben.

"I don't think so." He prodded the ground again, moving the trowel to a different spot.

Sally fell mute, watching as Ben poked around, trying out different locations. One time, after hitting something hard, he dug down only to discover an old tree root, the gnarled wood brown and twisted.

She yawned, suddenly bored, and wandered down to the edge of the lake. "It will be dark soon."

"I know."

"Don't you think we should build a fire?"

"Probably." Ben was still hunched over, engrossed in his search. "Why don't you collect some wood and bring it over near the tent. If I don't find anything soon, I'll give up for the night."

"Sure thing." Sally strolled along the shoreline for a while and then turned toward the woods when she reached the old BBQ grill. There was plenty of dry, dead wood here, and it wasn't long before she had a nice pile accumulated.

Ben looked up when she walked back toward the rock. "I can't find it."

"Come on, we'll search again in the morning." Sally rested a hand on his shoulder. "It's getting cold, and I don't want to spend the night in pitch darkness. Not to mention, we'll have to eat dinner cold if we don't get the fire lit."

"Fine." Ben pushed the trowel into the earth one last time, with the same result as all the others. "I'm not leaving until I find it though."

THEY SAT around the fire on a pair of small camping stools and watched the sky turn from crimson, to dark blue, and finally to black. It was a clear night, the wide band of the Milky Way slicing across the heavens like a celestial river. Low on the horizon, a full moon cast silvery white light across the waters of the lake, glinting highlights that danced atop the low waves stirred by a chill breeze.

Ben sat with his legs crossed, a paper plate of beans in his hand and a half-finished bottle of beer next to him. He dug a fork in and ladled the meal into his mouth, eating fast, until the plate contained nothing but streaks.

Beside him Sally finished her own meal and discarded her plate into the fire, watching the flames reduce it to nothing but ash, then swigged her own beer, licking her lips. She huddled close and rested her head in his shoulder, a contented look upon her face.

"I was hoping to find the box today." Ben threw his plate on the fire and stuck the plastic fork into the ground with the handle poking up.

"I know." Sally nuzzled into him. "We have all day tomorrow, though."

"What if it's gone?" Ben asked. "It's been fifteen years.

There must have been hundreds of people camping up here since then, thousands even."

"Let's worry about that when it happens." Sally poked at the fire with a stick, watching the flames leap into the air, sending sparks flying up into the heavens. "I wish we had marshmallows."

"Hmm." Ben closed his eyes for a moment. "That would be nice. We don't though."

"I need to pee." Sally put her beer down and climbed to her feet.

"Want me to come with?" Ben looked up.

"Nah." She reached into her pack, pulled out a flashlight, and glanced in the bathroom's direction. "I'm a big girl. I just hope it's not too gross in there."

"Why don't you just go over by the rocks?" Ben pointed. "It's much closer."

"I don't think so," Sally said. "It's not very ladylike."

"Up to you." Ben turned his attention back to his beer. "Don't forget to take the TP."

"Got it." Sally plucked the toilet roll up and took off toward the restroom.

Outside of the circle of light cast by the fire, it was dark and eerie. For a moment she wondered if she should just go back and make Ben's day by squatting down near the rocks, but then he would tease her about it for weeks, and she didn't want to give him the satisfaction.

She played the flashlight over the ground ahead, looking out for debris or holes that might send her tumbling, and picked her way forward. Once in a while she raised the flashlight and shone it around to make sure she was still heading in the right direction.

She reached the building and pulled the door open, wrinkling her nose at the putrid smell that wafted out.

This won't be so bad, she told herself, taking a tentative step inside, and looking around.

The room was small, with a toilet on one wall, and an aluminum washbasin on the other. A sign above the basin declared that the water was not fit for drinking. A metal box on the wall still bore the instructions, Diapers and Tampons Only, although heaven knew how long it had been since either of those items had found their way in there.

She choked back a snort of disgust when she saw the toilet. A thick crust of grime covered the seat. Black mildew crept up the sides, reaching from the floor like mottled tentacles. The water in the bowl was brackish, a rotting leaf floating on top.

She hesitated.

Squatting down to pee suddenly didn't seem so bad. And who cared if Ben made fun of her? Only, she was here now, and it seemed stupid not to do her business. Besides, it would only take a moment.

She took the toilet roll and pulled a wad of paper free, then folded it into a square several sheets thick before bending over and wiping the seat. The makeshift cleaning rag did a fairly good job removing most of the top layer of filth, although the seat was hardly clean. She dropped the paper into the bowl and tore off several more sheets, arranging them around the seat until she had a clean area to sit on. She inspected her work, and, noting that it was as good as it was ever going to be, tugged at her jeans, unbuttoning them and sliding them down.

She lowered herself onto the toilet, careful not to dislodge any of the arranged toilet paper, and settled down, letting out a sigh as she peed. The trickle of water splashed into the bowl like a mini waterfall, joining the mucky water already there. Sally leaned on her elbows and looked around, playing the flashlight over the walls.

The room was a mess of graffiti, a slew of badly scrawled messages blotting out other, older ones, like a spider had crawled across the wall depositing words. The number of crude slogans adorning the walls, a few of which she did not even understand, was evidence that the facility had been unisex. No girl would write anything that base. She read several of the messages, smiling at a few, disgusted by others, until the beam of her light picked out something else, something unusual.

There, high on the wall, out of reach to all but the tallest person, was a five-sided star—a pentacle—with sides turning inward upon each other to create a never-ending line. In the middle was a grotesque, crude rendering of a goat's head, the red paint used to create it bright and fresh.

Sally balked. Surely this was not what it looked like? But yet, she could not deny the proof of her own eyes. She noticed something else too. It wasn't old like the other graffiti. A shiver ran up her spine. Suddenly she didn't want to be here anymore. It was time to clean up and get back. She reached for the toilet paper, her fingers brushing it, almost closing on it. Then she heard the sound. Nothing much, a low whimper, but enough to get her attention.

Sally froze.

She sat there in the darkness, the beam of the flashlight wavering in her shaking hand, and listened.

Everything was normal now. Quiet. Maybe it was her imagination playing tricks. After all, it was easy to get spooked in a place like this, especially given the dubious nature of the art adorning the wall. Still, it was better not to linger. She tore off a couple squares of paper.

Something moved on the other side of the toilet door.

Sally stifled a whimper of fear, her heart pounding so hard she thought Ben would able to hear it all the way back at the camp.

It came again, a shuffling, dragging sound.

Sally dropped the squares of toilet paper. She stood, making as little noise as possible, and buckled her pants, then stepped toward the door. She reached out and rested her hand on the handle.

No sooner had she touched the handle, than there came another sound. A long, drawn out scrape, like nails on a chalkboard.

Sally pulled her hand away like it had been burned. What was that? It sounded like…

Claws running down the door, a slow, steady drag, deliberate and controlled. Whatever was on the other side of the door was no animal.

"Ben?" It must be him. It was the only thing that made sense. "This isn't funny."

No reply.

"Come on Ben." Sally contemplated opening the door, showing him that she was not afraid. There was just one problem. She was. "Say something. Please?"

Tap. Tap. Tap.

The sound was strange, almost like someone rapping on the door, but not quite. It had a weird timbre, and it set her nerves jangling.

Tap. Tap. Tap.

Sally backed up, a knot of panic rising in her throat. If it was Ben on the other side of the door he was taking the joke way too far, and she knew him well enough to know he would not do that. She looked around, frantic. The only other way out of the bathroom was a small window in the wall above the toilet. It was small, but maybe she could fit through.

Tap. Tap. Tap.

That sealed it. There was no way she was opening the door. The window it was.

She balanced the flashlight on the ground with the lighted end upward to provide as much illumination as possible, then set a leg on each side of the bowl and reached up. She ran her fingers along the window ledge, ignoring the gross things her hand touched, dead flies, roaches, and something that scuttled away as she brushed close to it. She found a latch and gripped it.

Tap. Tap. Tap.

She pulled on the latch, crying out with frustration when it didn't move.

Tap. Tap. Tap.

"Come on. Open." Sally hissed the words, mustering all her strength. The latch dug into her fingers, and for a moment she was afraid it might cut her, but then, suddenly, it gave way with a sharp crack.

She let out a grunt of satisfaction and pushed on the window. It tilted outward on rusted hinges, the movement slow and stiff. She raised herself up on tiptoe to look out of the window, but it was still too high, so she put a foot on the toilet seat and gripped the sill, intent upon climbing up.

From across the room, the door handle rattled.

Sally shot a look backward in time to see the handle turn. She gasped. It was coming in. Somehow it knew how to open the door. There was no doubt now. Whatever was on the other side of the door was not an animal.

Caution abandoned, she put a foot on the seat, praying that she would not slip into the nasty brown muck in the bowl, or worse, fall and sprain an ankle.

The door creaked.

She tested her balance, and then lifted the other leg to stand fully on the toilet, gripping the edges of the window frame, pulling herself up, ignoring the pain when her ribs grated against the hard edge of the windowsill.

A hinge squeaked.

Sally dared not look around. Instead, she redoubled her efforts to escape, pushing her arms through the frame and heaving upward until her head was through. It was a long drop to the ground below, and she could not tell if she would land on grass or rocks. It was too dark. With a groan she remembered the flashlight. She had put it down to pry the window open. It was sitting next to the toilet, useless.

The door slammed open.

Sally squealed and wriggled forward, her concerns about the drop secondary to her fear of what might come up from behind. She felt herself tip forward as gravity took over, her body sliding through the opening. She half expected something to grab her ankles at any moment, to yank her, screaming, back into the toilet, but then she was falling, the ground coming up fast.

She shot her arms out to break her fall, but even so, she slammed into the hard earth and fell sideways. Her breath came rasping and heavy. For a moment she lay on her back looking up at the open window, dazed, but then she remembered the sound of those nails on the door, the handle turning, the door slamming open. That was enough to galvanize her. She scrabbled to her feet and bolted around the building, going in the opposite direction to the door. With any luck whatever had burst in to the small room was still in there, and if it wasn't, well, she would do her best to outrun it.

That didn't stop her slowing for when she reached the corner, though. Better safe than sorry. She peered around, back toward the door, but all she saw was trash and an accumulation of dead foliage. Further away, across an expanse of loose sand and gravel that sloped toward the lake, were the tent, and the glowing red safety of the fire.

I can do this, she thought to herself, taking a deep breath. Then she was off again, her legs carrying her as fast as they could, her eyes scanning the ground ahead for anything that might trip her. Now she did risk a glance backward, toward the building, and was relieved to see nothing there, no crazy murderer in pursuit.

When she reached the camp, she barely skidded to a halt before ending up in the fire.

Ben glanced up. "You took your time." He saw the look on her face, her disheveled appearance. "What's wrong?"

"There's something up there," Sally said. She leaned over to catch her breath. "It tried to get into the rest room."

"What, like an animal?"

"I don't know." Sally glanced back over her shoulder. "I don't think so."

"Well, what then?" Ben hopped to his feet. "If there's someone poking around up here, scaring you…"

"I don't know if it was a person."

"You said it wasn't an animal."

"I know."

"Well it has to be one or the other." Ben stepped past her. "Come on, let's go see what is going on."

"Go back?"

"Yes," Ben said. "I don't like the idea of someone snooping around in the dark."

"Ben, stay here." Sally gripped his arm. "Please?"

"Don't be silly." He shrugged her arm away. "Won't you sleep better knowing there's no one around?"

"Yes, but…"

"Give me the flashlight." Ben held his hand out.

"I don't have it." Now Sally felt stupid. "I left it there."

"Great," Ben said. "We'll have to get that back, anyway."

"Can't we do it in the morning?"

"And what happens if one of us needs to pee again?" Ben took her arm. "I don't want to fall down out here."

"Please don't make me go back there." Sally resisted, hoping Ben would change his mind. When it became obvious he was not going to, she followed him. "Can we at least make it quick?"

"What, you think I want to be trudging around up here instead of enjoying the campfire?" Ben took it slow. Now that they were away from the glow of the fire, it was almost impossible to spot obstacles that might trip them without the flashlight. When they reached the restroom Ben stepped inside and picked the light up. He swung it around the small room and then turned to her. "There's nothing here."

"There was a few minutes ago."

"Well, whatever it is, it's gone now." Ben shook his head. "It was probably a raccoon or a possum."

"It was not." Sally could feel her anger rising. He didn't believe her. "There was somebody up here."

"Are you sure you didn't just spook yourself? It's pretty gross in here."

"Really?" Sally pointed to the window above the toilet, still stuck open. "You think I climbed out of a damn window just because I got scared for no reason?"

"Maybe," Ben said, but now his voice faltered. "Whatever, it's not important. If there was anyone hanging around, they've gone now."

"We don't know that."

"Do you see anyone?" Ben swung the flashlight in a wide arc. "It could have been some drunken idiot camping out somewhere close. They probably stumbled down here to use the toilet and disturbed you."

"Let's just go back to the tent." Sally didn't feel like arguing. It was pointless.

"Suits me." Ben pulled the restroom door closed and played the flashlight over the ground.

Together they made their way back to the camp. Sally was relieved to get back to the fire. The night had turned chilly and she was shivering.

"Did you bring a knife up with you?" Sally asked, as Ben picked up a couple of thick branches and threw them on the fire.

"No. Why?"

"I'd just feel safer knowing we had a way to defend ourselves." Sally warmed her hands, watching the flames lick at the new wood. "You know, if anyone comes around in the night."

"Nobody is going to bother us." Ben had a mischievous look on his face. "Except for the ghost that is."

"Come on. Don't say that." Sally glanced around, nervous. "There's no ghost."

"Sure there is. A crazy woodsman who died in this very spot and comes back each year to claim new victims." Ben held the flashlight under his chin so that the beam cast long shadows over his face. That, coupled with the dancing glow from the fire, gave him the countenance of a demon, just for a moment.

"That's enough." Sally punched Ben's arm. "You'll give me nightmares. I won't sleep a wink."

"Suits me." Ben grinned. "I can think of things we can do."

"Not a chance, not if you keep this up." Sally stretched, yawning. "What time is it, anyway?"

Ben glanced at his phone. "A little after ten."

"I don't know about you, but I'm beat."

"You want to hit the sack?"

"Maybe." Sally glanced toward the tent. "Can we leave the fire going?"

"Sure." Ben stood and took her hand. He pulled back the flap and motioned, guiding her in with a gentle hand on her back. "After you, my lady."

"Thank you. What a gentleman." Sally felt Ben's hand slide down to her rump. It felt good. "You know, if you apologize for earlier, I might still let you have some."

"Apologize, huh?"

"Yep." Sally turned to face him and peeled off her tee. The air was frosty on her bare stomach, but hopefully Ben would be keeping her warm enough pretty soon.

"Well then, I am very sorry." Ben feigned an apologetic look. It wasn't very convincing.

"Good enough." Sally grinned and unclasped her bra. "So, are you going to take those pants off or what?"

THE TENT WAS DARK NOW; the fire having burned down to little more than glowing embers. Sally was glad for the slight red light that filtered through the thin tent walls.

Next to her, Ben slept, his chest moving up and down in rhythm, a loud snore escaping his mouth on each exhalation.

She pulled the sleeping bag up and huddled down into it for warmth, briefly considering changing back into her clothes, and out of the thin negligee she'd pulled on after their fun. She couldn't be bothered though. It would require getting up and rooting around for the clothing, and she might wake Ben. So she lay there cocooned within the layers of fleece and nylon, listening to the breeze rustling the outer shell of the tent, and the fire crackle and pop as it consumed the very last of the wood.

She closed her eyes, thinking of Ben, and how good he'd felt. She could not believe it was only three months ago that they met, it seemed like so much longer. She sighed and stretched her toes to the end of the sleeping bag, relishing the warmth. She was about to drift off, was almost asleep, when something pulled her back.

She opened her eyes and lay there, listening, ignoring the gentle snores of her boyfriend. What had she just heard? It was a small noise, but out of place. Alien. It came again, a shuffling sound, as if someone was out by the fire walking around, and trying to be quiet about it.

She sat up, her ears straining.

From somewhere out by the fire it came, just like before. A strange clicking, knocking sound.

Tap. Tap. Tap.

Sally's eyes flew wide. She reached over and found her boyfriend's prone form. She shook him. "Are you awake?"

He snored and shrugged her hand away.

"Ben?" She tried again. "Please wake up."

For a moment she thought he was still sleeping, but then he rolled over and looked at her with half closed eyes.

"What is it?" He sounded groggy. "What's going on?"

"There's someone outside the tent."

"No there isn't," he mumbled. "Go back to sleep."

"Ben." Sally hissed the word. "I'm serious."

"Alright." Ben sounded irritated. He sat up and rubbed his eyes. "What did you hear?"

"I don't know. Noises." Sally bit her lip. "Out by the fire."

Ben rested on his elbows and together they listened, but the only sounds were the chirping of crickets and the lapping of the waves at the lake's edge.

"I don't hear anything," Ben said finally.

"I swear. I heard it."

"Like earlier in the restroom?"

"Yes. Just like that."

"Jesus Sally. You're just freaking yourself out," Ben grumbled. "There was nothing in the restroom. You're just hearing animals. We're in the woods."

"No, I'm not." Sally glared at him.

"This is the last time I bring you camping." Ben laid back down and pulled the sleeping bag up to his chin.

"Dammit Ben," Sally said, suddenly wishing she hadn't let him have his fun with her earlier. It wasn't her fault that Ben had heard nothing. If he'd been awake a few moments earlier he would have heard it just like her. She shook him again. "Why don't you believe me?"

"It's not that I don't believe you…" Ben was on dangerous ground now.

"Then what?"

"Well…" Ben shrugged. Then, obviously unable to come

up with anything plausible he changed tack. "Fine. I'll go look if it will make you happy." Ben unzipped his sleeping bag and found his jeans, pulling them on. Sally glimpsed his round butt, pale and toned, as he did so. He slipped his arms into a plaid shirt and buttoned it. "Stay here."

"Thanks." Sally felt better already. She watched him crawl to the tent flap and pull it open. As he was about to step outside, she added, "Be careful."

Ben shot her a backward glance and disappeared outside without uttering another word.

The tent became a different place in the blink of an eye. It seemed silly, but with Ben there she felt safe. Now though, on her own, she felt vulnerable. What if the intruder came around the back while Ben was at the front? Sally pushed the thought from her mind. That was the last thing she needed to be thinking about right now. If only Ben had brought his hunting knife up with him, she would feel so much safer. But he hadn't. She looked around for something to use as a weapon should the unthinkable happen, but the tent was sparse, and short of smacking any would be attacker over the head with a rucksack, she came up empty.

Ben will come back in a moment, she reassured herself, and he'll tell me again how silly I was, that it was just a cat or a raccoon. They were out in the woods. It was probably just a curious raccoon, or a squirrel. Except she didn't think the footsteps had sounded much like a small animal, just like it hadn't been an animal at the restroom earlier. Whatever Ben said, she knew what she had heard.

Another thought struck her. What if it was a bear? She'd heard stories of bears foraging for food at campsites, and Ben had been gone awhile now. Maybe he was in a mortal battle with a black bear. But no, if that was the case there would be a ruckus going on out by the fire, and everything was quiet.

Actually, it was a little too quiet.

She pushed the sleeping bag down and off, grimacing at

the sudden cold air that enveloped her, and crawled on all fours to the mouth of the tent. She pulled the flap back, just enough to see a swathe of the clearing, but not enough to see everything. She wasn't that brave.

"Ben?"

No answer.

A cold lump formed in her throat. "Ben, are you alright?"

A cricket spoke up, its chirp loud and close by, but still no answer from Ben.

"Ben." She called his name once more. He couldn't have gone far. How could he not have heard her? "Are you out there?"

"Sh." Finally. She recognized Ben's voice from somewhere off to the left of the tent. "Keep quiet."

"What's going on?" She whispered this time, taken aback by the urgency in Ben's voice.

"You were right," Ben hissed. He was closer now. "There is someone else up here."

"Oh, shit." Her heart missed a beat.

"We have to go." The tent flap opened, and Ben made a grab for her arm. "Now."

"What?" Sally drew back. "Why?"

"Come on." Ben made a grab for her.

Sally scooted back toward the pile of clothes in the corner. "Okay. Let me get dressed."

"There's no time."

"What? Why?" Sally said, shocked. She looked down at the knee-length sheer slip, the one she'd brought not because it was practical or warm, but because it was revealing and Ben liked it. "I can't go out there dressed like this."

"Jesus Sally. There's no time. Come on."

"Well, at least let me put my shoes on." Sally grabbed her sneakers and pushed one foot in, then the other.

"Fine." Ben looked nervous. "But for God's sake, hurry."

"I'm coming." Sally tied her sneakers and climbed from the tent, hugging herself against the cold. "What is going on?"

"We have to get to the Ranger's Station." Ben took her hand and pulled her toward the woods.

"Why?"

"There is someone up here, and they aren't here to camp."

"Oh God. What did you see?" Sally swallowed. A ball of fear curled itself in her stomach. She felt sick.

"I'll tell you when we get to the Station."

"It's that bad?"

"Less talking." Ben looked around. "We don't want to alert it we've left the tent."

"It?" They were among the trees now. Sally wished she'd at least grabbed a jacket. The nightgown was paper-thin.

"Keep it down." Ben led her out onto the trail and turned them left, back in the direction they had hiked from earlier.

"Fine." Sally whispered. "Will you please tell me what is going on?"

"Not yet." Ben's voice was horse, low. "Just keep moving."

He positioned himself at the rear and pushed her along the path and practically heaved her over the fence until they reached the fork in the trail. Straight ahead would be the official campsite, but that wasn't where they went. Instead, they turned right and took the narrow path back down to the parking lot. Sally tried to remember how long it had taken them to walk in earlier in the day. It didn't seem like it took much time, but she wasn't paying attention either.

The path was dark, and she soon wished she'd grabbed the flashlight on the way out of the tent, but it was too late now. All she could do was hope not to put her foot down a hole or trip on a root. They walked for about half an hour, with Ben looking over his shoulder every few minutes, as if he was expecting someone, or something, to come up behind them. He also insisted that they stay mute so he could listen for pursuers. But Sally heard nothing but the sounds of the forest. After a while she began to think that perhaps the whole thing was just some ruse to get her out in the woods in nothing but a piece of flimsy fabric. At least until he held up a hand and stopped, that was.

"Did you hear that?" Ben glanced around, first one way, and then the other.

"What? I didn't hear anything." Sally wished they would move again. The seeping chill of the night air was already finding its way back under her nightie, icy fingers that touched every inch of her bare skin.

"We are being followed."

"How do you know that?" Sally felt like crying. She wished Ben would tell her who was after them, and why.

"You didn't hear it?"

"No." Sally strained to detect any unusual sound, but everything was normal.

"Okay. I want you to listen to me very carefully." Ben gripped Sally by the shoulders. "We need to run now. You go first, and I'll follow. Get to the Ranger's Station. Whatever happens, keep going. Okay?"

"Okay." Sally nodded.

"Good girl." He glanced back over his shoulder, a look of fear on his face. "It's getting closer. We need to move. Now." He gave Sally a push and together they ran.

Sally barreled down the trail, her legs aching, calves burning from the exertion. Once, at a particularly narrow point, her foot jammed under a fallen branch and she stumbled, almost losing her balance, but then she regained her feet and took off again. Behind her she could hear Ben running, his footfalls a steady smack, smack, smack as he followed. She rounded a corner, slowing lest she veer into a tree, at the same time avoiding a low-hanging branch that threatened to knock her cold. It was then that she realized she could no longer hear Ben.

She risked a glance over her shoulder.

The trail was empty.

"Ben?" She stopped and turned, scanning the path, the trees and brush that crowded the side of the trail, but she was alone.

"Ben, where are you?" She kept her voice low, hardly daring to speak. She felt a wave of panic rise up. How could he have disappeared? He was right behind her.

She stood there for a moment, feeling lost, unsure what to do. Ben had said to keep moving, no matter what happened, but she couldn't leave him out here. What if he was hurt? She froze, locked by indecision, torn between running to safety and finding her boyfriend. Then the choice was made for her.

Something moved in the trees to her left.

Sally swiveled around, her eyes searching the blackness between the trees, but she saw nothing.

There it was again. The crack of a branch, the rustle of leaves, as something pushed past, stalking her, following her.

Sally backed up, wanting to run, wanting Ben to come around the corner even more.

Then she heard it, low and faint, barely audible.

Tap. Tap. Tap.

The same odd tapping she'd heard before. She stood still and listened, her heart thumping in her chest.

Tap. Tap. Tap.

The sound was much closer this time. There was no mistaking it now. Sally turned and ran, all thought of Ben lost from her mind, at least for the moment. In her haste she didn't notice a thorn bush, its branches half covering the trail, and soon the thorns were tearing at her skin, ripping through the nightie, but she didn't care.

Behind her, as if it were keeping pace, she heard it one more time.

Tap. Tap. Tap.

She let out a scream and found a jolt of speed; her legs

carrying her faster than she had ever run in her entire life. All caution thrown to the wind, Sally negotiated the last of the trail in a fit of blind panic, and was surprised when the trees fanned out and she found herself in the parking lot.

She staggered to a halt and gasped for breath, her lungs burning.

There was Ben's car, right where they parked it the day before. Up ahead was the Ranger's Station, a warm yellow glow pulsing through the window. She crossed the parking lot and hurried to the cabin door. Without a second thought, she pounded on the door.

"Help me." Her voice sounded strained, hoarse. "Please, open up."

For a moment she thought no one would answer, but then she heard a bolt being drawn back. The door opened a crack.

"Can I help you?" A face appeared in the space between the door and the frame. It was the Ranger she'd bought the camping permit from the day before. He looked tired. He held a flannel robe closed. He must have been asleep.

"Please, let me in," Sally pleaded. "Someone is chasing me."

"What the…" The door opened wide. The Ranger looked alarmed. "Get in. Tell me what happened."

"Thank you." Sally pushed past him and stood shivering in the small office.

The Ranger stole a glance in the trail's direction, then closed and bolted the door. "Alright young lady, what's all this about." His eyes roamed her body.

Sally looked down. The nightie was a mess. Here and there smudges of dirt soiled the white garment. The fabric was torn in places, exposing swathes of pale white skin. Not that it mattered. The nightdress was almost see-through, and even in the dim light of the office she could tell that it left little to the imagination. She folded her arms across her chest and met the Ranger's gaze. "My boyfriend is still out there. We need to call the police and look for him."

"Now slow down there. I'm going to need a tad more information before I go calling the cops up here." The Park Ranger plucked a dark green jacket with yellow badges on the sleeves from a coat rack and held it out to her. "Put this on before you freeze to death. My name's Arnie, by the way."

"Thanks." She snatched the jacket and pulled it on, covering herself. "Can we please find Ben now?"

"Well now, what makes you think he's missing?"

"We were chased. I told you." Sally could feel the tears coming, hot and wet.

"There's no need to cry." Arnie looked around. "Gosh, I don't have any napkins. Tell you what, why don't you come through to the lounge and sit down, and I'll make a few calls."

"Okay." Sally sniffed and followed Arnie toward a door at the back of the office, behind a service counter. Beyond the office were small living quarters. She found herself in a living room. It was sparse but comfortable, with two chairs and a bookshelf. The remains of a fire glowed in a stone hearth, the warmth from the embers still filling the cramped space.

"Sit down, please." Arnie motioned toward a chair near the fire. "Get warm. I'll take care of business and bring you a nice hot cup of cocoa."

"I don't want a drink." Sally slid into the chair, relishing the heat emanating from the hearth. "I just want to find Ben."

"I'll bring you a cocoa, anyway. Just give me a few minutes to throw something on." Arnie turned and left the room, leaving Sally alone. She heard him clatter around somewhere else in the building, and then things went quiet for a while. After that she heard the clink of cups and the whistle of a kettle. A few moments later Arnie returned, now wearing his crisp green uniform. In his hands he carried two mugs with the Park Service logo emblazoned on them.

"Here you are." He handed one mug to her.

"I told you, I don't want a drink." She took the mug anyway. "Did you call for help yet?"

"Just drink it. You will feel better." Arnie's mouth curled into a thin smile. "I put a call in to Williamsville. That's the nearest town. They are sending a squad car up here. It'll take a while, though."

"How long?"

"Gosh, I don't know. An hour maybe?" He placed a hand on her shoulder, just for a moment. "We're not exactly close to anything out here."

"An hour?" Sally knew the tears would flow again soon. "That's too long. We have to find Ben now."

"Do you know how hard it is to find someone out there?" Arnie gestured in the general direction of the woods. "Two thousand square miles of dense forest. No, we need to wait for help."

"But he's not lost in the forest. Someone took him, I told you." She felt like screaming. "He was right behind me on the trail, and then…"

"Be that as it may, we have procedures around here. If we are going to find Ben we need to follow them," Arnie said.

"You're sure the police are on their way?" Sally felt helpless.

"Cross my heart." Arnie raised a hand to his chest. "Now get that cocoa inside you, it will warm you up."

"Alright." Sally still didn't want the drink, but what else was there to do? Besides, she might as well keep her strength up. She raised the cup and sipped, the chocolate taste filling her mouth. It was warm and pleasant. She sipped again.

"There you go. That's a good girl." Arnie took a sip from his mug and relaxed back into his chair.

She gripped the mug with both hands and gulped. The cocoa was good, better than good, and Arnie was right, it was helping to take the edge off. She felt light-headed, tired. The cup slipped from her hands. She wanted to hold on to it, but it fell anyway, landing with a dull thud on the rough scraped wood floor.

This wasn't right. She was too tired.

She fought to stop her eyelids from closing, tried to stand up. She opened her mouth to speak, to ask Arnie why she felt so strange, but all that came out was a slurred mishmash of vowels and consonants.

Her vision grew dim, a black cloak closing in around the edges of her consciousness. And then there was nothing...

COLD.

A gnawing, painful cold.

Sally rose from slumber, just for a moment, and forced her eyes open, even though they wanted to stay closed.

Trees.

She saw trees above her.

She was moving too, although strangely she knew she was not walking. Someone was carrying her. She swayed back and forth as they walked. And then her eyes rolled back in their sockets and she passed out again.

SALLY DRIFTED BACK TO CONSCIOUSNESS.

Her head felt like a thousand hammers were pounding away inside it. She briefly wondered why everything looked lopsided, then realized that she was lying sideways on the ground. She felt loose gravel under her body, stones pushing into her, sharp and painful.

It was still light, but judging by how the sun hovered low on the horizon, it would not be for much longer.

She tried to move, but her hands were bound behind her

back. When she looked down, she found her legs tied at the ankles with a piece of nylon rope.

She let out a moan.

"Well, hello." Arnie was kneeling a few feet away with his back to her. "You've been out for a while. I was wondering if you would wake up before I left."

"What's going on?" Sally's voice felt thin. Her mouth was dry. She realized that she no longer wore the Ranger's jacket.

"You didn't follow my instructions did you, didn't do what the permit said. You just had to come up here, even though there's a perfectly good, perfectly safe campground on the other side of the lake." Arnie turned toward her, and for the first time she saw the figure propped up against the rock that looked like an elephant.

It was Ben.

His head hung low, his hair a matted, clumped mess. Something stained his shirt, something dark red and… With a shock she realized it was blood. A whimper escaped her lips. "What have you done to him?"

"Me?" Arnie looked shocked. "Nothing. He was like this when we got here. It must have dragged him back here. Poor guy."

"What are you talking about?" Sally pulled at the rope binding her wrists, but it held tight. "Is he dead?"

Arnie reached out, lifted Ben's head, and touched his neck, feeling for a pulse. "No, not yet. Pretty close, though. It tore him up real bad. His face looks like it went through a blender." Arnie whistled, as if he appreciated the damage to Ben's face. He stood and approached Sally. "I'm sure it will come back to finish the job tonight."

"Why are you doing this?" Sally could feel tears meandering down her face. She blinked them away.

"Me? You did it to yourselves by camping here." Arnie squatted next to her. "This land, this campground, it's cursed. This earth is soaked in blood. Has been ever since those damn kids came up here with that Ouija Board a few years back. They thought it was fun. Whatever the hell they conjured up had other ideas."

"What?" Sally wondered if Arnie was mad.

"Can't say I'm surprised though. Did you know they found a bunch of bones when they were building the restrooms? Some fancy folks from the university came up here afterward and poked around. They said the remains were Native American, said this was some sort of ancient burial ground." Arnie drew a long breath. "Now I don't know what those kids released with that Ouija Board, whether it was an angry spirit or something else. A demon, if you will. But it seems to me it must have been something to do with them bones. Regardless, they all ended up dead. Stupid kids. Cops were picking up pieces of them for weeks. Didn't stop there either. No, sir. A few weeks later a young couple went and got themselves torn apart. The cops blamed the deaths on animal attacks. Bears or some such nonsense. That's why the Park Service closed this place, moved the campground to the other side of the lake. Now I don't know a whole lot about such things, but it was no normal animal that killed those folks, I know that much."

"Please untie me." Sally pleaded. "I won't tell anyone what you've done. I promise. We need to call an ambulance for Ben. He's hurt."

"Sorry, little lady." Arnie shook his head. "You say that now, but you don't mean it. You'll have every cop in the county up here the minute I let you go. We both know it's true."

"Why are you doing this?"

"You think you are the first ones to camp here since we closed this place? Heck, no. Every year we get a few hikers that go wandering where they shouldn't, people like you that camp here, and every single time it ends the same. Folk ripped apart like they were rag dolls, torn limb from limb." Arnie lowered his head. "I have to give it to you though, you're the first to make it out alive."

"I don't understand." Sally squirmed, hoping to loosen her bindings, but it was no use.

"I like my job," Arnie said. "Do you know what would happen if folks found out that people are still dying up here?"

Sally shook her head.

"I'll tell you what would happen. I'd be out of work, that's what. They would close this park down for good. Not just move a campsite or two, but close it. We can't have that now, can we? I've got five years left until I retire and move to Boca."

"You're sick." Sally spat the words. She tried to sit up, but could not get enough leverage and fell back to the ground.

Arnie ignored her. "I always wondered what I would do if someone actually escaped." Arnie stood and wiped his hands on his trousers. "I guess now I know."

"Let me go."

"I'd love to, but I can't," Arnie said. He stepped toward the edge of the clearing. "This job, this place, it's all I have. If it's any consolation, it won't be long now. It will come for you once the sun goes down. I just pray it kills you quick. Of course, it probably won't. Dang thing likes the ladies. Sometimes, when the wind is just right, I can hear 'em screaming. It'll go on for hours, I'll tell you. Gives me the shivers, wondering what it's doing to them."

"Don't leave me here. Please?" A knot of fear churned in Sally's stomach. She tugged at her bindings.

"I'll come back in the morning to clear up the tent and such. Then I'll put you two with the others. Yes, siree. It's quite a little community of corpses we have going up here." Arnie chuckled. "Boy, if those university folks came back up here now, they'd find a lot more bones. Yes, sir, a whole lot more."

"Wait. Please don't do this." Sally couldn't see Arnie now,

but she could hear him pushing through the trees, picking his way back out to the trail. She called after him, begged him to let her go, but he didn't answer. Soon even his footsteps faded to nothing.

She was alone.

Except for Ben, and he was too far gone to be much help. The sun slipped behind the mountains, lighting the sky a bright crimson, which soon faded to dark blue, and then black. Darkness crept across the lake and stole the land. Sally struggled against the bindings on her wrists and ankles, twisting one way then the other, but it was to no avail. Arnie knew how to tie a knot. She called to Ben, begged him for help, but if he was still breathing, he made no show of it, and so she stopped trying. Instead, she cried. She wept for Ben, and she wept for herself.

The heat of the day gave way to a numbing cold that crept under her shredded slip and chilled the naked skin beneath. Her teeth started to chatter. The tent, and the warm sleeping bags contained within, were just as they left them the previous evening, but they might as well have been on the moon.

In the end she gave up and lay still, waiting for what would happen next, wondering if Arnie would come back to kill her. Not that he needed to. Given the way the temperature was dropping, she could very well end up freezing to death before morning.

She closed her eyes and let her mind wander. If she focused hard enough, she could pretend that everything was fine, that this was just a night spent camping under the stars. Even the numbing cold receded a little as she slipped into a fantasy that drew her away from the horror of the situation.

Tap. Tap. Tap.

Sally opened her eyes, a wriggling fear churning in her gut. The sound was faint but recognizable. She craned her neck, looked around, but she saw nothing. She shivered, only this time it was not just from the cold.

Tap. Tap. Tap.

Closer now. Just a little. She let out a small cry, a whimper of fear. She scanned the clearing, her eyes darting from the tent to the lake, and up to the trees, at least those she could see from her vantage point.

Tap. Tap. Tap.

Something was moving. She could hear it shuffling across the clearing behind her, drawing near. She called out to Ben, not because he would answer, but because she didn't want to face it alone.

Tap. Tap. Tap.

She sensed it right behind her, knew it was there, just waiting, savoring her fear. In that moment Sally realized that there was no escape, and so she closed her eyes and thought about Ben, about his smile, and the way she felt when they were together, because to think about the alternative would be too much. She tried to stay calm, tried not to let it know that she was afraid, even when its rancid breath touched her neck, even when she heard those terrible sounds right next to her.

Tap. Tap. Tap.

The Night the Starlight Burned

NANCY JACOBS SAVED my life the night the Starlight burned. She didn't mean to save it, but she did, none-the-less. That was also the night she broke my heart, and that she meant to do, I am sure.

She was my first true love, and the first girl I kissed, unless you count Gertrude Wells who ambushed me under the mistletoe at a Christmas party when I was ten.

I knew from the first moment I met Nancy that we were meant to be together. It was the fall of 1955, and the trees were turning orange and red, yellow and ochre, rendering the landscape alive in one last spectacular show before the onset of winter. Each evening after school I walked Nancy home, carrying her books even though my own did a more than adequate job of weighing me down.

Eventually, after a month of escorting Nancy to her door, which was precisely three blocks further than my own, I plucked up the courage to ask her out on a formal date. It was not a smooth proposal by any means, but more a stuttered, shambolic affair, that I was sure would result in a soul-destroying rebuttal. To my surprise however, she nodded, a smile passing across her lips as she spoke the words every young man wants to hear.

"I'd love to."

"Really?"

"Yes." Her eyes sparkled, catching the light of the waning sun. "I've been waiting for you to ask for weeks."

And that was how I found myself, a few days later, next to her in Timmy Thomson's old Studebaker, which he'd let me borrow on the promise that I would procure for him some liquid libations in the form of a six-pack.

If my father, a cantankerous curmudgeon of a man, noticed his beer missing from the fridge, he never said anything. It's possible he thought my mother had poured it down the sink to stop him drinking too much while playing poker with his buddies.

The movie was awful. One of those Busby Berkeley flicks with too much singing and dancing, but Nancy was enthralled by it, and that was all that mattered.

From then on the Starlight became our regular Saturday night date, thanks to Timmy Thomson's willingness to hand over his car keys for whatever hooch I could liberate without being caught, which sometimes only amounted to a single can of beer. The fact that I was aiding in the delinquency of a minor was of little concern to me.

Each week Nancy and I would drive his old jalopy and park center front, right under the screen, because she said the back rows were for fooling around, and she did not want to be seen there, lest some town voyeur spotted us and ruined her reputation. Once, while feeling particularly bold, I attempted to snake my arm around her shoulder after the movie started, my hand angled down toward the curve of her breast, but she was having none of it, and I soon withdrew. There was a time and a place for everything, she said, and the Starlight was neither.

We settled into a routine, and despite the fact that I would rather have gone to the late showing of horror flicks and sci-fi B movies with robots and ultraviolet death rays, I was happy to attend the early movie and watch musicals and romances, because it pleased Nancy. The fact that it left plenty of time to drive out to Willet's Overview, and park among the trees for an hour, helped a little too.

We didn't always go to the drive-in though. That was just our Saturday night thing. We went bowling, ordered milkshakes and fries at Sal's Malt Shop, and took long walks along the riverbank. In the winter, when the Starlight closed for the season, we joined the rest of the town ice-skating on Old Mill Pond, or at least Nancy skated. I fell over a lot and did my best to look nonchalant while doing so. Once we even played Bocce behind the Italian Restaurant. It was probably the only Bocce court within a hundred miles, and although the game struck me as old fashioned, I soon got into the spirit of things. It turned out I was worse at Bocce than I was at ice-skating. Nancy made short work of beating me, although I like to think I let her win, naturally.

And as such, things continued, through that year and into the next, and it was the happiest time of my life. In the summer of 1956, I gave Nancy my class ring, which she put on a gold chain and wore around her neck. She told me she loved me, and I told her I felt the same. I could not imagine being any happier than I was at that moment.

Time flew by and summer turned to fall once again. As the days grew shorter, and the nights stretched longer, we made our pilgrimage each Saturday evening to the Starlight, where we parked up to watch the weekly feature, all too aware of the approaching winter.

I was always sad when the Starlight closed each November, the screen dark until the following May. My parents had taken me there since I was a child. I would lay in the back seat of the car, with a blanket pulled up to my shoulders on cold nights and pretend to sleep while they watched horror flicks and low budget thrillers. I kept one eye open of course and had seen just about every horror picture there was by the time I was twelve.

Going with Nancy was something else though, despite the fact that I still did not like the early movies. It was on one such Saturday, toward the end of October, when everything changed.

Nancy was already waiting when I pulled up to her house, the Studebaker grumbling and growling as it neared the curb. When I slowed to a stop it belched a popping backfire, which was not an unusual occurrence.

I waved and reached over, releasing the door for her to climb in. Without a word she slid into the passenger seat and put her purse on the dash, then picked it up again, moving it from hand to hand as if unsure what to do with it.

It was not until I pulled away that she finally spoke.

"Wait." She put her hand on my arm. "Can we talk for a moment?"

"Sure." I eased my foot from the accelerator and turned to face her, noticing the look upon her face for the first time. "What's wrong?"

"Nothing." Her eyes fell to her lap. "Well that's not entirely true…"

"What's going on Nancy?" I knew her well enough to tell when she was upset. "What is it?"

"Gosh, I don't know how to say this…"

"Say what?"

"I…" She met my gaze for a moment, and then looked away once more. "I don't want to hurt you Jimmy, but…"

A strange crawling sensation overcame me. Nothing good has ever come from a conversation that started with those words. "Nancy?"

"I don't want to do this anymore."

"What are you trying to say?" I knew very well what she was trying to say, and if I didn't it was confirmed a moment later when she slipped the chain from her neck and removed my class ring.

She held her hand out, the ring sitting in her palm, mocking me.

I looked at her, then at the ring, and back to her again. A void of silence filled the space between us until she spoke again.

"Please, take it." A tear rolled down her cheek and fell between the seats.

"Why?"

"I've been wanting to tell you for a while. I'm not happy. I don't want to marry the first boy I date." She took my hand and pressed the ring into it.

"I don't understand." The ring felt heavy in my palm. It felt wrong. "You said you loved me."

"I'm sorry." She pulled the door open, a sob escaping her lips, and fled up the steps back into her house.

I sat in Timmy Thomson's car, the engine idling in the strange out of sync way an engine does when the sparks need replacing, and waited for her to come back.

She didn't.

As the sun dipped below the horizon and the long shadows of dusk claimed the street I pulled away.

I don't remember how long I drove around town, but I do know that eventually I found myself at the Malt Shop. It was while I was there, giving my untouched strawberry milkshake the cold shoulder, that I heard the bray of the sirens as the fire trucks tore down Main Street in the direction of the Starlight.

To this day nobody knows for sure what started the blaze that ripped through the old drive-in movie theater that cool October night, although all would agree that it started behind the screen, consuming the dry timber frame in minutes and sending it crashing down on the parked cars beneath. Some said a discarded cigarette was to blame, others that faulty wiring had caused the demise of the aging structure, but in the end all that mattered was the tragic outcome.

Twelve people died that evening, all in the front rows, trapped under the remains of the burning screen. Were it not for Nancy Jacobs deciding she didn't love me, we would surely have been among them.

Luck of the Irish

JACOB PULLED THE DOOR WIDE, pleased to escape the rain. His umbrella had done little to save him from the torrential downpour, the wind having turned it inside out within seconds. In the end he'd given up and closed it.

A wall of sound hit him from the far side of the room where a quiz night was in full swing, the participants hooting and hollering with each answer they got right. He glanced toward the noise before turning his attention back to the bar, catching the eye of a server.

"What'll you have?" She leaned casually on the counter.

"Guinness."

"Coming right up." The server collected an armful of empty glasses. She put the glasses in the sink before turning her attention to Jacob's beer. He watched as the black liquid flowed into the glass, all froth and bubbles.

While the Guinness settled, he took in his surroundings. The place was like hundreds of other Irish bars across America, a parody of the emerald Isle that packed more clichés into a thousand square feet than any building had a right to. Mirrored advertisements for Magners Cider and Harp Lager took up the back wall. A blackboard announced the food specials, Bangers and Mash, Corned Beef, fish and chips, the usual fare.

On the wall above the blackboard seven letters stood out in white against a green background. Slainte. Jacob had no idea what the word meant, but apparently it was law that all Irish bars display it prominently.

"Here's your Guinness sweetie." The server broke his train of thought.

"What do I owe you?"

"That'll be six bucks."

"This one's on me love." The voice belonged to a tall middle-aged man with blue eyes, dark hair and a leather jacket.

"Cheers."

"Don't mention it." The stranger had a lilting Irish accent. "I haven't seen you in here before."

"I'm just visiting. The girl at the hotel said this place served a decent pint."

"So you're a stranger to these parts."

"I suppose."

"Well you couldn't have found a friendlier place to spend the evening." The stranger held his hand out. "I'm Marty."

"Jacob."

"Pleased to meet you Jacob. You know, if you're hungry they have fantastic food here."

"I saw the blackboard."

"Best grub in town. Of course, it's the only grub in town, unless you count Thai Palace a couple of miles out on Route 6. They say the food there is excellent, if you like that sort of thing."

"Thanks for the heads up."

"Not me though. Give me good old meat and potatoes any day."

"Me too." Jacob took a swig of his beer.

"Well then, you're lucky you ran into me, or you might never have known about the best cottage pie in the country."

"Best in the country huh?"

"Absolutely. Say, talking of luck, why don't you take a look at this." Marty delved into his pocket and pulled out a small silver coin.

"What is it?"

"This here is a very special coin, a lucky coin. I got it from an old gypsy woman years ago in Ireland. It's over 350 years old."

"Really?"

"Sure is. I had it looked at by a professor at Harvard a few years ago. He told me so himself."

"So what does this lucky coin do exactly?"

"It keeps me safe from harm. In the thirty years I've carried it nothing bad has befallen me."

"I see." Jacob didn't believe a word of it, but the guy had bought him a beer, so he stopped short of voicing his opinion.

"Not so much as a scratch. But I sense a little disbelief."

"I'm not one for superstition."

"Well why don't you take it a while, maybe you'll change your mind."

"I couldn't."

"I insist. You can give it back next time we meet. By then you might be a believer."

"I really don't think I should." Jacob said.

But it was too late. Marty was already pressing the coin into his hand. "There you go, just don't lose it."

"I'll do my best."

"That's the spirit." He glanced at Jacob's glass. "Will you be having another?"

Jacob shook his head. "I should go. Early start tomorrow."

"Come on, one for the road."

"I don't think so."

"Well now that's a shame."

Jacob looked at the coin. A harp adorned one side, and on the other a crown. Both sides contained words that looked like Latin. "Are you sure you don't want to keep this? It looks valuable."

"Now would I show it around if it was worth a bundle?"

"I suppose not, even so…"

"Don't worry. I'll get it back from you soon enough mate."

"At least let me get your phone number, just in case."

"No need. It's fine, honestly. On my life."

"Well, okay." Jacob downed the last of his beer. "See you around."

He opened the door and stepped into the night. Much to his dismay the rainstorm had grown worse. He pulled up the collar of his coat and stepped from the curb.

Two blinding white lights lit him up. A squeal of brakes split the air. There was a moment of fear before the pain came.

Jacob lay in the road. Above him, swimming across his blurred vision, a crowd formed, they shifted in and out of focus.

He heard a familiar voice.

"I'll be taking that back now if you don't mind." The Irishman plucked the coin from Jacob's bloody hand.

"What happened?" Jacob rasped.

"It seems you had a slight mishap there, young fella," Marty said.

Jacob opened his mouth to reply but all that came out was a heavy gurgle.

Marty leaned in close. "I told you the coin was good luck. Well, for me anyway. It never fails to let me know when something bad is about to happen. All I have to do is pass it off for a while, and what do you know, my bad luck becomes someone else's." He straightened up. "Thanks for saving my bacon. You're a good sport." He pocketed the coin and pushed his way back through the throng of gawkers.

Jacob tried to call after him, but this time not even a gurgle escaped his lips as the blackness closed in.

The Carnival

IT APPEARED OVERNIGHT in Potts Field on the east side of town.

Mrs. Caldwell, who ran the hardware store on Main, said she went past the field before dusk, on her way to the Aimes Family Farm to play Bridge with Dorothy Aimes, and the field was empty. When she drove home later that night there it was, plain as the nose on her face. How a carnival had managed to sneak into town and set up, tents, rides and all, in such a short time was anybody's guess, but they had.

"She must have been drinking," my father surmised when he heard the story the next morning from Edgar Bailey, who lived next door to us. "Either that, or she's just crazy. Besides, if a carnival was coming to town there would be posters up, and I haven't seen anything."

And it was true, there were no posters hanging in the days prior to the arrival of the mysterious travelling carnival, but the next day there were flyers all over town, posted on telegraph poles, on fences, and even on a notice board outside town hall. These too had magically appeared overnight.

Not that I cared. I had bigger things on my mind, like getting to work. I'd recently landed a job as a waitress at the

Silver Spoon Diner out on Route 20 and my boss was a
stickler for punctuality. I also wanted to avoid Bobby Bailey,
son of the aforementioned Edgar, who had developed a crush
on me the previous year while we were still in school and had
been pestering me for a date ever since. The fact that he lived
a mere hundred yards from my front door made avoidance a
somewhat daunting feat, but one which I had become pretty
good at, even if I do say so myself.

I slipped from the house, ever vigilant, and hurried to my
car, sliding behind the wheel of the 1951 Oldsmobile 88 that
my father purchased as a bribe to ensure I graduated with
straights A's. This I had done, thereby foiling his plot to avoid
buying me a car. It was eight years old with a dent in the right
wing, but it drove like a dream and it was all mine.

My route to work took me out past Potts Field. It certainly
didn't look like the carnival could have sprung up in a matter
of hours. There were at least twenty stands and a bunch of
small tents, each painted in garish shades of red and green.
These were arranged on each side of the midway. Which in
turn led to a large white and red striped tent, not unlike a
circus big top. Then there were the rides, clustered up and
down the midway in between the smaller attractions. Tilt-a-
whirl. Carousel. The Caterpillar. Tallest of all, standing at the
end of the fair, the Ferris Wheel.

I didn't have time to ogle for long though. In no time I had
left Potts Field behind, and a scant ten minutes later pulled up
behind the diner, easing the car into a space between the
dumpster, and a beat-up old Chevy that belonged to one of
the busboys.

The Silver Spoon had been a town staple for over thirty
years, despite being two miles out of town. Built from a
salvaged dining car the building still retained much of its rail-
road heritage, and even had a set of rusting steel wheels
hidden beneath strips of white painted wooden trellis that ran
the length of the car. The one thing that was an obvious addi-

tion was the small hut attached to the back of the diner, which served as the kitchen and rest rooms.

I glanced at my watch.

I'd made it with ten minutes to spare. Not bad.

I pulled my apron from the back seat and hurried inside through the back door. My heart fell when I saw Bobby Bailey perched upon one of the red swivel top stools, his elbows dug into the countertop, a glass of soda going flat in front of him.

Jenny Bowers, two years my senior and the longest serving waitress at the diner, met me at the kitchen door. "He's been here for twenty minutes. Sorry."

"Dammit." I wasn't one to curse, but the situation seemed to warrant it. There was only one person in the place, and it had to be him. "Dad must have mentioned I was working today."

"I could tell him you called in sick." She raised an eyebrow. "Maybe he'd leave. You could hide out here for a few minutes."

"No. He knows I'm not sick. He lives next door, remember?" I wished getting rid of him would be that easy.

"He certainly is persistent."

"Tell me about it," I sighed. "He's asked me out twice this month already, and three times last month."

"Aw. Puppy love." Jenny pulled a face and laughed.

"Stop it." I was not amused. "How would you like it if he was following you around with those doe eyes?"

"Karen Winthrop, I swear, you're so picky." Jenny grinned, mischief dancing on her face. "He's kind of cute."

"No, he's not."

"Well, maybe not, but I bet he'd be good for a night out at the pictures. You might even get a large popcorn out of it."

"Didn't your mother ever tell you it's not nice to lead people on?"

"Yes, but I didn't listen. Hey, maybe you could go to the drive-in, I hear they have a horror double feature this weekend. You could cuddle up to him if you get too scared." She stifled a snort.

"Stop it. I'm not going to the drive-in with Bobby Bailey," I said. "He'd have his hand up my sweater quicker than you can say Boris Karloff."

"You're such a prude." Jenny glanced toward the counter. "You should get out there and see if he wants anything to eat. I bet he'll give you a huge tip. You can't say you object to that."

"No. That's different though." I lingered by the door, not quite ready to face Bobby.

"Well, whatever. You're going to have to deal with it sooner or later," Jenny said. "Honestly, the best way to get rid of him is just to go out with him. Act like a spoiled brat, spend a bunch of his money, and he'll soon lose interest."

"Thanks. With friends like you I don't need any enemies." I turned and entered the dining room.

"You're welcome." Jenny's voice floated back at me from the kitchen.

Bobby spotted me the minute I entered the dining room. He looked up, his face broadening into a wide smile. "Well, hello." He ran a hand through his slicked back hair. "I was starting to think you weren't coming in today."

"Don't you get tired of hanging around waiting for me?" I already knew the answer of course.

"Nope."

"Well if you're going to sit there you need to order something to eat." I pushed a menu over the counter. "This is a restaurant not a soda stand."

"What would you recommend?"

He knew the menu backwards of course. The whole town did. Walt Bolton, the owner of the diner, hadn't changed anything for twenty years. 'If it ain't broke, don't mend it,' he would say. The fact that most of his patrons would have welcomed some new items on the menu didn't matter. Even the daily specials had been the same for over two decades. "Just pick something, Bobby."

"How's the Catfish today?"

"Same as it always is, slightly overdone and a little too greasy," I replied. Had Walt been there he would have marched me out the back and scolded me for that one, but it was Friday, and he spent every Friday down at the river with his fishing rod and a six-pack.

"I'll take a cheeseburger then." Bobby put the menu down. "Extra pickles and ketchup."

"Anything else?" I scribbled his order down on a ticket.

"Maybe some fries."

"Cheeseburger and Fries. Got it. The same thing you always get." I ripped the sheet from the order pad and was about to run it back to the kitchen when Bobby spoke again.

"The carnival's in town."

"I know. I passed it on the way here." I knew where this was going. I wasn't disappointed.

"Want to go with me tonight?"

"I don't get off until seven. Sorry."

"That's alright. We can go after you finish."

"Well–" I hesitated. Maybe I should just go out with him and get it over with.

"It'll be fun," Bobby cajoled. "Besides, who else are you going to go with?"

"I wasn't intending to go at all." That much was true. "Doesn't look like a very good carnival."

"Haven't you seen the flyer?" Bobby reached below the counter and pulled up a dog-eared satchel. "Here, look at this." He dipped into his bag and pulled out a piece of paper, which he put down on the counter.

"It's a flyer, so what." I failed to see what he was so excited about.

"Look." He jabbed at the paper with his finger. "They

have a freak show. It's in that big tent at the end of the Midway. When was the last time you saw a freak show?"

"Never. And I'm not sure I want to now."

"Sure you do." His eyes glinted with excitement. "Man, I thought those things died out in the twenties."

"They did, because they are sick and twisted. They just exploit poor deformed people."

"Come on aren't you just the least bit curious?"

"Not really."

"Please? I'll drive and pay your entry."

"You're not going to give up on asking me out, are you?"

"Only if you say yes."

I knew when I was beaten. Maybe Jenny was right, I should just give in and let him see I wasn't the princess he believed me to be. I had no intention of being an obnoxious date – that was more her specialty – but maybe if he saw just how ordinary I was, it would dissuade him from pursuing me further. "Okay Bobby, I'll go to the carnival with you tonight."

"You will?" His face lit up like a tree on Christmas morning. "Gosh, I didn't think you'd ever say yes. This is great. Maybe afterward we can drive out to Inspiration Point and hang out."

"Don't push your luck." The carnival was one thing, but I had no intention of driving to some out of the way lover's lane with him.

"Oh. Well, we can decide on that later." He threw his satchel over his shoulder and slipped off the stool. "I'll see you tonight at eight?"

"Wait, what about your cheeseburger?" Great. Now I wouldn't get that fat tip out of him.

"I'm not hungry," He grinned. "See you at eight." And with that he bolted, leaving me alone in the diner.

I looked at the counter, at the crumpled flyer, wondering what on earth I had just gotten myself into.

EIGHT O'CLOCK CAME AROUND QUICKER than I would have liked. Bobby was punctual. In fact, he was ten minutes early. When I came downstairs, he was standing in the front hallway, a green jacket slung over one shoulder. His slacks looked a little wrinkled. I wondered if he had pulled them from the wash before his mother had time to iron them. My father lingered a few feet away. I wondered what they had been talking about.

"You look pretty," Bobby gushed as I reached the bottom step.

"Doesn't she though?" my father chimed in. "My princess."

"Oh, Daddy." I blushed. This was not the first time my father had called me his princess in front of a date. I suddenly felt self-conscious, despite my best efforts to dress conservatively, with a button-down white blouse and blue skirt that fell several inches below the knee.

"What?" He raised an eyebrow. "I can't be proud of my little girl?"

"Enough." I wanted to escape. It was bad enough to be going on a date with Bobby, but this was too much. I took Bobby's elbow and steered him toward the door. "We should get going."

"Hold up." My father switched to protective mode. "I want you back by eleven. You hear me?"

"Back by eleven, I hear you." I would be back by nine if I got a say in things.

"And no funny business." He fixed his eyes on Bobby. "You keep your hands to yourself, young man."

"Yes, sir." I thought I sensed a tremble in Bobby's voice. "You don't need to worry about me."

"Okay, see you later, daddy," I said, hoping to deflect any further conversation regarding my honor. I pushed Bobby through the front door before my father could say anything else, and then we were outside in the cool night air.

We walked to Bobby's car, which was even older and worse for wear than my own. He held the door open for me and I climbed in, noticing the slightly musty, damp odor immediately. I resisted the urge to wind down the window.

Bobby rounded the driver's side and hopped in. "Ready?"

"Sure."

Bobby turned the ignition key. The engine sputtered for a second, then roared to life. "Here we go." He grinned and pulled away from the curb.

Bobby didn't say much as we drove out to the carnival. I sensed that he was worried he might blow the date before it even got started. That suited me. I didn't want to spend twenty minutes making small talk with him anyway.

When we pulled up in the field, I noticed several other cars I recognized. Great. That meant there was a chance I would be seen with Bobby, and the last thing I needed was that getting around town. Before long there would be rumors of our impending engagement, our wedding date even. It didn't matter that none of it was true. I would be inexorably linked to Bobby by an invisible rope, forever to be 'in a relationship' with him. The town was small, and people loved to gossip.

"What would you like to do?" Bobby asked me as we walked the Midway.

"I don't mind," I replied, praying that he wouldn't suggest the Ferris wheel. Being trapped with Bobby atop a ride like that would be more than I was willing to put up with.

"How about I win you a stuffed bear." His eyes alighted on a shooting range game to our left. "I bet I can hit three of those targets easy as anything."

"It looks awfully hard," I said. "Besides, aren't those games rigged?"

"Nah." He pulled a coin from his pocket. "Watch this."

He paid the attendant and picked up an air rifle, inspecting it. Satisfied that it was worthy he raised it to his shoulder. The chain attaching the rifle to the counter went taut.

He squeezed the trigger. There was a soft pop and a hole appeared near the outermost ring of the paper target.

"Dammit. Went wide." Bobby aimed again and fired another pellet. This one missed completely.

"Three shots left, kiddo." The carney sounded bored. "You need a bullseye for a prize."

"I know," Bobby hissed. He raised the rifle and took aim again.

Pop.

A hole appeared below the target.

"Bad luck, son," the attendant smirked.

"I can do this." Bobby paused and took a deep breath, then took his fourth shot. The pellet hit the target to the right of the bull.

"Close, but no cigar. One shot left, kid."

Bobby raised the rifle one last time. He squeezed the trigger. The pellet pinged off a metal bar at the back of the tent, further from the target than any of the others.

"And that's number five." The carney clapped his hands. "Wanna go again, kiddo? You got real close a couple of times."

"Stupid rifle doesn't aim right." Bobby threw the gun back on the counter.

"Come on, son, don't be a quitter. Have another go and see if you can win something for the pretty lady?"

"Not a chance. What a rip off." Bobby turned to me, disappointment on his face. "Sorry."

"You did your best." For a moment I felt sorry for him. "It's no big deal."

"Yeah, it is." He folded his arms. "A real man would have won you something."

"Don't be so hard on yourself. I told you it was rigged, they always are."

For a moment I thought he was going to cry, but then he scowled. "There's no need to rub it in."

"I wasn't." I no longer felt sorry for him. Actually, I wished I could get rid of him. I changed the subject, hoping he would forget about the rifle range. "Why don't we go to the freak show?"

"Really? I thought you didn't want to see that."

"I didn't, but I've changed my mind. It might be fun," I lied. At least it would occupy him for a while longer, and then maybe I could claim to be tired and make him drive me home. Going out with Bobby had not been a good idea.

"If you're sure." He sniffed and rubbed his nose with the back of his hand.

"Come on." I took off in the direction of the large tent at the end of the Midway. Around us the sights and sounds of the carnival blurred into a flashing kaleidoscope of colors and mingled voices, shouts of joy and the cries of excited children. Black shapes cut across our path, silhouetted by the hundreds of garish bulbs lighting up the carnival. Smells assaulted my nostrils, from the sweet sticky odor of cotton candy to the aroma of bratwurst and onions cooking on hot plates.

When we reached the freak show Bobby paid quickly, as if afraid I would change my mind, and virtually pushed me inside.

Apparently, we were not the only ones who wanted to see the freaks. The tent was bursting with people. We jostled our way as close to the front as we could and waited. When Bobby tried to sneak his hand into mine, I brushed him aside and fixed my gaze on the stage. When he reached up and put his arm around me, I turned to him and growled. "Quit it."

He pulled his arm away, a wounded look upon his face. "Sorry. I just wanted to put my arm around you. You are my date after all."

"Maybe later." There was no way I was going to allow him to get his hand in position anywhere hear my boobs, but my white lie would keep him off me for a little while longer.

"Look, it's starting." Bobby pointed to the stage; a look of wondrous expectation plastered across his face. He seemed to have forgotten all about coping a feel.

A tall man dressed in a top hat and tails appeared.

He threw his arms in the air.

A hush fell over the throng of people in the tent.

He waited a while, the silence heightening the tension, and then spoke. "Ladies and gentlemen, boys and girls, welcome. Tonight, under this very big top, you are going to witness some of the weirdest, the most bizarre, and the most terrifying creatures ever seen grace a stage. They live to thrill you, they breathe to scare you. Brought together from the four corners of the earth, at great expense I might add, each one a unique and rare specimen of nature run amok."

A figure stepped from the shadows and into the light. It was a woman, her dress tight and revealing. Her hair flowed over her shoulders in a golden cascade. Upon her chin a thick matte of blonde hair spread upward to her ears, following the line of her jaw.

The announcer spoke again. "I present to you, Jemima, the bearded lady."

The audience remained silent, apparently unimpressed with Jemima, who played with her locks, running her hands through the mass of hair adorning her chin. From somewhere near the back a voice shouted, "get a shave."

A titter of laughter ran through the crowd.

"Ladies and gentlemen, please, have some respect for this poor creature." The announcer shook his head. "Now take your place, Jemima."

The bearded lady shrank back and lingered toward the edge of the stage.

"Next, I present for your approval Dorian, the strongest man in the world."

A second figure emerged from the gloom, a man, bare from the waist up. His upper body was a mass of tense muscle. In his hands he carried an iron bar, which he held up for the crowd to inspect. He gripped each end of the bar and squeezed, grunting as he did so. Slowly he bent the bar into a U shape and held it aloft in triumph.

"Is that all you've got?" A voice heckled from somewhere behind me. "We paid good money to see this."

"Not at all, there's plenty to come, I assure you." The showman raised his arms. "Behold Damian and Daniel. Conjoined at birth, they can never leave each other's company."

A strange figure took the stage, a man with a lump protruding from his chest. With a start I realized that the lump was actually the upper body of a second man, his head lolling upside down. What looked like the stump of a leg was fused to the upright gentleman's rib cage.

"Pathetic," Bobby said. "Look at the way that guy is just hanging there. It must be a puppet or something."

"I know what you are thinking." The showman threw his arms in the air. "How can this freak of nature exist? A monster for sure, but is he the genuine article?"

"Probably not." Someone heckled.

I glanced at Bobby. "This is terrible. Do you want to leave?"

"Suits me." He looked disappointed. "These freaks are lame."

I was about to turn, to push through the thinning crowd, when a voice boomed out across our heads. "Silence."

As one the crowd focused their attention back upon the stage.

A tall, rakish man stepped from the shadows. He wore a

white shirt and black vest. A cloak with red lining billowed behind him.

"What now?" Bobby whispered next to me.

The man spoke again. "Bearded ladies, strong men, conjoined twins. These things are old hat. The real freaks hide in the dark, waiting for the unwary traveler to pass by. Were-wolves, succubus, wraiths." He took a breath. "And vampires." He threw his arms wide.

Bobby snorted. "Really? What's he going to do, show us some fake teeth and climb into a coffin?"

"This isn't getting any better." I turned to leave.

"Wait." The man on stage spoke again. "Why are you leaving so soon?"

Bobby caught my arm. "I think he's talking to you."

"What?" I whirled around. Bobby was right. The *vampire* was looking directly at me.

He spoke again, his eyes meeting mine and holding my gaze. "Do you not like the show? Maybe you don't believe there is such a thing as the night stalker?" He grinned, displaying sharp canine teeth that protruded far more than they should. "And what about your young companion? Does he believe? Maybe I should bring him up here and drain him for all to see. He looks delicious." The newcomer licked his lips, his tongue circling in a long, drawn out gesture.

A nervous titter of laughter rippled through the crowd.

Bobby scowled and folded his arms. "You don't even look real. A cape? Come on. Gimme a break."

"I assure you I am as real as they come, young man. My name is Dmitri Scalokov. I was born in Budapest over five hundred years ago."

"You don't even have an accent."

Dmitri laughed. "Would it make you feel better if I talked like this?" The accent was thick and obvious, like the vampires that inhabited old black and white movies. When he spoke again, his voice returned to normal. "I came to America when

George III still ruled this land. That's a long time to keep an accent."

"So, if you're a vampire, prove it," Bobby said.

The tent fell silent. Everyone waited to see what would happen next.

"You are challenging me. Very good." Dmitri laughed; the sound more sinister than humorous. "Let me see what I can do." He spread his arms, his palms facing up. He looked to the heavens as if sublimating himself, and then, little by little he began to rise.

A startled gasp rippled through the expectant crowd.

Dmitri rose from the floor, his feet hanging freely in the air. Up and up he went, until he was six feet off the ground. He lowered his arms to his side and brought his head down. "Will this make a believer of you?" His eyes found mine once more. I tried to look away but could not. He held my gaze captive. Deep inside me a flutter of excitement pulsed.

"Wires. It's nothing more than a cheap trick." Bobby shook his head. "I'm out of here."

"Ok, let's go," I said, but somehow, I could not move, could not tear my eyes away from Dmitri.

Bobby took my arm. "Come on."

Still I could not make my feet work.

"What are you doing?" Bobby asked, his grip on my arm becoming more forceful.

On stage, Dmitri, still hovering high above the crowd, spoke once more. "Go if you must. I shall see you both later, perhaps?"

"Not a chance," Bobby snorted.

"Oh, but I beg to differ." Dmitri's mouth curled into a thin smile. "I can't wait to sink my teeth into you, young man."

A few of the spectators chuckled. Bobby's cheeks flushed. He glared at the fake vampire. "Why don't you pick on somebody else?"

"So much anger." Dmitri's eyes flashed with mischief. "Perhaps you feel threatened by me, yes?"

"Not really."

"Come now. You can admit it. Out on a date with such a beautiful girl… she only agreed to come here out of pity."

"That's not true."

"But it is, and deep down, you know it. She despises you."

"What do you know?" Bobby scowled and pulled at my arm.

"I know more than you would think. But don't take my word for it. Ask her."

"Screw you," Bobby hissed. "We're leaving now."

"Then go if you must." Dmitri kept his gaze upon me. "And you, young lady, I'll see you again."

A chill ran through me. I tore my eyes from the floating Dmitri and swiveled, as Bobby dragged me from the tent.

Outside, the cool night air was crisp and refreshing. I took a deep breath and did my best to calm my jangled nerves. The experience in the tent had been unsettling, strange.

"That guy needs a good thrashing." Bobby smacked a fist into his palm. "Vampire my ass. Why would he say I'm a pity date?"

"It's probably part of the act. You know. Rile up the audience," I said, but my stomach churned. How could that man possibly know how I felt about Bobby?

"Well then it's a pretty crappy act. You can't just go around insulting paying customers."

"He didn't really insult you."

"Yeah, he did. And the way he was staring at you…"

"Let's just forget it. Why don't we get some cotton candy?"

"In a minute. I want you to answer a question first."

"What?" The writhing unease in my stomach increased.

"Is this s pity date?" Bobby looked at me. "You have to answer the truth."

"Bobby, come on."

"Tell me."

"Of course not," I lied, then changed the subject, hoping he wouldn't press the matter. "Can we get that cotton candy now?"

"I guess." Bobby still sounded like he wanted to go back into the tent and punch the fake vampire. "That guy in there has it coming though. He's just lucky I'm with you."

"For goodness sake, Bobby, just let it go." I laid my hand on his arm. "It was only a show."

"Don't patronize me." He shrugged off my touch and stomped into the crowd.

"Wait up." I followed, darting between the throng of carnival goers, trying to keep up, but somehow, I'd lost him.

Bobby was nowhere in sight.

I stopped and turned full circle, scanning the sea of heads, but still could not locate him. I swore under my breath. How could he have disappeared so quickly? Why was he not coming back for me? After all his pestering to go on a date the least he could do is pay attention and not run off and leave me alone. Surely, he must have realized I was no longer with him. Or maybe he realized this really was a pity date and was even now heading back to his car, miffed because I lied. This was something Bobby would do, I was sure. Leaving me to walk home would be just like him. Well, if he thought I was ever going to accompany him on another date he'd better think again.

I stood there, unsure what to do. I could find the cotton candy vendor and see if Bobby was there, but I had no idea if that was where he had gone. On the other hand, if I stayed where I was, he might return.

The freak show must have ended. Laughing patrons spilled from the big top, merging with the crowd on the Midway. A sea of bodies washed around me. Suddenly I did not want to stay here, so close to that tent. Maybe I should find the cotton candy vendor. At least it would get me away from the freak show crowd. I took one last look around and then started off down the Midway. If Bobby was buying cotton candy, then all well and good. If he wasn't, I would have my answer. I would also have to walk home. I weaved through the throng of tightly packed bodies, finding my way to the edge of the freak show crowd. I'd almost made it when a familiar figure appeared before me, blocking my path. But it was not Bobby.

It was Dmitri.

He stood ahead of me amidst the teeming crowd, which flowed past him like a swift running stream parting around a static rock. The cloak was gone which somehow made him more intimidating. He fixed his eyes upon me. His lips pulled back into a sneering grin. I knew in that moment, that I was the sole object of his attention. Why he would fixate upon me, I had no idea. Perhaps he was mad that Bobby had heckled him so. Or perhaps he just found me attractive and wanted to pursue me. Either way, his gaze made my skin crawl. My step faltered. I felt alone and vulnerable. I looked around in the vain hope that Bobby was returning to me. When I looked ahead again, Dmitri was gone. The crowd had closed in once more as if he were never there at all. My thudding heart quieted. Was it possible I had merely caught a glimpse of the showman and misconstrued his intentions? Maybe he wasn't even looking at me at all. There were certainly plenty of other people around, and upon reflection, it seemed unlikely that he would even recognize me regardless of Bobby's earlier taunting. I started off again in the direction of the cotton candy stand. The crowd was thinning now, dispersing to the four corners of the fairground. I soon came up on the stand. Five or six people waited in line to receive their sugary treats, but to my dismay Bobby was not there. Either he had already purchased the cotton candy was now searching for me just as I looked for him, or my previous suspicion was correct, and he'd abandoned me. I turned back toward the middle of the fair intent upon retracing my steps.

And there was Dmitri again.

He stood across the Midway near the coconut shy and this time there was no mistaking the object of his gaze. If only Bobby had been at the cotton candy stand, Dmitri might not have felt comfortable in his pursuit. Alone, I had no doubt that he was stalking me. Had this been his intention all along? Drive a wedge between myself and Bobby to isolate me? But that was crazy. He hadn't seen me before tonight and even if he did have such a nefarious plan, it would require such an amount of good luck and coincidence to achieve that it became practically absurd to even contemplate the idea. Yet there he was. And whether by design or happenstance, I was alone and vulnerable.

I let out a fearful whimper.

My stomach clenched.

Dmitri took a step forward, his movements unhurried. He kept his eyes upon me, a predator focused upon its prey. Despite the presence of hundreds of people, I felt as unsafe as I ever had, perhaps even more so. I took a step backwards and turned to flee. And almost knocked Bobby to the ground.

He looked momentarily confused, standing there holding two fluffy clumps of pink cotton candy atop a pair of cones. "Whoa. Careful."

"Sorry." I felt a surge of relief.

"I was looking for you." Bobby held one of the cones out. "You're lucky this isn't all over your front."

"I know."

"What were you doing, anyway?"

"I was… I mean…" I was still shaken. I struggled to form a cohesive sentence. Eventually I got it out. "Dmitri. He was following me."

"What?" Bobby scowled. He narrowed his eyes and glanced around. "That loser from the freak show?"

"Yes."

"I don't see him." Bobby shrugged.

I turned and scanned the crowd, but no one was paying us any attention. Dmitri was gone. "He was right there. Watching me."

"Well, he's gone now."

"I know that. But he was here. I swear."

"You sure you didn't just get spooked and think you saw him?" Bobby took a bite of his cotton candy. "That freak show was creepy, but I'm pretty sure it was all an act."

I know what I saw," I snapped. "I don't care if you believe me or not."

"Okay. Fine. I believe you." Bobby rolled his eyes. "If he comes back, I'll bop him one. How about that. No one messes with my girl."

"Can we just go?" I couldn't shake the creepy feeling that had overcome me when I saw Dmitri slipping through the crowd toward me. The way he looked at me... it made my skin crawl. There was something weird about this carnival. Plus, I wasn't Bobby's girl. "Would you mind?"

"But there's so much left to do," Bobby said. "We haven't even ridden the tilt-a-whirl. That's my favorite. Although I got sick on it a few years back. Up chucked all over my shirt. I'd eaten a lot of hotdogs that day, though. You should have seen it. I probably wouldn't heave this time."

"I know." I would leave on my own if need be, but I hoped Bobby would come with me. "Please?"

"Fine. We'll leave." Bobby didn't look happy. "I guess I'll have to come back tomorrow night to do the good rides."

"There's no need to be snippy."

"You're right. I'm sorry." The annoyance dropped from Bobby's face and transformed into a puppy dog stare. "Please don't be mad at me."

"I'm not mad at you. I'm just creeped out." We started toward the exit, pushing our way through the crowd. I felt my anxiety dropping the closer we got to the turnstiles. As we neared the parking lot I slowed and glanced back toward the freak show tent, but it was closed up and dark now. The last show of the evening had finished. There was no sign of Dmitri. I breathed a sigh of relief. Maybe I had just imagined it? Only deep down I knew that I had not. I suppressed a shudder and followed Bobby to the car.

"What you want to do now?" Bobby asked as he reversed from the parking space.

"I think we should just go home."

"It's still early."

"It's nine thirty." I faked a yawn. "I have an early shift at the diner tomorrow."

"It cannot be that early. The diner doesn't open until eleven."

"And I have to be there by ten to do prep."

"Oh. That's still not early. Not really." We'd reached the edge of the parking lot, which was actually nothing more than the field. Bobby pulled the car to a halt and looked both ways. "I have an idea."

"What?" A flurry of panic welled inside of me. "What are you doing?"

"You'll see." Bobby flicked to the indicator and swung the wheel turning left onto the road.

"The town's in the other direction. You're going the wrong way."

"We're not going back to town. Not yet. I want to show you something."

"I told you I wanted to go home." I squirmed in my seat, uneasy.

"Don't worry about it." Bobby took a hand from the steering wheel. It came to rest on my knee. His fingers inched the skirt up until they were against bare flesh.

"Hey. Quit it." I slapped his hand.

He withdrew it with a startled yelp. "What was that for?"

"You know very well what that was for. Don't try getting handsy with me."

"I wasn't."

"You really were." We were far from the fairground now. I glanced back through the rear window but all I could see was a haze of light hanging over the field and the distant outline of the Ferris wheel. Pine trees clustered to the sides of the road. It was impossible to see in the dark, but I knew there was a drop to our left. We were driving up into the hills outside of town. It didn't take a genius to figure out where he was taking me. "I've told you already, I don't want to go to inspiration point."

"Come on. Just for a few minutes. You'll love the view. You can see all the way across the valley."

"I don't think that's the view you're looking forward to."

"If you didn't want me to bring you up here, you shouldn't have led me on." Bobby looked sideways toward me, then back to the road. "Unless you're just playing hard to get of course."

"I'm not playing hard to get. Turn the car around. Now."

"I can't. Not yet. The road's too narrow. I'll turn around when we get to the Point."

"Bobby, I'm asking you one last time, take me home. I don't want to go to the Point with you. Even if we do go there, nothing's going to happen. I assure you of that."

"Let's wait and see." Bobby switched the radio on. Elvis filled the cabin, crooning about being in love.

I reached out to turn it back off.

"Hey. I like that song." He pushed my hand away from the knob. "It's my car. I get to pick the music."

"Fine. Leave it on." I watched the headlights race along the road ahead of us and there, on the left, was a pull-in. I pointed toward it. "You don't need to go all the way to inspiration point. There's a turnaround right there. Take me back to town."

"Just come up to the Point for five minutes. Please?"

Bobby sounded like a petulant child about to throw a tantrum. "I've never been up there with a girl."

"And you're not going there with this one either." I reached across and grabbed the steering wheel as the turn-around raced toward us.

Bobby let out a startled cry and fought against my efforts to turn the wheel. "What are you doing? This isn't safe."

"Then stop arguing with me and do what I want." I refused to let go of the wheel. The car started to drift across the center line. Bobby wrenched the steering wheel back in the other direction and the vehicle lurched back into its lane. The passenger side wheels slipped off the road and mounted the shoulder, kicking up dust. Pine trees whizzed by, much too close. Afraid the car would leave the road entirely, I let go of the wheel.

Bobby wasn't expecting it. The sudden lack of resistance sent the wheel spinning to the right. The car started to turn into the trees. Bobby swore and tried to steer us back onto the road and for a moment I thought he'd succeeded. But instead of straightening up, the car kept careening to the left. The back now acted like a pendulum swinging us around.

I cried out.

The road slipped across my field of vision and as it did, I noticed a figure standing in the road, straddling the centerline. A figure I recognized with a jolt of fear.

Dimitri.

He smiled and watched the car lurch across both lanes toward the pull-in. I glanced toward Bobby, to see if he'd seen the carnival's freak show vampire too, but if he had, it was impossible to tell. His face was tense with fright, eyes bugging from their sockets. I turned my attention back to the road, but now Dimitri was gone. There was no one there. Had I imagined him? I had no idea, and there was no time to contemplate it. We were spinning dangerously close to the edge of the road, and beyond it a fifty-foot fall into oblivion. If we didn't smack headlong into a tree first, that was.

I screamed and screwed my eyes tight closed.

My stomach heaved upward into my mouth. I felt dizzy. The car's engine roared louder than ever in my ears. There was a high-pitched squeal and I imagined us smashing through the barrier and dropping. I waited for the final crunching impact.

Then I noticed we weren't moving anymore. The car had come to a halt.

"Hey." A voice cut through my terror. "Open your eyes."

I didn't want to. Who knew what horrific sight awaited me. Were we dangling half over the ledge, back wheels fighting for traction? Had we careened down and were even now balanced precariously against a pine trunk, ready to tip back into the void at any moment?

"Karen, sweetie. Open your eyes."

"Don't call me sweetie," I snapped. I was not Bobby's sweetie. Far from it. The fear gave way to annoyance and I opened my eyes. There was nothing but blackness beyond the windshield. Apparently, we had not gone over the edge. I looked toward Bobby. He sat unmoving with his hands on the wheel staring straight ahead. "Now will you take me home?"

Bobby didn't reply. He didn't even look at me. He just kept on glaring out through the windshield.

"Answer me, Bobby." I didn't care if he was mad because I didn't want to drive up to Inspiration Point and make out with him. If that was what it took to get through to him, then so be it. Come to that, I didn't care if I ever saw him again. I glared at the silhouetted outline of his head. "Ignore me then. See if I care. But if you don't take me home right now, I'm going to get out and walk."

THE MORNING SUNLIGHT streamed in through my bedroom window. I opened my eyes and sat up, the events of the night before lingering in my head like a bad dream. Bobby had turned out to be a heel, just as I expected. Still, I had fulfilled my obligation and went on a date with him. A liaison that had ended in chaos of his own making. If only he'd listened to me and driven us straight home the incident on the road to Inspiration Point would have been avoided. He was a jerk. But at least his puppy love had been vanquished. It was unlikely he would attempt to ask me out again, and even if he did, I had the perfect retort. Regardless, I felt a flicker of anger when I thought about his behavior. What was he planning to do up at Inspiration Point? I didn't believe for one moment that he just wanted to show me the fantastic view. He was a sad, pathetic individual. He was also dangerous. He had better stay out of my way from now on lest I tell my father about his antics.

I jumped out of bed and went to the bathroom where I freshened up. I'd slept later than I intended and did not wish to be late for my shift at the diner. I dressed quickly and hurried downstairs. On the way to the front door, I scooped up my car keys. Mother called out from the kitchen, telling me I should eat something. I declined, calling back that I would get something at work. As I hurried from the house, I waved a quick goodbye to my father, who was coming down the stairs behind me. It was Saturday, the one day when he slept in, and he would soon be ensconced behind the newspaper with a plate of eggs and bacon in front of him.

The car started on the first try and there was no sign of Bobby Bailey poking his head over the fence. I viewed both these things as fortuitous. My car was generally reliable, but possessed a sixth sense regarding my work schedule, and only played up when I was running late. Bobby's absence meant one of two things. Either he realized he'd gone too far the previous evening, or he was still asleep. Either way, I was glad to escape unnoticed. I pulled away from the curb and was soon heading down Route 20 on the way to the Silver Spoon. Which was why I noticed that the fair, which had occupied Pott's Field mere hours before, was now gone. I slowed and craned my neck to see any sign of the strangely absent carnival. That it had set up out of the blue overnight was weird, that it remained only one evening and then vanished as if never there, was downright baffling. It hardly seemed worth the expense to stay in town for a single night. But I didn't have time to ponder such things. I had a job and a boss who would dock my wages if I showed up even a minute late. I pressed on the accelerator and arrived at the diner with only moments to spare. I jumped from the car and donned my apron as I hurried toward the back door.

Walt was waiting near the kitchen. "About time, Miss Winthrop."

"I'm not late." Even so I glanced up at the clock to confirm my prognosis.

"Only by a hair's breadth." Walt shook his head and disappeared into the kitchen. As the double doors swung shut, I caught a whiff of fried fish and grease.

I glowered at the spot my boss had recently occupied and continued into the dining room.

"Walt's in a fine mood today," I said to Jenny, who was busy shining the knives and forks in a tub of lemon water.

"Isn't he though?" She shot me a sympathetic smile. "He complained about my apron not five minutes ago. Said it looked wrinkled. Like anyone would care in a dump like this."

"Speaking of which," I replied, nodding toward the pile of glistening cutlery. "Why are you bothering with that? It'll all be knee deep in fried food before you know it."

"Someone has to keep the standards up around here." Jenny glanced toward the kitchen. "And it ain't gonna come from the direction of Walt's cooking, that's for sure."

We laughed at that. Quietly. There was, after all, only a

thin wall between us and our boss. Jenny continued her chores, silently wiping down knife after knife and placing them in the correct utensil tray. I watched her for a moment, expectant, then spoke up. "You haven't asked me about last night yet."

"Last night?" Jenny raised an eyebrow. "What about it?"

"My date."

"You had a date?" Jenny put the washcloth down and turned to me. "You never told me you we're going on a date."

"You were right there watching from the kitchen when I agreed to go out with him. It was only yesterday. You can't have forgotten already."

"This again." Jenny put her hands on her hips and narrowed her eyes. "I wasn't even working yesterday. I haven't been in since Wednesday. If you don't believe me go look on the schedule."

"I don't need to look on the schedule. You were right here less than twenty-four hours ago. We had a whole conversation about Bobby Bailey, for Pete's sake. You're the one that told me I should go on a date with him."

"That's true, and I wish I hadn't."

"See. You do remember."

"I remember all right. But it wasn't yesterday. Goodness, we've had this conversation so many times. Maybe you should ask Walt for the day off and go home. I can handle it here."

"Why?" I didn't want to take the day off. I wanted to work my shift to make money. I was also completely confused. "What conversation?"

"That date with Bobby Bailey, the night you went to the carnival in Potts Field, it was over a year ago, Karen."

"What are you talking about?"

"I really think you should go home."

"Did Bobby put you up to this? Is this his idea of a joke?"

"Karen, Honey. I wouldn't joke about this. We're best

friends. I wish I'd never told you to go on that date. If I hadn't, perhaps this wouldn't be happening."

"Jenny, stop fooling around. If you don't want to hear about my date with Bobby, then I'm not going to tell you."

"You've told me, a hundred times. What he did, trying to take you up to Inspiration Point like that, it was wrong. I don't want to speak ill of the dead, but it is the truth." She reached out and placed a hand on my arm. "Bobby lost control of the car when you tried to make him turn around. You went off the road. He was killed instantly. You're lucky to be alive, what with the injuries and all."

"I don't have any injuries. And we didn't go off the road. We had an argument, and I grabbed the wheel. I know it was stupid, but I was so angry. After that he drove me home." I glared at her. "It was only last night."

"He didn't drive you home. He drove you into the ravine." Jenny wiped a tear from her eye. "The doctor said this would happen. It's the head injury. Just give it some time and you'll remember. You always do."

"I don't need to give it any time. I know what happened."

"Karen-"

"No." I shrugged her hand away. "I'll prove it to you."

"And how are you going to do that?" Jenny's face slipped into a mask of sorrow.

"I'll bring him here, that's how." My car keys were still in my hand. I only now noticed that I had tensed up, pushing them into my palm. I turned to leave, and saw Walt standing in the doorway, his face a match for Jenny's.

"I think we should call your parents," he said. "That's the best thing."

"No one's calling my parents." I pushed past him and fled into the parking lot. A moment later I was speeding back toward town, my wheels kicking up dust.

IF THERE HAD BEEN a cop sitting on Route 20, I would've left them no choice but to pull me over and write a hefty ticket. As it was, I barreled toward town without regard for my speed, and all but skidded to a halt outside of the house. Without even bothering to switch the ignition off I jumped out, raced up Bobby Bailey's path and banged on the door.

"Bobby. Open up." I waited.

There was a click as the deadbolt disengaged then the door opened. But it wasn't Bobby Bailey who stood looking at me. It was his father, Edgar. "What are you doing here, Karen?"

"I need to see Bobby."

"Not this again."

"Where is he?"

"You know very well where he is. You helped put him there." Edgar Bailey observed me with cool eyes. "I think you should leave now."

"Not until I see Bobby."

"Have you stopped taking your pills again?"

"Pills?" I shook my head. "Where's Bobby?"

"Honey?"

A hand fell on my shoulder. I recognized my mother's voice. I turned around. She stood on the Bailey's path with my father lingering a few steps behind. "I want to see Bobby."

"Come along." My mother gestured to me. There was sadness in her eyes. "You can't keep doing this. You have to leave the Bailey's alone."

My father stepped forward. "I think we should take you over to Dr. Mortimer. He always knows what to do."

———

DR. MORTIMER'S office was on the other side of town. He was, apparently, a psychiatrist. Despite my parent's assurances that I had been his patient for more than a year, I possessed no memory of such things. I told them this, in no uncertain terms. I also told them I was fine and was not in need of a shrink. They begged to differ and insisted in I see the doctor. The waiting room was stark and cold with a row of plastic chairs against one wall. A receptionist kept herself busy with paperwork while casting the occasional wary glance in my direction as we waited. This being a spur of the moment visit we had no appointment and as such were forced to wait for a break in the good doctor's regular schedule. When the time came my parents ushered me forward and through the office door into the unknown. This done they swiftly retreated, closing the door behind them.

I was alone.

Except for the doctor, who stood at the window with his back to me. For what seemed an eternity neither of us spoke. I did not wish to be here and even if the visit had been of my own doing, I had no idea what to even say. It appeared that my entire circle of friends and acquaintances knew more about recent events than I did, or so they said.

"We've had a relapse, I hear," Dr. Mortimer said as he gazed through the window.

"That's what I've been told." I shuffled from foot to foot, uneasy. "Personally, I feel great. If only everyone would stop telling me that Bobby Bailey's dead."

"And why would you want them to stop telling you that?"

"Because he's not. I saw him last night."

"Did you, indeed?"

"I did. We went to the carnival on Route 20."

"How was it? The carnival?"

"It was okay, I suppose." I shrugged. "Is this going to take a long time? Should I sit down?"

"Do you want to sit down?"

"I don't know. Are you going to spend the whole time standing at the window with your back to me?"

"That's a fair question. I am paying attention, I assure

you. But if you would prefer that we sit at the desk..." Dr. Mortimer made no attempt to move.

"It will be more comfortable, although I don't intend on staying long. I'm only here because my parents brought me."

"I'm aware of that."

"I should really be getting back to work. They need me."

"Ah. Yes. The Silver Spoon Diner if I'm not mistaken."

"That's right."

"The very place where Bobby Bailey talked you into going on a date with him."

"Correct."

"And you think this all happened yesterday." Dr. Mortimer turned around, finally, and met my gaze.

I felt a prickle of fear creep up my spine.

I knew this face. This was no doctor. He'd followed me after the freak show. He was in the road when Bobby spun the car out of control. Now he was here in this room. "Dmitri."

"I beg your pardon?" The man who claimed to be Dr. Mortimer crossed to his desk and settled in an oversized office chair. He pushed his fingers together and let them rest on the desk.

"What are you doing here?"

"My goodness. It's worse than I thought. You really are one confused young lady."

"I'm not confused. Why are you doing this to me?" I backed toward the door. Beyond it my parents waited. Beyond it lay safety.

"You can't leave." Dmitri smiled. His eyes twinkled with evil joy.

"Watch me." I turned and pulled on the door handle. Discovered, to my horror, that it would not open.

"See. It's just the two of us."

"Why am I locked in here?" I spun back to the fake doctor. "Let me out."

"I wish there were another way, but that's not going to

happen, Karen. Not until we talk about this. You've run out of here too many times."

"I've never been here before."

"So says you." Dmitri sighed as if he'd been through this a thousand times. "Now why don't you come and sit down like a good little girl."

"No." I pressed my back against the door, desperate to put as much space between myself and this imposter as possible. How was he even here? I felt my sanity spiraling into the void.

"Very well." Dmitri chuckled. "You can stand for our session, if you prefer."

"There is no session, because you're not a real doctor."

"Really, and who am I then?"

"You know who you are."

"Say it."

"You're Dmitri, the man from the freak show."

"Do you really believe that?" Dmitri raised an eyebrow. "Ask yourself this. What is more logical? That I'm a psychiatrist who has been treating you for post-traumatic stress and memory loss for the last year, or that I'm the bogeyman manipulating your reality for my own nefarious gain?"

"I think you're the bogeyman. I saw you on the road when Bobby lost control of the car. You were smiling at me. You caused us to crash."

"Did I indeed."

"You know you did."

"What I know is that a little over a year ago you got into a wreck with that boy who took you to the fair. He died. You didn't. Instead, you escaped with a few broken bones and a severe head injury. Now you're suffering from intermittent memory loss, and for whatever reason, you've convinced yourself that instead of a doctor, you're trapped inside this room with a man from the freak show. It's not the first time this has happened."

"I've never been here before." I turned back to the door and rattled the handle. "You need to let me out."

"Very well." Dmitri picked up the phone. He pressed a button before speaking into the receiver. "You can unlock the door now, nurse Monde. I think we're done for today." He replaced the receiver on its cradle and observed a long pause, then cleared his throat and spoke again. "We're going to be spending a whole lot of time together, you and I. Yes, indeed. You should accept the truth of your situation."

I tugged on the door. It was still locked. "And what truth is that?"

"That you are a damaged young lady with a severe mental disorder," Dmitri said. "And that I am your doctor."

"And why should I accept that?"

"Because it will make this all so much easier."

"I won't accept any of this. It's a lie. I know what happened to me."

"Ah, but do you?"

"Absolutely." I pulled on the door again and this time it opened, much to my relief. I could see my parents sitting in the empty waiting room. The nurse, who apparently doubled as a receptionist, looked on, her face blank and expressionless. Like a store mannequin posed in a frumpy yellow blouse.

I took a step toward them.

"One more thing, Karen," said the man who claimed to be Dr. Mortimer.

"What?" I peered back over my shoulder, a knot of fear twisting in my gut.

"Take care out there, my dear." The doctor's lips slid up into a sneering grin. His eyes narrowed. "You never know when the bogeyman will come a calling."

Cry of the Banshee

JOHN O'BANNON AWOKE, his eyes snapping open, an instant before the recollection of his surroundings rushed back to meet him. From across the room, through heavy lead paned windows, fingers of silver moonlight inched across the floor. Silhouetted against this pale reflected glow stood a chair, his clothes draped across it in such a way that when his eyes settled upon it he saw, briefly, a clawing, creeping shape that made his heart quicken, before common sense vanquished the terror. He breathed deeply, relieved to be alone. Nothing was coming for him, no skulking, looming demon, just trousers and a rumpled shirt. Plain. Ordinary.

Inside the shirt, in his breast pocket, a folded sheet of white cotton laid paper, the words upon it the instrument of bad news, a summons that had drawn him back to this bleak and dreary place.

It seemed an age ago that he had been at home in Manhattan, not merely two days. Since then he had requested a leave of absence from his lecturing position in New York, boarded a flight, made the long car ride from Dublin to Abbeyfeale, and out past the ruined walls of Purt Castle, in the direction of Diabhal House. A place he had not seen for more than twenty years. A place he'd hoped never to see again. The last few moments of the journey, as he walked across the driveway to the front entrance of the building, a sodden newspaper held above his head to protect from the winter downpour, had been the longest of his life.

He lay still, listening to the sounds of the house, the groans and creaks that had so terrified him as a boy. It was just the old place settling, his mother had said, but still it had the power to strike fear in his heart. Tonight though, a new sound joined the old familiar ones, a dry wail that rose on the wind, thin and distant.

His thoughts turned to his uncle, the man who had sent him the letter recalling him to this place, laying alone down the hall. He was dying, that much was evident. Gone was the robust man with the shock of flame red hair that had made John's life hell in the years after his parents died. Instead he'd found a pale shell of a man, his body ravaged by disease and the unforgiving grip of time.

Despite his reluctance to leave the warm cocoon of the bed, he felt compelled to check on his uncle, make sure the old man was sleeping, that he hadn't heard the distant shrieks and decided they were the call of the ghost that had plagued the minds of his family for generations.

John slipped from between the sheets, grimacing as the cold floor met his bare feet. He drew on a robe and padded down the hallway, pausing briefly before pushing his uncle's door open.

"Is that you boy?"

"Yes uncle." He was forty-two years of age yet was still a boy in the older man's eyes.

"Come in. Close the door."

John complied, wishing the man had been asleep. "Are you feeling alright?"

"Now what sort of stupid question is that?" The words degenerated into a bout of coughing.

"Did you take your pills?"

"Of course I did. There's no need to harass me so. You're as bad as the nurse that comes up from Kilkinlea."

"I just want to make sure you're comfortable."

"Comfortable? Bah, you're just like all the others, out for what you can get. Like that doctor that wants to shuffle me around to all those specialists, like that solicitor who keeps hounding me to get my affairs in order. What do I care, dead is dead. Why would I give a rat's ass about the living once I'm gone?"

"They're just trying to help you." John wondered why he'd bothered to come. His uncle was just as mean as ever. "Besides, you wrote to me, remember. You asked me here."

"I know, I know." His uncle's voice lost a little of its harsh tone. "Pass me those powders?"

"These?" John followed his Uncle's gaze toward the nightstand, to the painkillers. He picked up the sachet and poured a glass of water from the jug that stood nearby. He dropped the powdered medicine into the glass.

"Well mix it in then." His uncle studied him with narrow black eyes. "Make sure it's all dissolved. Use the spoon. Quickly now."

John stirred the concoction and handed it over, watching his uncle swig the medicine laced water. "Better?"

"Not really." He placed the empty glass on the nightstand. "I'm surprised you had the nerve to come back here."

"You're dying. I'm not that cold hearted."

"I'm dying, that much is true," the older man said. "Not too long now either. Do you hear the lament?"

"You don't actually believe that old story do you?" John had almost tuned out the sound, but now it seemed closer than before.

"I do, and so should you."

"It's nothing more than a barn owl, that's all."

"Barn owl. When did you ever hear a barn owl make a

noise like that?" The old man looked in the direction of the window. "She's coming for me. Wailed the last two nights she has. Time's short now boy."

"You should get some sleep. We can talk in the morning." John glanced toward the door. Despite his loathing of this place the bed down the hall was a welcome friend right now.

"She won't forget you know."

"Who won't?"

"The Banshee. Doesn't matter if you run away to America. She'll come to claim you just like she's claimed every O'Bannon for ten generations."

"I didn't go to America to escape the Banshee," John said. "I went there to escape you. Don't you remember what you were like? How you treated me?"

"Past is past."

"Except for the Banshee?"

"Except for her. She never forgets." The old man broke down in another fit of coughing. "I'm tired. You can go now."

John stood for a second. Silence filled the air. "Well then, I'll be down the hall if you need me."

"I'll not need you again tonight boy."

"Goodnight Uncle." John pulled the door closed and turned toward his own room. Outside, beyond the thick walls of the house, the harmonious keen carried upon the wind, close now. It's merely a barn owl out for the hunt, John told himself, but he couldn't help but feel a tinge of apprehension as he settled back into bed and closed his eyes.

———

THE SCREAM PIERCED the thin veil of John's restless sleep. He sat upright, the dying chords of the sound resonating in his ears. For a second there was silence, and then he heard a second cry, shrill and laden with terror.

John sprang up, the covers falling to the floor as he leapt

from the bed. He flung the bedroom door wide, barely noticing it slam into the wall with a sharp crack. He bolted toward his uncle's room, the source of the sound, and barged in, stopping dead in his tracks at the sight before him.

His uncle lay in the bed, but he was no longer alone. Upon the old man's chest, straddling him like a hideous jockey, sat a withered hag of a woman, her long hair grey and wispy, her skin like leather. Her hands were upon his chest, the fingers little more than desiccated claws.

"Help me." His uncle's voice was hoarse. "For the love of God, help me."

"Sweet Jesus." The words escaped John's lips before he could rein them in.

The creature swiveled and leveled her gaze upon him. A thin, mocking smile curled the corners of her mouth. The hag's eyes, set deep within dark rimmed sockets, burned an unholy yellow as they fixed upon him.

He backed up a few paces, his legs like ten pounds of lead, but he could not tear his eyes from the ghastly countenance they now looked upon.

The hag crept toward the end of the bed, her gaze never leaving his, and sat there for a time, watching him, daring him to run. And then, finally, he found the will to escape that room and the impossible creature it contained, but it was too late.

She leapt, a piercing shriek upon her lips, and landed on his back as he turned. Her claws dug into his shoulders, her legs whipped around his waist in a tight embrace.

He fell forward, reaching to break his fall with his arms, and rolled over. The hag, dislodged from his back, scuttled around and positioned herself upon him before he had time to collect his wits.

She lowered her face to his and he smelled the cloying, bitter stench of death upon her breath.

"You shouldn't have come back." Her voice was dry and broken.

"You're not real," he said, because to believe otherwise would have pushed him over the edge into a dark chasm of madness. "You're just a dream. A nightmare, that's all."

"How real is this?" The hag reared over him, lifting her arms, then plunged them down toward his chest. He felt her push within, finding his heart and curling her talons tight around it. Pain flared through his body. An empty blackness danced at the edge of his vision, closing in.

As the darkness ate the last shreds of his consciousness, and the agony ebbed away into the bleak nothingness of death, he heard his uncle's maniacal laugh. "She came for you boy. How do you like that? It wasn't me the Banshee wanted. It was you all along."

The Last Bus

CAROLINE CLEMENTS STEPPED out into the freezing drizzle and instantly regretted vacating the warm shelter of the Queens Head Pub. It was one of those wintery London nights. The kind of evening that made a person want to pull their collar high, hunker down against the wind and rain, and hurry home as fast as possible. Which was exactly what Caroline had in mind. Except that it was almost midnight on Christmas Eve, and in a couple of minutes the last bus would depart from its stop outside the Taj Mahal curry house on Knightsbridge Road. And she was still a block away, thanks to Melanie Jones, co-worker and party girl extraordinaire, insisting on one last round of holiday drinks - for the road, of course.

Now Caroline was late for her bus, and feeling a little woozy, not to mention how hard it was to run in heels. Sober, she might have slipped those shoes off and risked a barefoot dash to the bus, wet pavement be damned, but in her intoxicated state such obvious solutions did not spring to mind. So she ran through the rainy gloom, weaving around an alarmed pedestrian or two, until the Knightsbridge Road stop was in sight. And there was the bus already, idling at the curb on the far side of the street, while a line of holiday revelers boarded and paid their fare. A line that seemed too short given the distance she still had to cover.

"Dammit." She cursed under her breath, and put on an extra spurt of speed, reaching the curb opposite the bus and launching herself into the road with only a perfunctory glance to ensure the way was clear.

She didn't see the black cab, orange *For Hire* sign glowing atop the roof, until it lit her up with its headlights. The cab driver blew his horn, waved frantically through the windshield, and swerved left. For a moment everything was a blur of blinding light and screeching brakes. She felt a rush of air as the vehicle bore down upon her, and smelled the pungent odor of burned rubber as it came to a skidding halt. The driver shouted something, a panicked torrent of words, unintelligible and foreign. And then she was past the taxicab, a little shaken, but otherwise none the worse for wear.

The bus hadn't moved. Good.

She only had a few feet to go now, and not a moment too soon. The last of the passengers was boarding, a gangly twenty-something in blue jeans and a fancy shirt. He fumbled for some change and paid the fare, dropping the coins into the ticket machine.

Caroline was winded, her side burned from the exertion. She reached the bus, smelled the diesel fumes as she passed the engine compartment and made her way to the double doors at the front, pulling her purse out. And then, without warning, the doors slammed closed with a hydraulic swoosh.

"Hey." Caroline stumbled to a halt, glared through the glass door pane at the driver, who did his best to ignore her. She balled her hands into fists, intent upon pounding the doors to get his attention, but before she could do anything, the bus shuddered to life and slipped away from the curb.

"Come back." The words slipped from her mouth even though she knew it was pointless. The bus was already too far away. She watched her ride home disappear down the road as the rain picked up and the wind whipped at her sodden hair. If only she hadn't stayed for one last drink. If only that taxi hadn't startled her, slowing her down. Not that it mattered. There were no do overs in life. She might as well accept the situation. She would have to walk home, a trip that would take at least an hour. This would be a chore at the best of times, but in this weather, it would be miserable.

A thought popped into her head.

Take a taxi.

The words lingered there, a tempting alternative to a cold and wet trek through the darkened streets. But then her practical side kicked in. She only had a couple of pounds in cash, not nearly enough to get home. It would barely cover the tip, especially tonight, when cabs would be at a premium. She had two credit cards, but one was maxed out thanks to a last minute Christmas shopping spree the weekend before, and the other wasn't far behind. Next week, once she got paid, things would be different, but right now she might need the measly sum of available credit for groceries, or more likely, a few rounds of drinks on New Years Eve.

No. There was only one choice.

With a dejected sigh, Caroline turned away from the bus stop. She fished her phone out of her pocket, intending to send a text message to her roommate and let her know what had happened, but the phone refused to respond. A dark, lifeless screen greeted her.

Great.

Now her phone was dead too. She weighed it in her hand, fighting a silent rage that bubbled up from somewhere inside, and resisted the urge to toss the useless device into the road. She would regret that come morning.

Better to take a deep breath and let it go. She pulled her coat tight against the lashing rain and turned toward home.

And then something marvelous happened.

A trembling rumble reached her ears, the throbbing roar of a diesel engine. Caroline glanced back toward the bus stop, hardly daring to hope.

And then she saw it.

From out of the gloomy night another bus appeared, headlights blazing. A warm yellow glow escaped the vehicles windows, inviting and dry. She felt a wave of joyful relief. This never happened. They never put on a second bus at this time of night, even at Christmas. The jubilation turned to disappointment. It was probably out of service and returning to the depot. She readied herself for the bus to sail on past the stop, just another frustration in what had turned into a most frustrating evening.

Only it didn't.

Instead the bus slowed, came to a halt right next to her.

The doors parted with a well-oiled clunk. The warm and dry interior was an inviting alternative to her current situation. Even so, Caroline hesitated. There was nothing on the front of the bus indicating a destination, just a backlit oblong blank space where the route should be. What if it wasn't going where she wanted? She stood on the pavement, wavering between relief and indecision.

The driver turned and looked at her.

"Come along, miss," he said. "We have a schedule to keep, you know."

"Sorry." She took a step forward, climbed up out of the rain. "Are you going to Cromwell Road?"

"There's only one route served by this stop, miss." The driver sniffed and turned his attention forward again. "Take your seat, please."

"Fine." Caroline opened her purse, rummaged for the fare.

"Not necessary."

"I'm sorry?"

"No need to pay. Not tonight. This ride is on us."

"Oh." Caroline closed her purse, surprised. "Why is that?"

"Orders from the management." The driver hit the lever to close the doors. "This ride is free."

"Well, thank you very much," Caroline said, surprised but happy to catch a break. She wiped a strand of soaking wet hair from her forehead.

"My pleasure," the driver said, his tone contradicting his implied happiness. "Now, hurry along and take your seat. We don't have all night."

"Oh, of course." Caroline turned and made her way down the aisle as the bus lurched forward and began to move. She steadied herself and selected a seat near the back, happy to be off her feet.

Caroline glanced around.

The bus was almost empty.

A young couple occupied a bench seat two rows ahead, their arms locked around each other, heads bent close. They appeared to be sleeping. Across the aisle an older man with a sagging paunch spilling over the waistline of his trousers slumped across the bench. A days-old growth of stubble darkened his face and his hair hung limp and greasy against his scalp, circling an oval of shinny bald skin. He met her gaze with dull eyes set into sallow sockets.

She shuddered and looked away, uneasy.

The only other occupants of the bus were a pair of teens toward the front, hoodies pulled over their heads, and an elderly woman with wiry silver hair. She sat a row behind the driver, her hands folded into her lap.

The bus picked up speed, rumbling down the road past storefronts and office buildings.

Caroline yawned. The vehicle's motion lulled her into a drowsy state, her eyelids closing as she slipped into a light doze.

"Hello, my dear."

The voice jolted her back awake.

She jolted from her fugue and glanced up. The old woman from the front of the bus loomed over her.

"Can I help you?"

"You're a new one, aren't you?"

"I'm sorry?"

"I saw you get on at the last stop."

"Oh. Yes."

"It's so nice to have someone else to talk to." The old woman lowered herself into the seat in front of Caroline and turned to face her, arms leaning on the seat back. "People have been getting on and off so quickly that I've barely had a chance to get to know them. I do love to chat with the new passengers. My name is Cora."

"Pleased to meet you, Cora," Caroline said, wondering if the old woman was lonely, senile, or both. "I'm only riding until Cromwell Road, so I'll be getting off soon."

"No." Cora licked her lips, her tongue leaving a coating of glistening spittle in its wake. "You'll be riding with us for a while."

"I don't think so." Caroline glanced down the bus, hoping that one of the other passengers would come to her aid and distract the old woman, but no one paid them any attention. "A few more bus stops, that's all."

"Oh, I really don't think so." A mirthless smile cracked Cora's face. Her eyes twinkled. "You look like a keeper."

"A keeper?"

"A turn of phrase." Cora's smile widened to a grin, her lips pulling back to reveal yellowed teeth. "You will have to forgive me, I get so lonely. I've been riding for such a long time. I missed my stop you see. I was afraid to get off, so now I'm stuck here."

"Surely not." Caroline felt pang of sympathy. "Why don't you ask the driver for help?"

"No need." Cora cleared her throat, expelling a blast of

fetid air in Caroline's direction. "The bus will get back there in the end. I'll just ride it out until then."

"Are you sure? I can speak to the driver if you want. Maybe you can transfer, catch another bus back in the other direction."

"There are no other busses, silly." Cora shook her head. "This is the only one."

"Oh. Of course," Caroline said, remembering that it was past midnight. Nothing else would be running until morning. "I forgot."

"That's alright," Cora said. "I forget things sometimes. Comes with age, you know."

"I'm sorry to hear that."

"That's how I ended up on this bus in the first place."

"What is?" Caroline glanced out of the window, hoping to see her stop, but the street flashing past on the other side of the glass was unfamiliar. She turned her attention back to Cora. "Did you get confused and get on the wrong bus?"

"Oh no, nothing like that. I forgot the kettle on the stove and burned my house down. It was frightful. There were flames everywhere."

"That's dreadful, but I don't see what it has to do with the bus."

"Well, I couldn't stay where I was now, could I. Not after that," Cora said. "I wanted to, but then the bus came along, and the driver was so insistent. I didn't know what else to do."

"Of course. Makes perfect sense," Caroline lied. For the first time since boarding the bus, she wished she'd walked home. It might be warm and dry here, but Cora was obviously crazy, and Caroline was starting to feel uneasy. She turned her attention back to the window. Surely the bus must be near her stop by now. Except that it still seemed wrong outside. A flicker of panic ignited inside of her. It didn't seem like this bus was going to Cromwell Road at all. She stood up. "Excuse me."

"Where are you going, dear?" Cora reached out a hand, took hold of Caroline's arm. Her grip was surprisingly strong.

"I need to speak with the driver. I don't know where I am."

"You are on the bus, of course."

"I know that," Caroline snapped. "It's not the right bus."

"There is no other bus." Cora smiled up at her. "Just this one."

"You said that already." Caroline twisted out of the old woman's grip. "I'll get a taxi."

"No need to get in a tizzy," Cora said. "Better to sit down and wait it out. In the meantime, we can have a nice little chat to pass the time."

"I don't want to talk to you," Caroline beat back a surge of panic.

"Well, that isn't very nice." The old woman was reaching out again, this time with both gnarled, ageing hands.

"I don't have time for this. I need to get off this bus, right now." Caroline waited a moment longer, then pushed passed Cora's clutching hands into the center aisle. She took a step forward, toward the driver.

The man with the greasy hair struggled to stand. He grimaced as he heaved himself up and out of the seat, positioning his wide girth between Caroline and the front of the bus. He observed her with beady black eyes.

Caroline wavered mid stride, surprised. She came to a halt, unsure what to do next.

"Why don't you take your seat again, dear?" Cora cooed. "It's for the best."

"I don't want to take a damned seat," Caroline snapped back. "I want to get off this crazy bus."

"All in good time." Cora was on her feet. "Everyone gets their turn."

The other passengers, the young couple and the teens, had turned to watch the commotion.

Caroline edged forward. The greasy haired man folded his arms and set his legs. It was clear he had no intention of letting her pass.

From the front of the bus the driver spoke. "Alright now everyone, why don't we all settle down. Caroline isn't going anywhere until it's her turn."

"My turn? What turn?" Caroline fought to control her panic. She was close to tears. "I don't understand what is going on. You people are all nuts."

"Don't make a scene, dear." Cora said. "It's not so bad on the bus. There are worse places to be, believe me."

"I don't give a shit about…" Caroline spun around, ready to put the old woman in her place, except that there was something wrong. Cora was not Cora anymore, at least, not like she had been. Her face had morphed into a skull, blackened and charred. Where her left eye should have been there was nothing but a darkened empty pit. The remaining eye, pupil milky and white, remained in its socket despite a lack of flesh to hold it there. Her clothes were burned tatters. Scorched, blistered skin showed through, wet and oozing yellow puss.

Caroline fought to stifle the scream that struggled to escape.

"I'm so sorry, my dear," said Cora, or at least, the thing that once was Cora. Her jawbone moved up and down, held in place by nothing more than two knots of raw sinew and connective tissue at the joints. Flakes of charred ash puffed from the space between her jaws when she talked. "I really thought we'd have more time."

"Time?" Caroline could feel the vomit rising in her throat. "This can't be real."

"Oh, it's real, alright." The greasy haired man spoke now. "It doesn't get any more real than this, sweetie."

Caroline turned toward him, unable to stand the sight of Cora's rictus grin any longer.

She wished she hadn't.

The man's flesh was pallid and colorless, as if he were molded out of lumpy, wet clay. His clothes were dusty and moth eaten. A stench of decay wafted from him, pungent and cloying. But this wasn't what froze Caroline in place. On his forehead, above the bridge of his nose, was a round hole, powder burns blackening the edges. She sensed, rather than saw, the gaping exit wound at the back of his skull.

The young couple, their clothes sodden with blood, let out a low snigger. She stumbled sideways, between two rows of seats, and slumped down on a bench, partly because she felt faint, and also because her legs didn't feel quite right anymore.

She risked a glance downward, recoiled at the sight. Her legs were twisted and broken, a piece of gleaming white bone sticking out through torn, bloodied flesh.

"Oh my, I think she remembers," Cora said, a tinge of regret in her voice. "I do hate this part."

"Remember what?" Caroline asked, but she didn't need an answer, because it was all coming back to her now. The frantic dash for the bus, not bothering to look when she crossed the road, the swerving taxi. She winced when the agony of hitting the windshield, of bouncing up over the roof, came back to her. She whimpered at the recollection of slamming into the unyielding road with a sickening crunch of breaking bones, and never getting up. She cried when she realized that this was the last bus - if indeed it was really a bus - she would ever catch. She wept because she knew that when it stopped, when her time came to disembark, what lay beyond the doors might be more frightening than the vile creatures lingering in here. Unless she didn't get off, stayed with Cora, the man with a hole in his head, and the rest of the passengers, another lost soul trapped in the eternal void between life and death.

Whiter than White

MRS. BARBARA PORTER, Barb to her friends — who numbered precisely one — tore the package open with a zeal usually reserved for Christmas and birthday presents. She plucked the contents from the box, a round plastic container, and squealed with delight.

"It's here. Finally."

"What is?" Emily West, the sole recipient of Barbara's friendship, knew what would be in the box, what was always in the box, but there was a ritual that had to be observed.

"For all your whites, to keep them bright, Whiter than White." Barb recited the slogan on the plastic container.

"That stuff from the infomercial on Channel 10, oh Barb, you didn't?"

"I most certainly did. They got red wine out of a white shirt with this. Oil too. You should see what it does to counter tops."

"I'm sure it doesn't work half as well as they make out," Emily said as her friend fawned over what was surely the latest disappointment in a parade of underperforming products that had made an appearance in Barbara's kitchen over the years. "Why do you always have to watch those infomercials?"

"And just what would you have me watch dear?" There was a hint of condescension in Barb's voice.

"Why can't you just watch quiz shows like all the other middle aged women instead of wasting your money on that stuff?" Emily wished she hadn't agreed to come over for coffee. To tell the truth she rarely had the fortitude to visit her friend these days. That had not always been the case though. Barb had been different before, back in college. It was not until years later that the cleaning fetish had reared its ugly head.

"Quiz shows? Why ever would I want to watch those?"

"I don't know. It's better than infomercials."

"Is it?" She placed the tub of cleaning powder on the table as if it were the most precious thing she had ever owned. "I can't wait to try this stuff."

"Why don't you sit down and drink your coffee?" Emily looked at her own drink, at the white plastic spoon and oblong packet of sugar her friend had placed on a folded napkin. This was a new development. Barb had decided that no one could touch her silverware for fear of contamination. Apparently germs were everywhere.

"Nonsense my dear, there's cleaning to be done."

Emily sighed. The kitchen was a picture of perfection, scrubbed Formica surfaces, gleaming floor tiles, appliances that looked like they had just come out of the box. "The place is spotless, please sit down, you're making me nervous."

"Well, just for a few minutes."

"Thank you." Emily reached toward the plate of ginger cookies, her hand hovering as she decided whether to take one. It was a trap of course. There was always a plate of cookies. But where there were sweet treats there were crumbs, and crumbs would not be tolerated. She withdrew her hand and looked wistfully in the direction of the door, toward the umbrella that sat propped against the wall, waiting. The same umbrella she'd dared not open on the way over despite the rain. Drips of water on Barbara's floor certainly would not do.

"So my dear, what's new with you?" Barbara asked, finally settling into a chair, her hand resting on the tub of Whiter than White.

"Nothing much. Harold, my oldest, is going to college in the fall. He got into UCLA." She could feel hives breaking out on her face. She always got hives in stressful situations, and coffee with Barb more than qualified.

"Really? UCLA. That's a good school." Barbara said.

"Yes. It was the first one he applied for."

"You must be very proud."

"I am. He's grown so much since you saw him last. Would you like to see a photo?" Emily reached down toward her purse.

"Well of course I…" Barbara paused, her eyes shrinking to deep narrow slits. "What's that?"

"What?"

"That." Her voice rose in pitch, a faint tremor creeping in around the edges. "Those red marks on your face."

"Oh, it's nothing. Just hives, that's all."

"Well they look dreadful."

"I'm sorry." Emily had no idea why she was apologizing, but it seemed like the right thing to say.

"Don't be sorry, get rid of them."

"I can't. It happens sometimes when I'm stressed."

"Stressed?" Barbara pushed the chair back and sprang to her feet. "Why would you be stressed? Make them go away."

"Don't worry about it, they will go down soon," Emily said. "Just give it a few minutes."

"I don't have a few minutes." Barb drummed her fingers on the table. "They're not clean. Oh my, just think of the germs."

"There's no germs, and getting mad at me won't do any good." Emily wondered if it was time to leave.

"Of course there are germs. Make them go away this instant."

"Barb, I can't, you're making them worse."

"Well if you won't make them go away, I will." Barbara lunged across the table, sending the plate of cookies crashing to the floor. She fell upon her startled friend, gripping her by the hair. With her other hand she reached out and found the tub of cleaning powder.

It only took a second for Emily to regain her senses. She lifted her arms, pushing back against Barbara, trying to dislodge the heavier woman, almost doing so.

But not quite.

Instead, Emily's chair shifted and started to tilt, the front legs lifting from the floor. It teetered for a few seconds, fighting gravity, and then toppled. She let out a brief scream before her head cracked hard on the gleaming white floor tiles. The thud reverberated around the kitchen.

Barbara sat astride her dazed friend and pried the top off the tub of Whiter than White, throwing it to aside. She reached in, her fingers finding the round abrasive scrubber and closing over it. Next, humming a tune that had been rattling around her brain for days, and with a wide grin on her face, she loaded up with powder and went to work...

BARBARA SAT ON THE FLOOR, her chest heaving from the exertion.

The screaming had finally died down to a wet gurgle, and then stopped altogether. It was funny how she'd noticed all those other blemishes once she started scrubbing, a mole here, and a freckle there.

The tub of Whiter than White lay half empty on the floor next to her, it's top lost somewhere under the table. It had certainly done its job though.

She admired her handiwork, studied the gleaming white skull that stared up at her without so much as an ounce of appreciation. At least Emily would not have to worry about those unsightly hives now. Not that she had said thank you of course, that would be too much.

Barbara looked down at herself, at her dress, her legs and arms, all covered in her friend's blood. That would never do. She picked up the tub of cleaner and dunked the scrubber down into the powder once more, and went to work. She rubbed, moving the pad over her knees, her thighs, ignoring the pain that flared with each pass. Soon she'd be spotless just like Emily, and it was all because of her new tub of cleaning powder. Thank heaven for Whiter than White…

The Cellar

ETHAN TURNER STOOD STRAIGHT, stretched and leaned against the shovel. A trickle of sweat weaved its way down his brow and into his eyes. It stung. He blinked the salty fluid away.

"Mr. Turner?" A voice drifted from above. "Are you down there?"

Ethan glanced up the stairs, to the open cellar doorway, where Jed Thomas, the contractor hired to refit the plumbing, stood waiting, his burly frame blocking the light.

"Is it knocking off time already?" Ethan asked.

"I'm afraid so." Jed nodded. "It'll be getting dark soon. The wife doesn't like me to work late, not these days. Says it's not good for me."

"Well, I wouldn't want to upset your wife. That would never do," Ethan said. "How far did you get?"

"The bathroom is all finished, and I made a start on the hot water tank in the attic," the plumber coughed, a hacking dry expulsion of air that came accompanied by a few flecks of spittle. "I turned the water back on, so you can wash up if you like."

"Thanks, Jed. I appreciate that."

"All part of the service." Jed rubbed his greasy hands together. "I'll finish up on Thursday, if it's all the same to you. If you need me before then just give me a call. You have the number, right?"

"I do." The plumber had asked that same question twice this week already. "You wrote it on the quote."

"Alright, then." Jed nodded. He lingered a moment, as if expecting Ethan to say something else, and then stepped back. The plumber's large form disappeared; the door swinging closed now that there was no one there to stop it. The hallway light shrank until it was nothing more than a sliver. Ethan heard the heavy pad of footsteps crossing the floorboards, and then the thud of the front door.

Ethan was alone.

He stood a while listening. The now silent building felt different with the plumber gone. Less welcoming. Ethan felt a prickle of apprehension.

"Best get on with it," he mumbled to himself, breaking the eerie silence, if for no reason other than to hear the sound of his own voice. He glanced down at the pile of earth, newly removed, and then toward the concrete mixer. Just a few more days and the floor would be level enough to lay a slab. Then he would be done with carting the sandy mix of soil and ancient debris up the stairs, through the house, and outside. God alone knew how many generations had added to the junk content of the soil down in this depressing dark hole. Yesterday he'd found a pair of rusted spectacles, the oxidization sure proof of their age, and of bad drainage. He hoped whoever lost the specs had also cured the drainage problem. The last thing he wanted was cracked and sinking concrete.

The light flickered and for a moment Ethan thought it would go out entirely, but then it found a second wind and brightened again. That was something else the house needed. New wiring. The more he worked on the old place the more he wished he'd went with the more expensive, fully restored property, instead of the *bargain* fixer upper. In short, the fixer upper, due to a myriad of suddenly developing faults, was going to be more expensive in the long run - A fact that caused him to wonder about the validity of the home surveyor's qualifications.

The shovel shifted in the loose soil and Ethan stretched once more. It was already past 9PM, and Jenny wasn't going to like it if he worked himself into the ground, which was, ironically, exactly what he was doing. He smiled. Good old Jenny with her battered VW Bug and ideas on the validity of life. Good old Jenny whom he had met on the sociology course a few years before - the same course he had dropped out of in utter boredom just about the time when the lecturer was filling their heads with Emile Durkheim and Max Weber. To Ethan, the course was a depressing insight into humanity's unyielding pessimism.

He pushed the shovel deep into the earth, determined to finish one more bucket load before heading out to pick Jenny up from her spin class. The shovel bit into the compacted ground. Ethan scooped up a load, deposited it in the bucket. He was about to lift a second shovel full when a light touch of stirred air jostled his hair.

He glanced around.

The cellar was cold and drafty. The old coal chute badly needed new doors. The wood was rotten in places. The hinges corroded and loose. A window, caked in grime, sat high toward the ceiling, its warped frame no doubt contributing to the shifting air.

The breeze pushed at the light, a bare bulb hanging from a cord, and made it sway. Soft shimmering shadows moved ghostly over the rough walls. The stonework was older than the rest of the house - Older, in fact, than most of the houses in the village. Some said that they were from a Norman castle that once stood on the site, others thought they dated all the way back to the Roman conquest, which was, of course, impossible. Did the Romans even build cellars like this? Ethan didn't think so.

The light bulb flickered again, and then the cellar was plunged into darkness. Only the blue and red retina burn of the bulb remained imprinted on Ethan's eyes, and soon that faded.

"Really," he yelled in the general direction of the bulb. The agent who sold him the place said it was last wired in the sixties, but Ethan had a suspicion that it was probably more like the forties. The fuses were square and chunky. The light switches were mounted on wood backboards, a sure sign of old wiring techniques. He decided to call the electrician in the morning to nail him down on a date. This was the third time this week the lights had failed. This wiring job was an emergency. If it wasn't taken care of, the rotten wiring was going to cause a nasty accident sooner or later.

He waited, counting the seconds off, expecting the light to return any second. The other two times the lights had gone out they had come on again within thirty seconds. His eyes grew accustomed to the blackness, but he could make nothing out. Darkness flowed like a cape around him and engulfed him, whispering dark promises of childhood fears, and forgotten nightmares, in his ears. He groped in his pocket for a lighter, but the pocket was empty. It was probably upstairs, on the kitchen table. Or out on the back stoop near the flowerpot containing a dead Geranium. He was always leaving it somewhere. He decided to wait for the light to return rather than risk breaking his leg in the darkness, making a mental note to bring a flashlight down with him next time.

There was no point in holding on to the shovel. He pushed it deep into the earth floor, expecting the blade to part the soil easily, but instead it hit on something hard buried a few inches beneath the surface.

Surprised, Ethan knelt and felt around the half-buried shovel blade. It wasn't long before his fingers brushed against wood, and old wood at that. Whatever this was, it had been buried a long time.

He began to brush dirt away from the spot, then scooped it in his cupped hands and threw it to one side. He traced his fingers along the edge of the object and until it disappeared back into the dry soil of the unfinished floor.

He scooted along on his knees, following the wood until he found the edge of the object. Sweeping away loose particles of soil he revealed more and more of the buried object, until he'd cleared a space at least six feet by two feet wide. Clearly a box of some sort, it had odd angles, not so much oblong as…

A sudden, unwelcome thought crept up on him. Was he down here with a coffin?

All of a sudden Ethan did not want to be down here in the dark anymore. His mind conjured up all sorts of images of what might lay beneath him in the coffin - the possible coffin, he reminded himself – and none were good.

He tried to think happy thoughts. He remembered a birthday party, children singing, laughing, but the voices changed and became brittle, terrifying, the children themselves becoming grotesque gargoyles cast from living flesh. He thought of holidays, but the coffin crept in, unwanted. In the end he thought of nothing, just to dispel the phantom that had crept upon him. And then the light came back on...

It stung his eyes for a second and he closed them, letting the red and blue colors that danced, proof of the fact that his pupils had not reacted fast enough, fade to inky black.

The faint blare of a car horn sounded outside.

Normality drifted back. Already the light had purged the terrors of his isolation and he laughed out loud, the noise clattering from the walls and echoing noisily in the cellar. He stood and brushed the traces of dirt from himself with a flicking motion, then rubbed his hands together briskly.

The coffin - of course it had not really been a coffin, he chided himself - lay partly exposed to one side of the shovel.

It was wood though, and it looked old. In fact, it looked ancient.

The wood was black with age, its surface pockmarked and gouged, probably by hungry rats or even someone else's shovel. Maybe he was not the first to find it. Ethan knelt and rubbed the surface with his palm, feeling muck remove itself from the surface. He began to push soil from the object, sweeping it away and uncovering more and more. Then his hand hit something else. Something cold and sharp. Metal...

It was a hinge. Rusted and red, but, nonetheless a hinge, and where there was one hinge, there must be another. He moved faster now, his mind reeling. Had he found an ancient chest? A trove of some kind? He would never be that lucky. If indeed the buried object was a box it probably contained the once fashionable dresses of some old spinster, or a pile of moldy old papers, lumped together by mildew and age.

He found the partner to the first hinge. If anything, this one was worse. He wondered if he would be able to open the lid, those hinges looked rusted tight. He moved to the other side of his find and began to work on that, all thought of time slipping his mind. Jenny far from his thoughts.

The surface was almost clear now. There was a crack where the object ended, and beyond that, what appeared to be stone pavers.

The floor was not dirt after all. It was stone.

Why would anyone go to all the trouble of laying stone, and then cover it with three feet of earth to give the appearance of a soft floor? It did not make sense. He realized the roof must have been much higher before someone imported a few tons of dirt down here. Unless the cellar was older than the rest of the building, meaning whoever built the cellar was not the same person who later disguised the floor with dirt. He wondered why none of the previous owners had noticed the floor and cleared the dirt out. Maybe they hadn't looked hard enough. Maybe they didn't care?

He brushed more earth aside, sweeping it away with his hands, and then stood and looked down at the larger uncovered patch that included a wooden square set into the floor with rusted hinges on one side and a round iron handle. All at once, he knew what he was looking at. A trap door. Which meant there must be something underneath.

His curiosity burning, Ethan gripped the handle and pulled.

It moved, but only slightly. Ethan felt the muscles in his arms begin to reach to their limits of endurance. He let go and breathed the stale air, his chest heaving, lungs trying to supply the oxygen his system was demanding. He took hold once more and pulled upward with all his strength. The trap door seemed to lift a fraction but nothing else. He realized that only the handle side had lifted, using the slight play still left in the old timbers. The hinge side was rusted so badly that it prevented any movement. It occurred to him that he needed something to lever the door open. He looked around, saw an old broom sitting in the shadows, trying to merge with the cobwebs and almost succeeding.

The broom handle was brittle and past the age it should have retired as firewood, but it might work. He pushed the handle under the iron loop and fed it through so that it rested on the earth beyond the trap door hinges and tentatively pulled up on it. The iron loop stood, taut, and the broom handle held. He applied more power and felt the door move a little, reaching the point where it had stopped before, and then the hinges gave way with a gratifying creak. A little more power and the door eased upward. Stale air wafted from the black pit beneath. He wondered if he had found an old sewer service entrance or some such thing. Judging from the smell he could have found hell itself. Then the broom handle snapped, sending the trap crashing back into place with a belch of rotten air and dust.

Silence rushed in to fill the gap left by the sound of the

thudding door. Ethan stood and looked lamely at the broken half of handle still in his grip. So much for that. The dust settled around him. He reached out and took hold of the iron handle and pulled up. The trap wheezed open on its arthritic hinges, easier than he had expected this time, and he almost toppled into the dark chasm below.

He needed a flashlight, something to lighten the pit. He went upstairs to the kitchen and rooted around in the cupboard, finding the flashlight. It shone a feeble glow then the bulb faded into inaction. Great. The batteries were dead. He could not remember the last time he had used the flashlight. Possibly six months before, maybe longer. He thought quickly, looking around for anything he could use, and then he remembered the utility light he kept in the back of his van.

The utility light was orange plastic, its handle sprouting a cord and plug at one end, and a bulb protected by a wire cage at the other. A metal hook dangled from the cage end so that it could be hung up to free both hands. It was better than the flashlight and would light the chasm up like day... hopefully. There was no socket it the cellar, and so Ethan took the extension cord from the van as well and plugged it into one of the kitchen sockets, trailing it behind as he descended the cellar steps. When he reached the open trap, he plugged the light cord in and the bulb glowed brightly, lighting the edges of the stone in which the door was set.

He dangled the light down, letting it hang over the edge, and peered below. He looked directly into another cellar, no, not another cellar, but a sub-cellar. A wooden ladder descended from the trap to the floor of this second cellar and Ethan saw a stone pillar at the edge of the vision granted him by the trap entrance. He swung his legs over the edge and tested the ladders strength.

The sub-cellar was not as large as the one above. A slightly vaulted ceiling arched into darkness at the furthest corners of the room, and square metal plates, now almost eaten away, where the remnants of chains hung like metal tentacles, told Ethan that even if the cellar above did not belong to a castle, this surely had at one time.

The pillar he had seen from above was positioned directly in the center of the small room and blossomed out at the top to form four ridges which traversed the ceiling to the edges of the room. The disfigured faces of gargoyles, their eyes looking blankly at the same view they had seen for hundreds of years, pushed out, as if trying to escape, from the stone walls at the end of each ridge. Cobwebs hung from the ancient stone and the smell, which had been awful before, was almost overpowering. It smelt like something had died here... Which it probably had.

He looked around in awe, his nose wrinkled at the stench. It would be better to breathe through your mouth to avoid the smell, he reminded himself. He cast his eyes over the sub-cellar and noticed the floor. This one really was dirt, but it was what lay in the dirt that caught his eye.

Bones.

And not just any bones. These were human. He saw a pair of skulls half buried in the earth. One was face down, only the cranium showing, the other looked up accusingly from dark and empty sockets.

He stood there, shocked by this discovery, unable to tear his eyes away. All this time he'd been living on top of... Of what exactly? Some sort of mediaeval torture chamber? An ancient and long forgotten tomb?

He steeled himself and counted to ten, resisted the urge to turn and flee. There were bones here, which was alarming to say the least. But that was all they were. A heap of old bones no more dangerous than those from yesterday's roast chicken. The fear abated, at least a little.

He studied the skulls in morbid fascination. And now he saw something else. There were scratch marks below the eye holes and on the cheeks. Deep uneven gouges that looked more animalistic that anything else. Almost like they were made by claws.

There was only one culprit that sprang to mind. Rats. They were voracious chewers and were not picky, gnawing on whatever was at hand.

Ethan shuddered. He hated rats.

Those evil red eyes and black fur. The way they scurried in the darkness.

Now he really felt good. Not only was he living on a mausoleum, but a rat infested one at that!

He raised his eyes and inspected the walls, peered beyond the scattered charnel, and into the room's murky depths. And found himself looking at a door set into the ancient stonework.

He took a step forward, approached the unexpected find.

The door was old. It was made of wrought iron that had turned black with age. Set into the frame was a panel of vertical bars. They reminded him of—he hated to admit it—the door to a jail cell.

He stood a moment, contemplating this new discovery. He peered through the bars but saw nothing. Whatever lay in the room beyond the door was obscured by darkness, and there was only one way to find out. So, in the end he reached out and touched the door, even as his own common sense told him to turn around and walk away. He gripped the bars and gave them a pull.

The door didn't move.

He pulled harder, grunting with the effort.

Now it moved. Opening, inch by inch, with a squeal of tortured hinges. Until it came to a jarring halt. Ethan glanced down, saw the problem. A sturdy chain wrapped around the bars and looping into a hasp on the doorframe. A large padlock hung low, keeping the chain in place.

He lifted the chain, tugged.

No joy. It was not going to give.

He peered into the gap between the door and the frame, pushed an arm inside. Maybe he could slip through? But it was useless. He could barely get arm in, let alone the rest of him.

There was a hammer up in the main cellar. The chain might not give way on its own, but it looked rusty, the metal weakened by years of dampness. A few good whacks would take of it. He turned and hurried up the rickety ladder. A minute later he was back with the claw hammer in his hand. It only took two blows to send the chain clattering to the ground. And he was in.

The utility light did nothing to illuminate the newly revealed space. It remained shrouded in inky blackness. Worse, a rotten smell wafted out toward him. The scent of decay.

He took a tentative step inside the room, put a hand to the wall and followed it until he reached a corner. Another ten feet and the wall turned again. The room was small and square. He now had no doubt. The sub-basement was a dungeon, the remains of a structure much older than the one built above it. And this room was a cell.

Ethan didn't want to be here anymore. He glanced toward the door, a rectangle of light that beckoned him to safety. He took a step toward it eager to escape the stygian darkness. But before he had gone two steps, his foot snagged an object in the soft earth. He almost tipped forward, steadied himself\ at the last moment and regained his balance.

There was something down here, buried in the soft earth below his feet.

Nathan glanced toward the door, contemplated ignoring his find and running back upstairs, and outside into the fresh air. Never looking back. But now his curiosity had gotten the better of him. He knelt, reached down. His finger brushed against a spongy, soft lump half covered with dirt. He brushed the soil away and felt around. It was cloth. And there was more too. Something hard underneath the brittle fabric. He ran a finger along the fall of the cloth and underneath, his skin touching what felt like parchment, hard and rough. He followed it along, tracing the edge of the object until it turned in a gentle curve. Then he felt the teeth...

He whipped his hand away in disgust.

Sweet Jesus.

A skull. And not just a skull. This one still had skin. It was leathery, desiccated, but it was there. A corpse somehow mummified, waiting in the black confines of the cell. How long had it been here? Who was it? The question rolled through Ethan's mind, but at the same time he didn't want to know the answers. He did know one thing though. He wanted to escape this horrific place. This charnel house. He jumped to his feet and backed away. Then turned and fled for the door.

Then he heard it.

A scraping, rasping noise. Like breath escaping a thousand-year-old set of lungs.

Ethan froze. He stopped outside the doorway and turned, afraid to look. Just as afraid not to.

At first, he saw nothing, but then it came into view.

A corpse.

Pulling itself from the blackness, hand over hand as it dragged its body from the cell. The head emerged first, swaying from side to side as if it had been in a long, long sleep and was trying to clear its mind. The remains of what might have been long hair hung limply from the scalp and the eye sockets. Dear God. That was the worst of it. They burned the color of cold blue flame. The creature looked up and fixed Ethan with a cold, dead stare. Then it gripped the doorframe and heaved itself erect. Its mouth gaped open and Ethan saw the teeth he had brushed against only moments before, and his chest tightened.

He had awoken something down here in this dank cellar,

something evil and ancient, maybe even as ancient as the Earth itself.

He scrambled away in fear, even as the creature watched him retreat. It stood on spindly legs that looked too weak to support it, one hand gripping the frame, long dried fingers curling around the stone. It opened its mouth wide and emitted a let out a warbling, angry shriek.

It watched him dispassionately and he wondered for a second if the monster before him really was there, or if he were hallucinating. Maybe there was sewer gas in the cellar. But Ethan knew he was not seeing things. This was real. And if he didn't move now, he might not get another chance. Ethan hesitated for a moment longer, his eyes locked on the creature, then he turned and ran for the wooden ladder.

Behind him, the creature let forth another shriek.

Ethan was at the ladder now. He gripped the rungs and hauled himself up. He scrambled up the ladder, reached the trap door set into the ceiling and pushed his head through. For a brief moment he felt a surge of hope. He might make it after all. Then something slammed into his back. A mummified hand slipped over one shoulder, then the other. Talons dug into his flesh sending white hot flashes of pain searing thorough him. He tottered on the ladder, fighting to keep his balance, but it was futile. The creature was too heavy. With a cry of dismay Ethan lost his grip and tumbled back into the sub-basement, with the creature on his back, riding him all the way down like some demented jockey.

He hit the ground hard. The wind exited his lungs in a mighty whoosh, but there was no time to recover. The beast was already scrambling on top of him. Ethan rolled out from underneath the living corpse and tried to stand. The creature leapt with incredible speed and latched onto him, wrapping its arms around him in a macabre lover's embrace. He fell back once more and his head smacked against the ground, stunning him. The creature arched its head back, the bones of its neck showing through the parchment colored skin. It let out another long, inhuman howl. A cry of hunger.

Ethan tried to twist away, but it was no good. His attacker was too strong. Sharp talons ripped through the fabric of his shirt, slicing into his chest. Blood gushed from the wounds. The corpse opened its mouth and licked its lips, then lowered its head toward his throat.

Ethan saw the two long teeth, needle sharp. He felt its rancid breath on his face. Then the creature bit down and this was the worst pain of all. He struggled, tried to dislodge the nightmare that was slurping the blood from his veins. But he was growing weary now. A tiredness enveloped him. He felt a cold chill spread throughout his body, but Ethan didn't care anymore. All he wanted to do was sleep. As his vision blurred to blackness under the vampire's feast, he remembered he had to pick up Jenny after class.

It dropped his body to the floor and looked up toward the trap door. From above, came sounds of movement.

A woman's voice drifted down into the cellar. "Ethan, Honey? I finished early so I caught a cab. Are you done down there? You must be starving. Would you like to get a bite to eat?" There was a pause, then the woman spoke again, closer now. "Ethan? Are you down there?"

The creature paused a moment, sniffing the air, breathing in her scent. Then it leapt up the steps and filled the house with screaming...

The Frequent Visitor

I HAVE ALWAYS FOUND train journeys to be tedious, and particularly so at night, when not even the scenery is visible to distract the wandering mind from lapsing into a stupor.

I was finding this particular train journey, from Manchester to London, particularly uneventful. This might, perhaps, explain why I ended up making conversation with the rakish gent with whom I occupied a small first class cabin.

He was reading a book of ghost stories, one of those leather bound volumes that are so good to consume in front of an open fire on a cold winter night, which was what made me think of my own story, something that had happened to me years before, the memory of which had been rekindled by a recent newspaper article.

"Have you ever seen a ghost?" I inquired, hoping to stimulate at least a few precious minutes of conversation to save me from the awful monotony.

He peered up, his eyes examining me over his book. After a few seconds, as if deciding that I was not a lunatic, or a bore he would be obligated to entertain for the duration of the journey, he set the book aside. "No, but I have heard several supposedly true ghost stories, none of which I am inclined to believe, and some of which are so utterly predictable that they become tiresome within the first few lines."

"Would you like to hear another," I said. "I can guarantee that it will, at least, be interesting enough to while away a few minutes, and I can assure you that it is true."

He looked out of the window, watching the rain lash the panes of glass. Beyond this the darkness was almost absolute, only the occasional lights from some far away town or lonely farmhouse, breaking the blackness. "Well, it is certainly the night for ghost stories." He shifted in his seat and placed his hands neatly on his lap. "Go ahead, and we will see if your tale is as interesting as you promise."

I closed my eyes, gathering all the details of the events I was about to recount, gathering the happenings from my far-flung childhood memories. At length I recounted my tale. "This occurred when I was a child, maybe nine or ten years of age. I was living in Manchester. My parents are Irish. They had come over to England like so many other poor Irish families to escape the same poverty and unemployment that sent so many Irish immigrants to the New World. I don't remember much about my life in Ireland. I do remember how bleak and rocky County Mayo was, how the wind scoured the land until only the hardiest of vegetation could take hold. It was a different world in Manchester."

I slowly drew breath. "We lived in a three floor house on Maypole Street, which was in one of the poorest districts of Manchester. There were seven of us including my parents. I had two brothers and two sisters. I was the youngest. Due to lack of space my brothers doubled up in a room on the second floor, as did my sisters. My parents occupied a room on the first floor, between the lounge room and the parlor, which was not uncommon in those days among large families. I occupied a small attic room on the third floor. I thought myself lucky to have a room of my own, even if the walls did slope, following the line of the roof. As I recall, the room was always dark and full of long shadows. There was only one window that barely let a drop of light in even on the brightest of days. My imagination created many a demon out of those shadows during the long winter nights I can tell you."

"It sounds like the perfect setting for a ghost story. I do hope this spirit isn't going to turn out to be the conjuring of a small boy's imagination," said my companion.

"I assure you that the apparition in question was no imaginary ghost raised from my subconscious, although that is not to say that the room itself didn't create a few imaginary monsters for me at times. No, she was real, of that I am one hundred percent sure."

"She? So the ghost was a lady then?"

"Female yes, though not a lady, a little girl with piercing blue eyes and an adorable face. At least she had an adorable face in the beginning, but we shall come to that. As I said, at first she had an adorable face... I remember the first time I saw her as if it were yesterday. It was midweek, a Wednesday evening I believe. I was reading in bed by the light of a small gas lamp. This was before the house had electricity, at least on the upper floors. It was common in those days for houses not to be fully wired. I don't know why I looked up from my book, but something drew my attention, perhaps the room turned colder, I don't know. They say that a ghost will create a chill in the air, but I can't recall any change in temperature when she appeared."

My traveling companion shifted in his seat, eager to hear more.

I took a breath and continued. "The room was dark beyond the glow of the lamp. At first I didn't see anything. Flickering shadows licked at the darkness, but one shadow seemed more intense, brighter than the others, and it was moving strangely. I was accustomed to the way the shadows moved, the way the flicker of the gas lamp made them dance over the walls, but this shadow didn't dance. It had a fluid movement all its own. It glided. I watched it for several seconds, although to me the time felt longer. My heart was beating very fast, and I remember wanting to cry out, but I couldn't, my mouth opened but no sound came out. Of course, at this point I didn't know what the strange shadow was, but I knew it was something different, and that scared me."

I cleared my throat, pushing back the tight knot of fear I always experienced when thinking back to that time, and the ghost. "The shadow appeared to be growing darker, and more solid, until I could make out a shape, a human shape. An arm reached out from the shadow, and gradually the arm became clear, it pulsed into focus. The rest of the shadow became clear moments later and I saw a pretty young girl standing translucent before me, dressed in a long billowing white night-dress. I could see my wardrobe through her, or at least the outline of it. I could actually see through her! I remember she had long blond hair, locks of which curled down over her fore-head. I noticed her mouth was moving, but could hear no sound. I was terrified. Then, no sooner had she appeared, than she was gone."

"What did you do?"

"I buried myself deep under the covers and stayed that way until morning, by which time I had convinced myself that what I had seen was merely a trick of the light, maybe a bad dream, or some such thing."

"But it wasn't."

"No. I saw her again several times after that, although not every night, maybe once every few weeks. After a while I got used to seeing her, and she never harmed me, so my fear disappeared. It's amazing how easily you accept things like that when you are a child. The world hasn't taught you that they are impossible yet."

"Did you tell your parents what you had seen?"

"No, I thought they wouldn't believe me, and they probably wouldn't have. I don't think I have ever told them anything at all about the ghost."

"Is that all that happened? I must say, that is not the tale you promised me!" My companion reached for his book again.

"Oh, there is more. Like I have said, the apparition came to me every few weeks on average. At first she was just a sweet child. Sometimes I wished I could understand what she was trying to say, but I could never hear her words, all I could see was her mouth moving. I always thought she was trying to tell me something important, but could never make out the words."

"So when did she stop becoming just a sweet child?" I could see I had aroused the interest of my companion once more.

"That happened later. It must have been about six or seven months after I first saw her that she began to change."

"In what way did she change?"

"It was slight at first. Her hair was a little unruly, her nightgown smudged with dirt. Then the changes really began."

My companion observed me for a minute, taking this in, then bade me continue.

"Like I said, at first the changes were small, but soon they became unsettling. It was a cold night in December when I first felt uneasy. I know it was December because I had been wrapping Christmas presents that evening and had just climbed into bed, later than usual. She appeared at the end of the bed and began to speak silently, as usual, frantically trying to say something. I watched this with fascination as always, but then I noticed that something was different. There was smoke, or at least what looked like pale wispy smoke, rising from her nightgown. Of course, I could smell no smoke, or even see any flames, at least not yet."

My companion raised an eyebrow, but said nothing.

I continued. "The next time she appeared, about a week later, I could clearly see flames around her. In fact, it looked like her nightgown was on fire. She was frantic this time, much more than normal, although she did not seem to notice the flames that were licking up around her, catching her alight. Then she vanished, as suddenly as always."

"What did you do?"

"What could I do? Of course I was rigid with fear at this development. The ghostly visits had been something of an amusement, once I had accepted them, but now they were frightening. She was burning up in front of me." I wiped my forehead, removing a bead of sweat. "She appeared several more times after that, and each time her condition grew worse, until in the end all that remained was a ball of flames. It was quite disturbing, I can tell you."

"And you never told your parents any of this?"

"No. I don't know why. I just had a feeling that even though the apparition was a grotesque sight, the little girl meant me no harm. I never felt threatened. I came to the conclusion that she was desperately trying to tell me something. That I could help her, if only I could have understood what she was trying to say. Of course, by the time the visits stopped there was no way of telling even if her mouth was moving, all one could see was flames."

"How terrible. When did you stop seeing her?" My companion was sat on the edge of his seat.

"Oh, it must have been about ten months after I first saw her. In the end there was nothing recognizable as a human shape appearing, just a mass of flames, and then the flames started to get less each time she appeared, until the apparition literally burned itself out."

"And that was it? You never found out who she was, or why she was appearing to you?"

"Yes, I did find out who she was, but only recently. I had forgotten all about the ghostly visits of my childhood, or at least pushed them out of my mind, until last month. My family moved away from Manchester about two years after the ghostly visits stopped, and I only returned to the city last month when my job required me to start attending meetings there. It is my habit to buy a newspaper each morning, and on the morning in question I took my usual trip, from the lodging house, to the paper shop. When I arrived a headline in the local paper caught my eye, so I bought it, even though I prefer the national publications. The article concerned a house that caught fire and burned the previous night. The upper floors were completely destroyed. The sad thing was that the attic room had been turned into a play room and the eight year old daughter of the house owners had been up there playing before bed. No-one could get to her in time to save her. She was a pretty girl. They printed a photograph."

"But what has that to do with the girl you saw so many years ago in your attic bedroom?"

"Well you see, the house that burned down was on Maypole Street, in fact, it was the very same house that my family owned when I was a boy. That poor girl that burned up in the attic last month was the very same girl that appeared to me as a ghost all those years ago. Her spirit appeared to me thirty years before her birth, to try and warn me of her death, in the hope that I could save her..."

Secrets

WILLIAM LARSON RAN a finger around the rim of his whisky glass, peering deep into the amber liquid within, before lifting it to his lips and downing it in one fluid gulp.

"I'll take another one." He pushed the tumbler across the counter and watched the bartender fill the glass for the fifth time.

"You're really going for it there, buddy."

William glanced left, his eyes settling on the man who occupied the next bar stool over. "So?"

"Just sayin', is all."

"Yeah, I guess I am," he said. "It's been one of those weeks. Hell, it's been one of those years."

"Life's a bitch, ain't it?" The stranger chuckled. "Name's Floyd. Floyd Arnold."

"William, but my friends call me Bill."

"So, what's the deal, Bill? What brings you to a lowly establishment like this?" Floyd waved an arm in the general direction of their surroundings.

"Just looking for a place to stop a while and drink away my sorrows." William looked around. The bar was dark, with threadbare carpets, tables that looked like they had been in the place since Reagan was president, and a small stage near the far wall. Above the stage an ultraviolet strip light bathed the space in a strange purple glow, although there was no band, and no one dancing. An old man, his shirt glowing under the ultraviolet light, a beer bottle clutched in his hand, shuffled his way toward the restrooms, his movements drunken and shambolic.

"Want to share? I can be a good listener."

"I don't think so." William motioned the bartender for another drink.

"What, is it a secret?"

"Yeah, something like that."

"I don't hold with keeping secrets." Floyd took a swig of his beer and slammed the glass down, a little too hard, on the bar top.

"Sure you do. I bet you have secrets. Everyone has secrets."

"Now that you mention it, maybe I have a few things I wouldn't want to get out. Tell you what, you tell me your secret, and I'll let you in on one of mine."

"Nah, I'm not falling for that. You just said you don't hold with secrets. How do I know I won't tell you mine and then find out you've got nothing in return?"

"Alright then. Why don't I go first?" Floyd said, his eyes narrowing.

"Well, that seems acceptable."

"So here's my secret. Bocce. I play Bocce."

"What the hell is that?" William asked.

"It's a game, like bowling, only different. My father came over from Italy in the fifties. He loved playing it. He taught all us kids how to play. He was a bear when he didn't win though, a real sore loser if ever there was one."

"Well, that's not much of a secret. If you want me to tell you anything you're going to have to do better than that." William sipped his whisky, relishing the burn as it made its way to his stomach. "Tell me something more personal. What's the worst thing you've ever done? Something so bad you never told a soul."

"The worst thing?"

"Yeah. That's a real secret. I want to hear that. The worst thing."

"Alright then." Floyd hesitated, looking around the bar to make sure some drunken voyeur had not taken an interest in them. He leaned in close. "I killed two people."

"No way." William shook his head. "You're making that up."

"You said you wanted a secret. You got one."

"Okay then, if you really killed a couple of people, then tell me about it."

"Well now, that wouldn't be too smart of me, would it? Confessing my sins to a total stranger."

"You're the one making the wild claim, not me."

"You still think I'm bullshitting you?" Floyd leaned in, his elbows on the bar. "It was a few years ago when I was still living back east, not that I'd call that filthy flophouse in the Bronx living. There was this club, The Republic. I'd go there every Friday night with the boys." He paused and ran a hand through his hair, dislodging beads of sweat that crawled down his forehead. "You ever been to New York?"

"Sure," William replied. "I lived there for a few years."

"Small world, huh?"

"It sure is." William finished his drink and waved the bartender for a refill.

"Bet you never got out to the Bronx much though, eh? You look more like the Manhattan type to me. I bet you used to drink in those tacky tourist places with fake street signs on the walls and photos of the Statue of Liberty in the bathrooms."

"I got around. But you're getting off track. Remember the deal? I don't tell you my secret until you tell me yours."

"Right. So where was I?"

"The Republic Club." William looked down into his whisky, watching the ice shift as the heat of his hand melted it.

"Oh yeah. So anyway, me and the boys went out this particular Friday night and hit the clubs. Man, did we party hard. Not just booze either."

"So?"

"Well, like I said, we were pretty messed up that night. So anyway, this young couple came into the place. You could just tell they were out of their element, you know, rich kids roughing it, looking for a little excitement. Maybe they were bored with the clubs in Brooklyn Heights and Soho. Hell, maybe they were just lost, who knows." Floyd shook his head. "The girl was a stunner, though. That was what started the whole thing." Floyd paused, a distant look on his face.

"What happened next?"

"What do you think? It was just some fun at first, a couple of comments. The boyfriend didn't take it well at all, thought we were disrespecting his girl, which I suppose we were. Things got a bit heated. We exchanged words. The girl was trying to drag her boyfriend toward the door, begging him to let it go."

"So things got out of hand?"

"Real quick. If it had been any other night, things might have ended differently. That night though, I was on a roll, high on beer and coke. I followed them out, caught up with them a few blocks away. It was late. There was no one about. The boyfriend turned around and saw me, tried to fight, but I had a knife. It didn't take long to finish him. It took even less time to stop that damned girl screaming."

"You killed them both."

"Didn't mean too. Not at first. Just thought I'd scare them a bit, show them the knife, but…"

"Well, it certainly is a secret worth keeping."

"You still don't believe me?"

"Oh, I believe you." William downed the last of his whisky and slid from the barstool. "Well, it's late. Guess I should get along. Thanks for the company."

"Hey," Floyd protested. "You can't leave yet. You haven't told me your secret."

"Maybe next time." William turned and walked toward the door. "I'm sure we'll bump into each other again."

FLOYD ARNOLD PULLED his coat tight against the bitter wind and moved from the protective shelter of the doorway, leaving the bar behind. Despite the best predictions of the weather girl on channel 36, the night had turned wet and wintry.

He fumbled for his car keys, digging deep into his pocket. He was about to pull them out, his fingers closing over them, when he felt an arm wrap around his neck. He was jolted backwards.

He stumbled, fighting to regain his balance, but it was no use. He tumbled to the ground, head smacking the concrete with a dull thud that sent a shock of pain coursing down his spine.

He blinked, clearing a fine mist of rain from his eyes, and looked up, startled to see William looming over him. "What the…"

"Told you we'd bump into each other again." William kneeled and reached into his jacket, drawing out a long knife.

"What are you doing?" Floyd tried to rise, but William's fist shot out, sending his skull crashing back to the pavement again. Blinding white light flared before his eyes for a moment. Blood trickled from his nose.

"I realized after I left the bar, it was wrong not to tell you my secret. Fair is fair, after all."

"Huh?"

"We've met before, you see."

"I don't understand." Floyd slurred his words. The pain in his head was unbearable.

"That's my secret. We've met before." William put the knife to Floyd's throat. "But it hardly seems adequate in light of the weighty secret you told me, so I'll pad it with a word of advice."

"What?" Floyd squirmed, trying to inch away from the blade, eyes wide with terror.

"When you try to kill a man, make sure he's actually dead." William drew the knife across Floyds throat, the blade digging deep, tracing a crimson line.

WILLIAM WATCHED the pool of blood spread around Floyd's head, mixing with the rain and flowing toward the gutter. He pulled a photograph from his pocket, looked at it for a second, at the face of the girl smiling out at him from the old Polaroid, and then slipped it back inside his coat. A single tear fell from his eye and hit the pavement next to the lifeless body of Floyd Arnold. In the distance the wail of police sirens, drawing closer each second, carried on the breeze.

The Apartment

JACK BRANNAN SAT in the small New York City park with his arms stretched across the back of the bench and waited. A gaggle of children, excited cries drifting on the breeze, played near the fountain where two pathways intersected. Their parents lingered nearby, deep in conversation and paying no heed to their raucous offspring. Further afield, a clutch of older boys tossed a ball between themselves, full of youthful exuberance. His attention thus distracted, Jack didn't notice the woman's approach until her shadow fell across the bench.

"Are you here to feed the cats?"

"I beg your pardon?" He shifted his gaze from the impromptu football game. She stood in the glare of the afternoon sun, her body little more than a black outline against the powder blue sky. He raised a hand and shielded his eyes. It didn't help much, but at least it allowed him to make out her features, a deeply lined face, gray wispy hair flowing over her shoulders, thin lips and deep set eyes.

"Are you the man that wants to feed my cats?" She asked again, fixing him with a penetrating stare, as if she could drag the answer forth merely by burrowing into his head.

"I'm sorry, you must have me mistaken for someone else."

"I don't think so." Her tone was crisp with a slight nasal quality. "You're wearing a blue shirt."

"Of course." Realization dawned on him. He'd told her what he'd be wearing. "The apartment. You must be Emily Waltham." He jumped up and extended his arm.

"That's the name my mother gave me." She looked at his outstretched hand as if he were offering her a piece of moldy bread. She made no move to reciprocate. "You'll want to see the place I assume?"

"I'd love to." He dropped his arm.

"Excellent." She waited for him to scoop up his laptop bag. "It's not far. Follow me."

JACK MISSED the tranquility of the park. He stood on the sidewalk, the New York traffic assaulting his ears with beeping horns, his nostrils burning with the acrid odor of exhaust fumes. He'd always wanted to visit the Big Apple, to spend time there like a real writer. This place, this sprawling metropolis, had inspired more stories than any one city ever had a right to do, yet now that he was here he wondered, briefly, if he'd made the right decision. It seemed somehow different from the New York of his dreams, a little dirtier, and a lot Noisier. It was certainly a far cry from the snow-capped mountains of Colorado, where he'd grown up skiing and hiking.

Emily pulled a heavy set of keys from her pocket and unlocked the apartment building's double doors. A blast of cold, dank air met them as they stepped over the threshold. It smells a bit like a tomb in here, Jack thought as he waited for his eyes to grow accustomed to the gloom. "You keep the building locked?"

"Always. You're in the city now Mr. Brannan. One can't be too careful."

"Please, call me Jack." He let the door swing shut behind him.

"I prefer to keep things formal, if you don't mind."

"Fine with me." Jack really didn't care what she called him as long she was letting him stay in her apartment free of charge, just for feeding some cats. It seemed fortuitous that he'd seen this place come up online mere days after getting the call from his agent that *Red is for Murder*, his latest thriller, had been picked up by a big five publisher. Even better, they wanted to see the sequel as soon as possible - The unfinished sequel. What better location to finish the book than the city that inspired the likes of Jack Kerouac and Ernest Hemmingway? So here he was, one leave of absence and a six-hour plane flight later, standing in this building that was to be his home for the next month.

"You're a writer?"

"Yes." He took in his surroundings. The lobby was expansive, with alternate black and white tiles that gave the impression he was walking on an oversized chessboard. Rows of ornate bronze colored mailboxes were set into the wall immediately to the right of the front entrance. A couple of them gaped open, one missing its door entirely. Dust bunnies gathered around the legs of a chaise longue that had seen better days, its once bright red fabric patchy and worn. The lobby had a musty smell that reminded Jack of dirty socks.

"What do you write?"

"Fiction mostly. Thrillers."

"I've never heard of you."

"I write thrillers, I never said people read them," he joked, smiling. "I also teach English at a small community college in Colorado. I took a month off to finish my latest book. I couldn't believe it when I saw your ad. It's a perfect situation."

"Now don't be making your mind up so quickly. You should wait until you see the building before you commit yourself. We're not exactly the Ritz you know, the poor girl's seen better days."

"I'm sure the accommodations will be fine. All I need is somewhere quiet to write, free of distraction. Besides, the price is right."

"Ah yes. Just because I'm not taking your money doesn't mean I don't expect certain duties to be carried out."

"I know, feed the cats, make sure the furnace stays lit, water the plants, and generally keep an eye on things," Jack said, paraphrasing the text of the ad.

"I've lived here for over thirty years Mr. Brannan, and this is the first time I've left the building in the care of another soul. I wouldn't leave now if it were not absolutely necessary."

"Your mother's passing. I'm so sorry."

"These things happen, Mr. Brannan. She was a very old woman. Regardless, her affairs do need to be taken care of now that she has gone to the other side, so to speak."

"Of course."

"Mother hated this building. She said the tenants annoyed her. She was always trying to get me to leave, to join her in New Jersey. Now she finally has, if only for a short period." Emily touched his arm. "Would you like to see the apartment now, Mr. Brannan?"

"I would. If you don't mind."

"We shall take the elevator. The stairs are so steep and dark, and my legs are not what they once were. I should have the place rewired, but it's just too much money."

Jack had noticed the elevator already. A great hulking thing enclosed in an iron cage. It looked original to the building, with two gold colored scissor gates that guarded an ornate wooden elevator car. He had assumed it was a relic, left in place for nostalgia purposes, but apparently it was not.

Emily spoke again, as if reading his mind. "It's perfectly safe, I assure you." She pulled the grates back and motioned for him to enter. "After you?"

THE ELEVATOR PROVED to be as ponderous as it looked. The cables creaked and moaned as they heaved their load upward. Jack immediately wished he'd taken the stairs, bad wiring or not. He wondered when it had last been inspected. There did not appear to be a safety certificate anywhere in sight.

A vision of the cables snapping, the two of them plummeting to their deaths amid the splintered wood of the shattered car, refused to vacate his mind. Sometimes having a vivid imagination had its downside.

Emily, clearly immune to the nuances of the aging elevator, did not seem to share his fears. "This place has been in my family since 1924. My great grandfather bought it as an investment. The building itself dates back to 1903."

"Really?"

"The place started life as the Hotel Roosevelt. It was quite the place to be until a fire gutted the top two floors. That was 1943, if I remember rightly. The fire nearly bankrupted my great grandfather. It took him many years to repair all the damage. It wasn't converted into apartments until the fifties."

"How did the fire start?" Jack's interest was piqued. He'd come here to finish a story, but maybe he'd find an idea for a new book too.

"The police suspected arson, but they could never prove anything. Twelve people died. It was a sad business."

"That's dreadful." Jack wished he could write this down, but it might seem odd, or worse, rude, to pull out his phone and make notes while she talked. He wasn't here to interview her.

"It's an old building Mr. Brannan, and as such has seen its share of tragedy. It's the way of things."

"Still-" Jack was about to press her further on the fire, but at that moment the elevator came to a shuddering halt.

"This is it. Floor five." Emily pulled the gates back.

Jack stepped into the corridor, all at once aware of the bone-gnawing chill that hung in the air.

THE APARTMENT WAS SURPRISINGLY MODERN. The paint seemed fresh, and the musty smell that permeated the rest of the building was absent, for which he was grateful. The living room was spacious. Two large picture windows flooded the space with daylight. Gorgeous polished hardwood floors took second place only to a large brick fireplace that boasted a dark cherry mantle. The furniture, although not to his taste, was well kept and clean.

"This is one of the largest apartments in the building." Emily said. "There is a larger one on the floor above, but I don't like it. That floor burned in the fire, and even though it was all repaired many years ago, I can't stand to live where so many people lost their lives. I keep everything above floor five closed off, and hardly ever go up there."

"I understand completely." He smiled. "I think this will be just perfect."

"Good. Now let me tell you about the cats." Emily gripped his arm, a little too tightly. "They really are rather finicky little things, and they will take advantage of you, if you let them."

"I see." How hard could it be to feed a few mangy cats?

"You won't let them will you?" Emily asked, her face furrowed with concern.

"No," Jack assured her. "I will make sure the cats know their place. You have nothing to worry about."

"Good." Emily seemed to relax. She led him to the kitchen and opened a small door set into the wall to reveal a tight walk in pantry. She pointed to a shelf with a large bag of dry food on it. "The cat food is in here. Please make sure you seal the bag each time, otherwise the air gets to it."

Jack nodded.

"You probably won't need to top up the water more than once a day. Their bowls are outside in the hallway. They come and go as they please." She pointed to a small cat flap set into the door.

"You let them roam the whole building?" Jack asked, surprised.

"They like it that way," Emily said. "Besides, they keep the mice at bay, so they earn their keep."

"Ah." Maybe it was better that the cats were free to go where they chose. He wouldn't have to share the apartment with them.

"Do you have any questions?"

"I don't think so," Jack answered. Everything seemed pretty straightforward.

"Excellent. I shall see you tomorrow then. Ten o'clock sharp?" Emily put a hand out and steered him toward the door.

"Ten it is," Jack nodded. It seemed their meeting was abruptly over with.

"I'll walk you out." Emily followed him to the elevator.

"There's no need. I can find my own way out."

"Nonsense," Emily said. She waved an arm in the air. "I shall see you out. After all, someone has to lock up after you leave."

"Well in that case—" Jack held the elevator door open for the strange old woman. She shuffled past him and waited in the car until he stepped in behind her.

"Besides, I need to show you the basement. If there is an issue you will need to know what to do."

"Right now?" Jack said. "We can do it tomorrow if you like."

"No time like the present." Emily pulled the elevator door closed with a clank. "Unless you have somewhere else to be?"

"No." Jack tried his best to look at ease. "Not at all."

"Good." She reached out and pressed the button marked with a large red letter B, and soon the elevator was clanging and clunking its way back toward the ground. As the creaky old elevator descended down through lobby and kept going, gears and cables moaning and grinding, Jack wondered just what he had let himself in for.

JACK CHECKED out of his hotel a little before ten the next morning. With a backpack full of clothes slung across one shoulder, his laptop bag hanging from the other, he walked the two blocks to the apartment building, pausing only briefly to purchase a cup of hot coffee. When he arrived at the apartment building, he found Emily at the curb waiting next to an idling taxi. She watched him approach with a mirthless gaze.

"You are two minutes early, Mr. Brannan."

"Better that than two minutes late."

"Quite so." She pushed a set of keys into the palm of his hand. "The silver one is for the front doors. The bronze key opens the apartment. The others are for the rest of the building. They are numbered by apartment. I doubt you will have a need for those. Please remember to keep the downstairs doors secure and locked at all times."

"And this one?" Jack fingered a tarnished old key, larger than all the others.

"That opens the door to the equipment room in the basement."

"Okay."

"Here. Take this." Emily pressed a crumpled slip of paper into his hand. "If you need me for any reason you can call this number. It's for my mother's house in Wildwood. I'll be staying there while I settle her affairs. I don't have a cell phone I'm afraid, never had the need, but mother has an answering machine. If you leave a message I'll get back to you as soon as possible."

"I doubt that I'll need to call you." Jack slipped the note into his pocket.

"Well, if anything happens, just call. Any time, day or night." A look of concern flashed across Emily's face, just for an instant, and then it was gone. "I've left an extra bag of kitty food on the kitchen counter."

"The cats will be fine, you don't need to worry."

"I'm sure they will, Mr. Brannan." Emily climbed into the taxi. She looked up at him through the open back window. "One more thing–"

"Yes?"

"Try to keep out of the way of the tenants. They really don't do well with strangers."

JACK SPENT the day settling in. He went to the store and bought some basic groceries. He also bought a six-pack of beer and several chocolate bars. He always worked better when he had chocolate around.

Back at the apartment he set up his writing area, dragging a stout wooden desk from its nook near the bedroom door and placing it facing one of the large picture windows. He set his laptop upon the desk and sat back, taking in the view of the city. A perfect place to finish the book, he thought. He could feel it in his bones. This publishing deal would change everything. He could feel his earlier misgivings fading away. This was where he was meant to be, where he should be.

New York.

Later, as dusk spread across the sky, he popped a beer and sat on the overstuffed couch. A nagging voice inside his head told him he should be writing, but he ignored it. The book could wait one more day. Besides, a few beers would help him sleep. He always found it hard to relax the first night he was in a new place.

He was about to start on his second beer, was halfway across the living room with the open bottle in his hand, when he was interrupted by a single sharp knock. He turned and looked at the apartment door, surprised. The silence in the wake of the sudden sound seemed almost palpable.

Seconds ticked by. Jack waited, listening. The hairs on the back of his neck stood up and he was suddenly aware of the sound of his own breathing.

He held his breath.

When the second knock came he almost dropped the beer. "Hello?"

Stony silence answered him.

"Can I help you?" He reached out and touched the latch, unsure if he should open it. He wished there was a peephole, one of those things that let you see whoever was on the other side of the door before opening it, but there was not. New York City was hardly known for its safety. He briefly considered peeking out through the cat flap, but then realized how ridiculous that would look. Instead he called out. "Is there anyone there?"

No answer.

He took a deep breath, pulled back the latch and pulled the door open, just a crack.

"You're not Emily." An old woman stood on the other side of the door, with her hands on her hips. She couldn't have been more than four and a half feet tall. Her face was a roadmap of old age. She wore a blue patterned dress with a white collar. A knitted shawl was draped over her shoulders, which she held tight to her chest.

Jack took a step back, alarmed. "No I'm not."

"Where is she? What have you done with her?"

"I haven't done anything with her. She had to go away for a little while."

"Away? What right has she to go away?"

"Her mother passed on."

"Well isn't that a fine thing." The old woman shook her head. "So who are you?"

"I'm Jack. I'll be staying here for a little while to take care of the place." He wondered if she was senile or just plain rude. "And you are?"

"Crantz. Dorothea Crantz," she replied, looking past him as if she thought Emily might somehow magically appear.

"Can I help you with something?" he said, opening the door a little wider, while at the same time hoping she would not try to come in. "I really am very busy."

"Busy drinking." Her eyes lingered on the beer bottle in his hand. "Alcohol is the devil's vice you know."

"So I've heard," Jack said. He shuffled his feet, anxious to be done with the conversation. "But it's an awfully fine tasting vice."

"All the worst ones are." Dorothea clasped her hands together as if she was about to pray for him. "That's why they are so tempting to sinners."

"Well I'll try and make this my last one for the evening." He humored her.

"Make sure you do." Dorothea didn't look like she believed him. "I'll be on my way, since Emily is not here."

"I won't hold you up then. It was a pleasure meeting you, Mrs. Crantz." Like hell it was. "You should drop by again sometime."

She turned and took a step toward the elevator, then turned back, looking at him with unblinking dark eyes. "Theodore would like you."

"Theodore?"

"My husband. He doesn't like Emily, so he won't visit with her. Maybe I'll bring him to meet you though."

"You do that Mrs. Crantz." He could only imagine what poor Mr. Crantz must have gone through over the years married to this oddball. It was no wonder he had little interest in accompanying his wife. Emily was hardly a model of sanity herself. The two of them together must make quite the double act.

"Well, goodbye then."

"Goodbye." Thank god. She was leaving.

"Don't forget to feed the cats." Mrs. Crantz was apparently on Emily's payroll. "They always get their food at ten sharp, and not a minute later."

"I won't fogrget."

"See that you don't." With that she turned and walked briskly in the direction of the stairs, disappearing amid the blackness that lingered in the stairwell.

Jack stood in the doorway and took a sip of beer, relishing the cold bite as he swallowed the liquid.

The corridor was silent as the grave. No sounds emerged from any of the other apartments. No TV, no music, not even the low rumble of muted conversations behind closed doors. A crack of light under a door would at least prove that some of floor five's other occupants were at home, but he could see none. The building seemed to have a blanket over it, shutting out the light and swallowing the sound. He could not even hear Mrs. Crantz's footsteps as she made her way back downstairs. He suddenly felt very alone.

"Pull yourself together Jack," He mumbled under his breath. It was a fine time to get the hebejebes.

He looked at his watch. It read a little past 9:30 p.m. Screw it. The cats could get their supper a little early. Not that he had seen hide nor hair of them. Maybe they were pouting about the temporary departure of Emily too.

He left the door ajar and found the bag of cat food. A scoop lay beside it, which he used to fill the waiting bowl.

He placed the food on the floor outside the apartment door. Should he call to the cats? Would they find the food on their own? Calling to them would be useless anyway, since he didn't actually know their names.

He was about to make his way back into the apartment, and his beer, when he saw two silent figures standing in the shadows near the bend of the corridor watching him, a young woman and a little girl of perhaps ten years of age. The child clutched a rag doll in one hand, and held on to the woman with the other.

"Hello?" he called, his voice echoing. "Can I help you with something?"

He waited for the woman to reply. When she didn't he decided to try another tack.

"I'm looking after the place for Emily. She's out of town for a while."

Still the pair never made a sound, never moved.

The hairs on Jack's neck and arms stood up. He felt a tickle of fear. There's nothing to be afraid of, he thought, it's just a couple of the other tenants. They are probably curious, that's all.

He lifted his hand and waved, forcing a wide smile.

They stared, immobile, their eyes boring into him.

Nice, he mused, real nice. It appeared they didn't take too well to strangers in this building. Well too bad. He was here now. Besides, he had better things to do than make social with the neighbors. There was a book to finish.

He turned away from the bowl of cat food and pushed the apartment door open. Before he stepped through, he glanced back down the corridor, but it was empty.

The woman and child were nowhere in sight.

———

JACK AWOKE EARLY the next morning. He lay there for a moment, with the covers pulled up to his chin, processing the remnants of a dream that lingered in his mind, broken and

196 • ANTHONY M. STRONG

fragmented. What he did remember though, was dark and sobering. Visions of gloomy hallways, of flitting figures that skulked at the edge of his vision, reaching for him with clawed skeletal hands, and a dead eyed woman with long blonde hair, her skin pallid, flesh soft and doughy. She wore a tattered dress, ripped in several places, and stained crimson. He wondered who she was, why his subconscious would conjure up such things. Her face was not familiar, and he was sure he hadn't met anyone that looked like her recently. Eventually, unable to piece together anything more than disjointed flashes, he swung his legs from the bed and padded to the bathroom, where he relieved himself and brushed his teeth.

Pushing the strange dream from his mind, he dressed and went to the kitchen. He threw together a quick breakfast of scrambled eggs and bacon, and two slices of hot buttered toast, and then settled down to write. For the first time in a long while he felt motivated and ready to go, despite the lingering effects of the bad dream. If he was lucky he could get a good nine or ten hours of work done, maybe even more.

He opened the laptop and waited for the screen to light up, then entered his password. The manuscript was ready and waiting, just where he'd left off yesterday. He took a moment to read over the last few pages he'd written, and then started to type. He hadn't managed more than three lines when there was a dull thud from above.

Jack glanced upward, toward the sound.

The ceiling light, hanging by a short cord, swayed back and forth. He watched it lose momentum and slow, while at the same time listening for any further sound.

None came.

He turned back to his work and started to tap away at the keyboard once more, his fingers flitting over the keys, a staccato soundtrack to accompany his writing. No sooner had he gotten back to work than he forgot all about the sound from above, his whole attention focused on the manuscript.

Then the ceiling shook a second time.

Jack leapt to his feet, startled.

This thud was louder than the previous one. Jack looked upward, annoyed, and then crossed the room and picked up the wad of keys. He'd been under the impression that the apartment above was unoccupied, yet clearly there was someone up there.

He moved to the door and opened it a crack, peering out for a moment, then stepped into the hallway. He moved down the corridor. Had anyone else heard the thumps?

It appeared not.

The place was deserted, silent.

He felt a pang of disappointment. He'd hoped to run into another occupant of the building, someone who might accompany him up to the sixth floor.

He stopped at the elevator, placed a hand on the cage door, his fingers lingering on the latch, but decided against it. Better to take the stairs. If there was someone up there fooling around he didn't want to alert them that he was coming, and the elevator made enough sound to wake the dead. Besides, he didn't trust the thing as far as he could throw it. Who knew when it had last been serviced?

He came to a heavy fire door marked Emergency Exit, and peered through the small pane of safety glass to confirm it was the stairs, and then pushed the door open. He began to climb, taking the steps two at a time, keeping his footfalls light and even. Even so, the noise reverberated in the enclosed space, and he was glad to reach the landing one floor up and exit the stairwell.

He paused for a moment, listening, but the corridor was silent. Still, someone had made those noises. Maybe they were still in the apartment.

He hurried along until he located the correct door, walking off the distance, a mental map of the floor below in his mind. When he reached out and turned the handle, the door did not budge.

Locked.

Thank goodness he'd had the foresight to bring the set of keys along. He looked at the large ring of keys, which easily numbered twenty, not counting the ones he knew were for the building's front door, the apartment below, and the basement. He flipped through them, noticing the numbers engraved on the fob of each key - 610, 611, 612.

He glanced upward to the door, noticing the faded gold leafed number on the door. 613.

Of course it was.

Jack was not superstitious, but even so he felt a tingle of apprehension as he found the correct key, the one with 613 engraved on the hilt, and inserted it into the lock. He hoped it would not work, thus relieving him of the duty to further investigate the strange bumps, but to his dismay it turned easily, the deadbolt sliding back with a faint click.

He took hold of the knob and turned, letting the door swing inward on worn hinges, then stood for a moment, peering into the space beyond, before taking a tentative step across the threshold.

The apartment was dark and gloomy. It smelled of moth-balls and something else, a rotten, cloying odor that burned his nostrils. Jack did his best not to gag, and reached for the light switch, his hand fumbling across the wall, searching.

After a few seconds he located the switch and flipped it up. Weak yellow light illuminated the room. It was not much better, but it did at least push the darkness back into the corners.

He took a deep breath. If there was anyone lurking in these dank and oppressive rooms, they knew he was here. Only Jack had the feeling that there was no one in the apart-ment. He couldn't explain it, but the place just felt empty. Even so, he should check the place out, make sure. Emily had left him in charge, and even though security guard was not on the list of duties, he felt an obligation to keep her building safe.

Jack padded across the room, noting the lack of furniture, and approached the closest door, peering inside.

This appeared to be a bedroom, with a closet built into the far wall. For a moment he considered taking a peek inside the closet, but then thought better of it. He'd seen too many horror films. That was the kind of thing that ended badly.

Instead he turned and made his way to the next door and opened it. This was a bathroom with a claw foot iron tub and a shower. A tattered shower curtain hung from a rusting chrome bar. A roll of toilet paper lay on the cracked tile floor, no longer round, but instead sagging and formless as the damp air took its toll.

Apart from that, this room was also empty.

Finally Jack turned his attention to the only other room in the apartment, a small kitchen separated from the main living area by a wide arch. Dirty yellow cabinets hung on the walls above a chipped porcelain sink. One hung open to reveal a tilted shelf, a lone drinking glass perched precariously as if it might slide off at any moment. There was no stove or refrigerator, just empty spaces where the appliances should have been, with peeling, stripped wallpaper and dirty baseboards.

In the middle of the kitchen sat a huge rat.

Jack took a step backward, startled, his heart pounding in his chest. A wave of revulsion caused him to let out a slight whimper before he realized that the creature was not moving.

It was dead.

He took a step toward the furry corpse, than another, stopping close enough to see the crushed skull, the crimson circle of blood, still wet and glistening in the weak light.

Jack recoiled. Suddenly he didn't want to be here anymore. Even so, he hesitated for a moment. Should he pick the thing up and dispose of it? Rats were vile, filthy things full of disease, even when they were alive, and the thought of returning downstairs knowing it was rotting right above him, separated only by the apartment ceiling, drywall and wood, gave Jack the creeps. On the other hand, something had killed the rat, caved its head in, and that would take quite a bit of force, and in a locked room no less. Was this the source of the twin thuds that shook his apartment and sent him up here in the first place? Had he heard the rat being dispatched?

If so, that meant someone must have been in this very room, despite all the evidence to the contrary. They might still be around, skulking in one of the other apartments on this floor. They could be watching him right now for all he knew.

A shiver ran up Jack's spine.

It took him all of two seconds to make up his mind. He turned and fled, a tight knot of fear balled in his stomach. He reached the hallway and slammed the apartment door closed, eager to put something solid between himself and the grisly dead thing in the apartment. He hurried toward the stairs without bothering to lock the door. The place was empty anyway, so what could anyone steal? The moldy old roll of toilet paper? The rat?

When he reached the stairs he hurried down, not caring that the strike of his feet on the concrete steps echoed in the narrow stairwell. When he reached the floor below he almost ran toward his apartment, eager to slam the door and hide out.

Only he wasn't alone.

Standing in the corridor was a slim, attractive woman with shoulder length brunette hair. She wore a thin white dress with a floral pattern, and held her hands across her waist, her fingers intertwined.

"Can I help you?" Jack briefly wondered if this was the intruder, the person who had dispatched the rat, but then decided against it. She was much too demure and waiflike. Besides, if she'd just killed a rat there would be some evidence on her dress, at least a spatter of blood or two, given the violent end the creature had endured.

"I heard we had a new tenant in the building," She said. "so I thought I would come by and say hello."

"Temporary tenant. Just until Emily returns later this month," he corrected her. "I'm Jack."

"Eliza." She smiled and Jack noticed how young she was, no more than twenty-five years of age. "Pleased to meet you Jack. Mrs. Crantz told me all about you, and I just had to swing by and see you for myself."

"Ah yes." A thin smile touched Jack's lips. "Mrs. Crantz."

"She is a bit of a busybody, I'll admit." Eliza leaned on the doorframe. "But she knows everything that goes on in the building."

"I bet. Maybe she can tell me who is running around on the sixth floor killing rodents," Jack said.

"What?" A flicker of concern crossed Eliza's face. "Oh dear."

"It's probably nothing. Someone caught a rat in the apartment upstairs." Jack tried to make light of the situation, not wanting to scare her.

"I hate rats. Such vile creatures." Eliza shuddered. "At least we won't have to worry about it paying us a visit in the dead of night now."

"I suppose not." Jack glanced toward the door, eager to go inside. Under normal circumstances he was all for passing the time with an attractive young woman, but right now, at that very moment, he felt ill at ease. The image of the rat, head smashed in, white shards of bone poking through tufts of blood soaked hair, played over in his head.

Eliza may have noticed his mood, or perhaps she was already done, but either way she said, "I'm sure you're busy. I'll leave you in peace."

"It's fine." Jack hoped he hadn't offended her.

"I have to go." She backed up, a wry smile on her face. "But I'll see you again, no doubt."

JACK CLOSED the door and leaned against it, relieved to be back in the relative safety of the apartment. He stayed like that for a long while, listening to the empty silence in the corridor beyond, wondering if the rat killer was out there, creeping through the hallways looking for more hairy victims to dispatch. This sort of thing must happen all the time in these old buildings, he reasoned, otherwise the vermin would overrun the place. It was probably just one of the other tenants taking care of business.

Taking care of business with a hammer.

That thought made him shudder, so he pushed it from his mind.

It was only after his phone rang that he moved, the sudden sound making him jump. He snatched it up from the desk, almost spilling a half empty can of Coke in the process, and answered. He recognized the voice of his agent, Bob Thomson, immediately. How was he doing? Had he settled in? When would there be more pages?

Jack answered all of these questions with calm precision, and by the time he hung up he felt normal again, ready to work, as if Bob's voice had put things in perspective, brushed away the cold fingers of paranoia that had gripped him so easily before. So he wrote, for the rest of the day and well into the evening. He didn't even stop for food, only stepping away from the laptop twice. Once to pee, and once to get a cold soda from the refrigerator. In fact he was still writing like a mad man, the words pouring onto the page in a hailstorm of vowels and consonants, when the lights blinked out.

Jack sat there, the white light from his laptop screen the only relief from absolute darkness. He reached out and toggled the switch on the desk lamp, as if this small action would somehow restore things to their erstwhile state.

It didn't.

He looked out over the city and was surprised to see the windows in the surrounding buildings still lit up, so it wasn't a power failure. That left only one other option. A breaker must have tripped.

It appeared that he would have to go down to the basement, to the rows of fuses located near the back of the building. If he was very lucky it was just this apartment that was out, if he was slightly less lucky, the whole floor. Worst of all would be if the entire building was dark, which meant the master had been tripped and would need resetting. Unless it wasn't a fuse at all, but something else, something worse, which would mean starting up the generator. He was not sure he remembered how to do that, even though Emily had gone over it with him. No point in worrying about that now though, not until he got down there and checked things out.

He stood and stumbled to the kitchen, stubbing his toe on the side of a chair along the way. He opened the cabinet under the sink and retrieved the sturdy black flashlight he'd seen there the evening before. He clicked it on, relieved when the narrow beam of light fanned out across the room. The batteries were fresh.

He picked his way back through the apartment, avoiding the chair this time – his toe throbbed enough from its first encounter – and stepped into the corridor, shining the flashlight in both directions.

The hallway was empty.

He padded toward the stairs. This time the elevator was not even an option, not that he would have taken it anyway. Apart from the clamorous noise the thing made as it descended, he still could not get the image of the cables snapping, the car dropping eighty feet before smashing itself apart in the very basement he was now heading toward, out of his mind.

When he reached the stairwell he lingered at the door, his hand resting on the knob. All of a sudden he didn't want to go down there. The thought of trudging down six flights of stairs, in a cramped space at night with the lights out, gave him pause. He was not even sure why he was the one responsible for getting the lights back on. Didn't buildings like this one usually have a maintenance man, someone who got cheap rent in exchange for doing this kind of thing?

Then it occurred to him that he was the maintenance man, and that he was, in fact, getting free rent for doing this. That still didn't explain who would have taken care of it if he weren't around. Surely Emily didn't do this kind of thing herself. Either way, it was irrelevant. He would just have to suck it up take care of it.

Taking care of business.

The phrase popped back into his head, along with an image of the dead rat.

Stop it, he chided himself, think of something else, something fun, like skiing on Copper Mountain after a fresh fall of snow, or drinking cocoa in the ski lodge next to a roaring fire.

That seemed to work, if only a little.

He cracked the door open and slipped through, the flashlight bobbing off the walls and ceiling as he started down toward the basement.

He reached the landing below and turned the corner, his footsteps hollow and dull. The stairwell was cold, much colder than the rest on the building, and he wished he'd put his jacket on. He briefly considered going back, it was only one flight up after all, but that would mean plucking up the courage to enter the stairwell all over again, and it took nerves of steel to do it the first time. No, he would just have to suck it up and press onward.

When he reached the second landing he paused to catch his breath. Only then did he hear it.

A hiss.

It was barely audible, but a hiss none-the-less.

He froze, listening, his ears straining to detect the sound, to find out where it came from, but all was still.

After a moment he breathed a sigh of relief. It must have been his imagination, or perhaps the wind pushing through a crack somewhere. He took a step forward.

The hiss came again.

This time there was no mistaking it.

He swung the flashlight around in wild arcs, seeing nothing at first, but then the narrow beam picked out a shape in the darkness. Actually it picked out two shapes.

Standing above him, hovering on the next landing up, stood the little girl with the rag doll, and next to her, a black cat with green iridescent eyes that caught the light and threw it back.

He stumbled backwards, alarmed, his foot finding the edge of the stairs. For a moment he thought he might fall as his heel slipped. He teetered, neither on nor off the step, throwing his arms forward to regain his balance.

The cat opened its mouth, wide and yawning, and emitted a long, drawn out yowl that made Jack's skin crawl. The little girl, her doll clutched tight to her chest, watched as he fought with gravity, and then the flashlight beam slid upward, draping the pair in darkness once more. At the same time, with one last effort, he managed to arrest his backward momentum and stood shaking, his breath coming in large heaves, relieved that he was not laid flat on the next level down with his neck cocked at an unnatural angle.

When he lowered the flashlight back to the spot where the little girl and the cat had been standing, they were gone, only empty space greeting him.

JACK DESCENDED the rest of the way to the basement at a faster clip than before. Nothing to be afraid of, he told himself. It was just a kid and a cat, perfectly ordinary. Yet somehow he was afraid.

He reached the ground floor, the door that blocked access to the basement, and fumbled to pull the ring of keys from his pocket, then found the larger brass key, the one he'd hoped he wouldn't need, and inserted it into the lock.

He swung the door inward and looked down into the darkness, which seemed a little denser, more cloying, than it should.

Almost like soup, he thought, darkness soup.

He stood at the brink of the basement, unwilling to cross the threshold into that dark place, knowing that he must. Then, after sweeping the flashlight around the lobby just to make sure he was still alone, Jack took the plunge.

The basement was damp and frigid. By the time he reached the bottom of the steps, he could feel goose bumps breaking out over his arms. He glanced back up, toward the open door, half expecting to see the little girl there, with that doll held tight to her chest. She was not, which filled him with a fleeting sense of relief.

He still had to get the power back on though, and that meant picking his way through the dank basement to the far wall and locating the main fuse. That should not be any big deal, after all, he'd been down here with Emily already and he didn't feel nervous then.

That was in daylight, with another person.

Now he was alone in the dark, and somehow everything was just that little bit creepier.

He edged forward, trying to remember the way. As he went he swept the flashlight back and forth, picking out objects that loomed from the darkness. There was a stroller with one wheel missing, which now sat tilted to one side, a pile of old paint cans, some with lids so rusted he doubted they would ever open again, and several objects under dusty tarps, none of which he could identify by their shape alone. He hurried past all these things, until he came to the far wall, and was relieved to see the large fuse box, its metal door already open as if was expecting him.

It didn't take long to locate the problem. As he suspected, the main breaker was in the off position. He reached out to flip it back to on, and at that moment the basement door crashed closed.

Jack almost dropped the flashlight.

He swiveled around, his heart racing, eyes searching the basement. He appeared to be alone, which was some small mercy, but what caused the door to slam shut? There was no breeze down here, and even if there were, he doubted it would have been enough to do that. It might have swung back on its own, but with such force? That didn't seem likely. Maybe that damned creepy kid had followed him? He'd seen her in the stairwell not fifteen minutes ago, so it was not much of a stretch to imagine her creeping after him and doing something like that as a prank. She was probably laughing up in the lobby right now. That must be it, he reasoned, convincing himself.

If he saw her mother again he would have something to say, for sure. In the meantime, he still needed to address the power situation.

He turned back to the breaker board, reached out, and flipped the switch, relieved to see the bulb at the top of the stairs light up. Thank god it was just a breaker. At least he wouldn't have to climb back up to the apartment in the dark.

He pushed the panel door shut and hurried across the basement to the stairs, taking them two at a time, eager to be out of there. As he reached out to open the door, a thought flashed through his mind. What if it was locked? He would be trapped down here, and who knew how long it would be before he was found. A vision of his desiccated corpse, skeletal hand still clutching the knob, weaved through his mind. He turned the handle, almost convinced that he would end up a prisoner in the basement, but the door opened with ease, much to his relief.

He entered the lobby, felling sheepish all of a sudden for overreacting. In the cold yellow light of the incandescent bulbs set high in their sockets on the ceiling, his fear seemed just a little silly. Still, he wasted no time in getting back to the apartment, and when there, opening a beer and downing it in one, just to calm his nerves.

THE NEXT MORNING Jack awoke to the chatter of a jackhammer somewhere on the street below, its rhythmic beat mixing with the vague sounds of honking horns and revving engines. He glanced at the clock on the bedside table.

6 A.M.

What in gods name were they doing digging up the road at this hour? Come to that, why were so many people leaning on their horns? Not once in all of recorded history had sounding your horn ever made a traffic-jam go away, and yet people still blew them as if their particular horn was the one that might somehow achieve that state of vehicular nirvana.

He turned over and wrapped the pillow around his head, pressing it into his ears, which only served to mute the sound. It was also uncomfortable, so in the end he crawled from bed, dressed, and left the apartment. It would do him good to get out for a while. There was a diner down the block, and a stack of pancakes, dripping in butter and Maple Syrup, just might get the creative juices flowing.

And they did.

By the time he left the restaurant, his belly full of

pancakes, he felt rejuvenated and ready to write. This would be a better day. He could feel it in his bones. This was his day.

He sauntered back to the apartment building and skipped up the steps. The jackhammer was still pounding the asphalt, but Jack no longer cared. He slipped inside the building and made sure the door closed behind him, Emily's warnings about the big city echoing in his head.

He turned toward the stairs, and there, standing in the corner near the basement door, half shrouded in shadow, was the same girl, with the same tattered rag doll in her hand.

"Well hello." Jack forced a smile, resisting the urge to flee. "You get everywhere, don't you?"

She stayed mute, her eyes boring into him.

"Shouldn't you be in school?" he asked.

If he was expecting a response he didn't get one.

"Okay then," Jack said. He crossed the floor in the direction of the stairwell, all too aware of those eyes following his every move, pulled the door open, and entered. The feeling of unease had returned now, creeping back like an old enemy. The pancakes sat like lead in his gut. He glanced upward, took a deep breath, and started to climb.

BY THE TIME Jack reached the fifth floor any humor left within him had dissipated. He stepped into the corridor with his breath ragged from the ascent and legs burning. He turned toward the apartment, and then stopped, his eyes picking out a familiar shape.

In the middle of the hallway, right outside his door, was the dead rat.

A feeling of dread came upon him.

What was that doing there?

He moved closer, never letting his eyes stray from the furry black corpse, hoping against hope that it was not the same rat, but rather another rodent that just decided to pass its last breath on his threshold.

Only it wasn't.

Jack could clearly see the caved in skull, the blood, now dried and dark, coating the poor thing's mangy fur.

Someone had placed this here, put it there for him to find. Unless…

Maybe one of Emily's cats had picked the thing up, brought it down as a gift. He'd heard of cats doing that kind of thing. But for that to happen the cat would need to get into the upstairs apartment somehow, and the last time he checked, cats could not open doors.

So that brought him back to the only logical conclusion. The rat had been left for him to find.

"Dammit." He muttered, stepping over the carcass into the apartment. He went straight to the kitchen, found a five-gallon trash bag under the sink – it was rather too big but it would do - along with a pair of yellow kitchen gloves, and returned to the scene of the crime.

He pulled on the gloves, wrinkling his nose against the smell that wafted up, and reached down.

The first time he tried, he could not touch it. He stood straight and took several deep breaths through his mouth, then bent over again.

He grimaced and closed a gloved hand over the lifeless rat, scooping it up off the floor. Disgusted, with the pancakes rising in his throat and threatening to make an encore, he dropped the corpse into the trash bag. He stripped off the gloves, which joined the rat, and then twisted the top until he could tie the bag shut.

He hadn't used the trash chute yet, but it was easy to locate, tucked away within a tiny beige room at the far end of the corridor. Soon the whole package, rat, gloves and all, were speeding down to the dark depths of the building to join all the other nasty stuff. When he arrived back at the apartment he was surprised to find Eliza waiting for him.

"Hello again." She smiled, her eyes sparking despite the gloom.

"Hi." His own greeting was not quite so enthusiastic.

"What's wrong?" A worried look passed across Eliza's face.

"Just the damn rat again," Jack told her. "Some joker decided to leave it outside my door."

"That's awful." She narrowed her eyes. "Have you got any idea who would do such a thing?"

"Beats me." Jack had his suspicions. "It was probably that weird kid with the filthy rag doll. She probably thought it would be funny."

"What, Katie?" Eliza shook her head. "I can't imagine."

"Well someone put it there." Jack opened the door. "Would you like to come in?"

"I don't want to intrude." Eliza shook her head.

"Nonsense. I don't think I'll be able to write anything of any consequence right now anyway," he said. He didn't want to be alone, not at that moment, and Eliza's company eased his apprehension regarding recent events, the basement, the dead rat, and the creepy kid with the rag doll. She was also easy on the eyes, and he wasn't complaining about that.

"Well, alright then. Just for a short while." She followed Jack into the apartment and looked around, her eyes wide with curiosity. "I haven't been in here before."

"Really?" That was odd. Emily was the building's owner, the landlord. It seemed like Eliza should have been in the apartment at least once or twice, if only to sign her lease or complain about a plumbing issue or some such thing. "That seems odd."

"Emily doesn't like the tenants coming into her personal space. She says it is an invasion of her privacy." Eliza wandered over to the picture window and gazed out over the city. "Most of us abide by her wishes."

"Most?"

"There are a few who don't heed her requests." Eliza turned back to face Jack. "Not all the tenants are as nice as I am."

"I see." A creeping, crawling sensation wriggled its way up Jack's spine. There was something about the way she spoke, an edge to her voice, which set alarm bells ringing in his head.

"I don't think you do." Emily glanced toward the door as if she expected someone to appear, and then turned back toward him. Her eyes alighted on the laptop, a sudden fire dancing in them. "Mrs. Crantz said you are a writer."

"That's correct," Jack replied. "Thrillers mostly."

"Can I see?" she said, her eyes widening. "I haven't read a book in such a long time, but I used to read all the time."

"Sure."

She positioned herself behind him. "Well? Can I see it?"

"Sorry." Jack reached down and tapped the keyboard. The screen came alive, but something was wrong. The page on the screen should have been filled with words, but instead all it contained was one line. He frowned. "That's not right."

"What?" Eliza leaned in.

"This document, it's wrong. This isn't my book." He read the words out loud. "I am watching you." He looked up at her. "Someone must have come into the apartment while I was out and messed with my laptop. What the hell?"

"Oh no." Eliza backed away, a strange look upon her face. "I was afraid of this. I should have known."

"What were you afraid of?" Jack narrowed his eyes. "What do you know?"

"Please don't be mad." Eliza was shaking. "It's him."

"Him who?" Jack could feel the anger rising inside him like a black wave. Someone had entered his personal living space and fooled around with his stuff, touched his laptop. And what was with that strange message, I am watching you?

Who was watching him, and why would they bother? Surely it wasn't that creepy kid. "Tell me."

"Harold," She gulped. "Harold Creach."

"Who the hell is Harold Creach?"

"One of the other residents. He's not a nice man, not nice at all." She turned toward the door. "I have to go now."

"Now hang on." Jack moved to block her path. "Just what exactly is going on in this building? Tell me."

"Just leave it. Trust me, you don't want to make him mad at you." She was at the door now. Her eyes flitted to the cell phone on the desk. "You should call Emily, tell her that you can't stay here."

"Why? Who is this guy?"

"I've said too much already." And with that Eliza turned and fled, leaving Jack all on his own.

He sat for a moment, stunned at the strange turn of events, then reached out and picked up the cell phone. Eliza was right. He should call Emily, but not to tell her he was leaving – he would not be frightened off that easily – but rather to find out with who he was dealing with, and why someone seemed hell bent on scaring him.

He found the slip of paper Emily had given him and dialed the number, waiting while the call connected. When it did, the phone rang four times, then clicked. An automated voice answered.

Damn. She wasn't there.

Jack took a deep breath and waited through the greeting, recorded by the recently passed Mrs. Waltham senior. This is a dead woman, he thought, listening to the scratchy, phlegm filled voice. Even from beyond the grave she still wants people to leave their name and number.

And that was exactly what he did as soon as the greeting played out, adding that Emily needed to call him back right away, that some unsettling things had happened and he must talk to her. He was about to mention the dead rat, but then thought better of it. No point in upsetting her needlessly.

After hanging up he sat for a long while, waiting for Emily to return his call, which she didn't. Then he wrote for a while, but he was distracted and his mind kept wandering. The words refused to come, and he found himself deleting everything he had written, then starting again, only to repeat the process. After three hours he gave up and went to the kitchen, finding enough ingredients to pull together a chicken salad, and ate it at the small dining table. He felt frustrated. Afterward he cleaned up and went back to the computer, where he sat for what seemed an eternity, just staring at the screen. He knew there was no hope of getting any work done now. Worse, he was overcome by a heavy tiredness, possibly brought about by his lack of sleep the night before. In the end he gave up entirely and made his way to the bedroom, where he flopped down on the bed, thoughts of the dead rat, and the strange message on his computer screen, swimming around in his head.

Despite his unease he must have fallen asleep, because when he opened his eyes again it was dusk. Long shadows crept along the floor. The apartment was dark and oppressive. He reached out and fumbled for the switch that turned on the bedside lamp, squinting for a moment when the light came on, then stood and made his way back to the computer, checking his phone on the way. There was still no call from Emily, which surprised him.

He settled at the desk and brought up the web browser. An idea had struck him. It was a long shot, but he might be able to find out a little more about his unwelcome visitor.

When the browser opened he typed a name into the search bar.

HAROLD CREACH.

He hit enter.

The computer pondered his request for a moment, and

then returned a page of results. He clicked each one, looking for answers.

The first two were irrelevant. A plumber in Cleveland, Ohio caught cooking the books, and a high school student in Los Angeles. The third result caught his attention. It was an article from the New York Times dated June 3, 1943. The headline read:

TWELVE KILLED AS FIRE BREAKS OUT AT HOTEL ROOSEVELT.

But it wasn't the headline that piqued his interest, but rather the article itself, and a name that stood out among the text.

Harold Creach.

He read the brief article, and then read it once again just to be sure he wasn't seeing things.

FIRE BROKE out today at the grand old Hotel Roosevelt on Park Street. The inferno, which spread quickly, consumed much of the top floors of the structure. Twelve people lost their lives before the blaze could be brought under control. The NYPD have released the names of several of the dead, including local businessman Harold Creach, and an elderly couple from New Jersey, Theodore and Dorothea Crantz. The identities of the other victims have not been released pending notification of their families, but it is believed a mother and daughter were among those trapped inside the building. A full inquiry into the cause of the blaze will be carried out.

JACK LEANED BACK in the chair and exhaled. This couldn't be correct. Was it a different Harold Creach that died in the fire? That seemed unlikely. So what about the Crantz's? Dorothea seemed very much alive when he spoke to her just hours before, so if she were at the Roosevelt in 1943, she must have been very young. Besides, the article quite clearly reported her death, so young or old, how could she have spoken to him last evening, unless there was a second pair of Crantz's living here all those years ago. Now things were getting into the realm of the impossible. The odds of that happening were staggering. And yet…

He leaned over the laptop. He hit the back button and watched the screen change to the list of search results once more. There must be something else, something he was missing, but what?

Jack's eyes scanned down the list of results, but he saw nothing else on the first page. He clicked the link for page two and perused these as well. He was about to move on to page three when he saw another headline. This was also from the Times.

DECEASED BUSINESSMAN HAROLD CREACH MAIN SUSPECT IN DISAPPEARANCE.

Jack clicked through to the article.

LOCAL BUSINESSMAN HAROLD CREACH, who lost his life in the fire at the Roosevelt Hotel on June 2nd of last year, has been implicated in the disappearance of long-term girlfriend, Eliza Bright. Miss Bright disappeared without a trace in May of last year, a month before the tragic blaze, from the suite of rooms the couple shared at the Roosevelt. The NYPD interviewed Mr. Creach three days after his girlfriend was reported missing by her parents, but dismissed him from their inquiries. That changed last month with the discovery of several bodies, in various states of decomposition, on a rural plot of land owned by Creach, in upstate New York. Miss Bright's body was not among those recovered, but police did find articles of clothing and personal effects that link Creach to the disappearance.

· · ·

JACK LEAPT TO HIS FEET. One coincidence he was willing to believe, two would be strange, but still within the realm of possibility, but three? Despite how crazy it sounded, he was sure that the woman he'd spoken with earlier that day was the same Eliza who went missing all those years ago. There was something very wrong in this apartment building, what with the dead rats and weird tenants that should have been dead and buried years ago.

He didn't want to be here anymore. He paced back and forth, wondering what to do, how to proceed, and then came to a decision.

He would gather up his belongings and leave right away, find a hotel for the night. The cats would be fine if he left a bowl of food for them and topped up their water. He would call Emily once he was safely tucked up in a warm hotel room far away from this place and let her know what happened, tell her that she would need to find somebody else to mind the old building and care for the cats.

He hurried to the bedroom and gathered up what few clothes he'd already removed from his backpack and stuffed them back inside, then unplugged the laptop, closed it and slid the computer into its thin black case, pushing the cord down into the front pocket and zipping it shut. He went to the kitchen, intending to grab the groceries he'd purchased a few days before, but thought better of it. It was just some eggs, milk and a few bottles of beer. It was not worth his time.

He hitched the backpack and computer bag over his shoulders and hurried to the door, drew back the deadbolt, and stepped into the corridor.

"Don't tell me you're leaving so soon?" A male voice, low and full of gravel, echoed down the hallway. "I'm so disappointed."

Jack spun around.

There, standing with his hands on his hips, was a burly man in a white cotton shirt and dark slacks held up by black suspenders. His hair was greased back over his scalp. A five o'clock shadow darkened his jaw line.

Somehow Jack knew who he was looking at, and the realization sent a chill through him. "Harold Creach?"

"The one and only."

"You're dead." Jack was aware of how odd that sounded even as the words spilled from his mouth, but he knew, just absolutely knew, that it was the truth.

"We're all dead here," Creach replied, his eyes glinting with unholy light.

That sentence, those four small words, each so innocent on their own, but somehow terrifying when spoken together, made the hairs on Jack's arms stand straight up. But that wasn't the only thing that made his hairs stand on end. Behind Creach, half hidden in the dark hallway, were the undeniable, familiar outlines of people. Vague at first, almost wispy, they seemed to solidify, to pull themselves together from within the blackness, and take form right in front of his eyes. He didn't recognize most of them, but he did pick out the familiar face of Dorothea Crantz, and next to her, with a look akin to sadness on her face, Eliza.

A freight train of cold, hard fear slammed into him. His knees threatened to give way. He fought to stay upright, reaching out and using the wall for support. This could not be real. Surely he must be dreaming. Any moment now he would wake up in his bed, warm and comfortable under the covers, and this would all fade away into the ether, soon to be nothing more than a few half remembered snatches. Only it wasn't a dream, some deep part of him knew that, no matter how much he wished it were. He opened his mouth, and for a moment nothing came out, but then he found his voice. "What do you want with me?"

Creach grinned, a wide smirk that wrinkled his face in all the wrong places and gave him the countenance of a demon. "We haven't had anyone new to talk to for such a long time."

"Better make the most of it." Jack inched backward toward the stairs, never letting his eyes stray from the tall man and his cohort of ghosts. "I won't be staying."

"We'll see about that." Creach seemed closer now, despite Jack not having seen him move.

"I don't think so." Jack finally found the will to run. He turned and bolted for the emergency exit at the end of the hallway, and tugged on the door. For a moment it didn't budge, and he wondered if it was locked, but then it swung open and he almost fell through.

Fighting the urge to glance backward, knowing what he would see, Jack bounded down the steps, taking them two at a time, until he reached the floor below, then turned the corner and started down the next flight.

"There's nowhere to run." Creach's voice reverberated down the concrete stairwell. "Nowhere you can hide."

We'll see about that, thought Jack, rounding the third floor landing and continuing down at a breakneck pace.

"Come back to us Jack. Eliza is waiting for you Jack."

Yeah right. The lobby was in sight now. Just one more flight of stairs and he would be safe. Jack catapulted himself down the final steps and ran toward the main doors, his feet loud on the tiled floor. When he reached the entrance he almost crashed into it, pulling up just short. He turned the latch and pulled on the doors.

They did not budge.

He tried again, frantic.

Still they remained firm in their refusal to open, which made no sense. They always opened from the inside. It was only from the street side that a key was needed.

"The building doesn't want you to leave Mr. Brannan. It likes you."

Jack swiveled in the direction of the voice, and was horrified to find Creach less than three feet away. Crantz and the others huddled behind him like a flock of ghastly sheep.

"Get away from me." He tugged at the doors, beads of perspiration dripping down his forehead, his breath labored.

"You really are making this so much harder than it needs to be." There was a hint of satisfaction in Creach's voice. "Why can't you be more like the rat?"

"What?" Jack pounded his fists on the doors, one last-ditch attempt to force them open.

"The rat knew when its time was up. It just sat there and let me crush its skull," Creach said. "It accepted its fate."

"I'm not a rat." Jack looked around, desperate to find another escape route.

"Oh, I know you're not." Creach moved closer, the others fanning out behind him to form a semi-circle around Jack, trapping him against the unyielding door. "That's what makes it so much fun…"

EMILY WALTHAM INSERTED the key into the lock, turned it, and pushed the heavy double doors open. The pale early morning sunlight spilled through them onto the polished tile floor of the lobby, as if it had been lingering, waiting for a way in.

She picked up her overnight bag and turned to the taxi, which idled a few feet away, waving him off, then watched the cab nose its way back into the thick city traffic.

When she stepped over the threshold, into the building, she stopped in her tracks. The bag fell from her grip and she let out a long, drawn out wail. "Oh no. No, no, no."

She'd had a bad feeling ever since receiving Jack Brannan's message the afternoon before. If only she could have gotten back sooner, but Wildwood, New Jersey, was a long way away.

She shuffled across the floor, over to the crumpled shape that lay near the elevator doors. She bent down, noticing the thick, dark halo of blood around the man's head, and raised her hands to her face, wiping away a tear.

"I'm so sorry Mr. Brannan. I should never have left you alone here with them." She whispered the words, her voice laden with remorse, and then she raised her head and spoke again, this time loud and angry. "Harold Creach, I told you to leave him alone. I warned you not to do this. You were a monster when you were alive, and you're no better dead."

She straightened up and went back to the front doors, pushing them closed and turning the latch, then focused her attention on the man standing in the shadows, the man who stared in silent disbelief at the sprawled corpse.

She reached out, beckoning to him. "Come now Mr. Brannan, let's find you an apartment. You're going to be with us for a very long time…"

Excerpt from The Haunting of Willow House

Continue reading for an excerpt from the novel, The Haunting of Willow House, available in paperback and E-book, and free on Kindle Unlimited.

Prologue

December 1958

SOMETHING WAS WRONG. Very wrong.

This single thought lingered in Father Christopher Halloran's mind as he steered his cherry red 1952 Plymouth along
the narrow country road a few miles west of Salem, Massachusetts. He drove with the reserve of a man who wished he
were tucked up in bed rather than outside on a cold and
wintry New England evening, but none-the-less, he drove.

Halloran hunched forward, his hands gripping the wheel
so tight his knuckles drained of blood. He loathed driving
after sunset, and more so when the weather was inclement.
Any other time, a storm such as this would have tempered his
desire to venture out, but not so on this occasion. The nagging
feeling that things were not right had bothered him for days,
and finally, unable to dispel the quiet doubt, he resigned
himself to this journey.

Grimacing, he stared into the snow-laden darkness beyond
the windshield, his eyes searching for the gnarled oak that
stood at the edge of the trail leading to Willow Farm.

For a moment, he wondered if he might have gone too far and missed the landmark entirely. But then, as he was about to turn around, he saw it loom out of the night like a wraith, limbs twisted and bent upon themselves. The oak was a grim sight, devoid of life since the summer of forty-eight when a mighty bolt of lightning had cleaved the tree almost in two.

He threw the steering wheel hard to the right and touched the brakes, feeling the back of the car slip on the icy road. It threatened to careen into the tree, but then he wrestled the heavy vehicle under control again, and was soon heading up the narrow dirt trail toward a faint glimmer of lights beyond the fallow fields.

By the time he pulled up in front of the farmhouse, he was cold and tired, but at least his trip was not to be in vain. Frank Walker's white Oldsmobile, the same one he drove to church every Sunday morning, stood like a silent sentinel near the old barn. The glow from within the farmhouse, once a barely perceptible flicker, spilled onto the driveway through half parted curtains.

Father Halloran opened his door and climbed from the driver's seat, gasping at the sudden cold that drilled into his bones. He hitched his coat collar up against the wind, blinking away snowflakes that drifted under his glasses and into his eyes, and slammed the car door.

For a while he stood still, stared up at the old house, and then trudged toward the front entrance, gripping the brass knocker and letting it fall three times. He listened to the dull thud of his knocks reverberate through the hallway beyond and waited.

At first, he saw no sign of life within the dwelling, but soon the sound of a drawn latch greeted his ears.

The door creaked open.

The woman who stood inside seemed surprised.

"Father Halloran, what brings you all the way up here?"

Her accent carried the hard edge of a born and bred Boston New Englander.

"Well now, Mrs. Walker, I was just passing by and thought I would stop in and say hello." Halloran's own Irish accent, unchanged by his years across the Atlantic, stood in stark contrast.

"Really?" Mrs. Walker glanced past the priest, toward the Plymouth, which was already catching a gentle cover of snow despite the fading warmth from the engine. "You thought you'd drive up here in a blizzard, on a whim?"

"Well, yes. The Lord requires that I tend my flock regardless of circumstance." Father Halloran smiled, his eyes straying beyond the doorway into the house. "How is Mr. Walker?"

"Bullheaded, as ever."

"I see." Halloran paused, weighing his words. "I didn't notice him at mass last week."

"He's had a sniffle. Waking at the crack of dawn every day, tending to the farm in weather such as this, it takes a toll." She shifted her stance. "It's nothing to worry about. He'll be fit as a fiddle in a day or two, you mark my words."

"That's good to hear." Halloran nodded. "I am well aware of the ills of foul weather. May I step inside for a moment, Mrs. Walker?"

"What?"

"May I come in?" Halloran rubbed his hands together. "I won't keep you, I promise, but it will be much better to talk in the warm."

"Of course. Where are my manners, keeping a man such as yourself outside on a night like this?" Mrs. Walker said, but even so, she did not move to allow him passage until the priest mounted the front steps.

"That's better." Halloran brushed the melting snow from his coat and pushed the door closed. That done, he spoke again. "I have to tell you Mrs. Walker, I am a little concerned."

"Really? Why is that?" She raised an eyebrow.

"Like I said, your husband, Frank, was not at church on Sunday, and neither was young Thomas. You came alone."

"Thomas?"

"Yes."

"Why would you be concerned with him?"

"Your son is one of my best altar boys, Mrs. Walker. He was absent on Sunday, along with your husband, and he missed practice today. May I inquire, is he sick also?"

"It's that time of year." Mrs. Walker said by way of explanation. She wiped her hands on her apron. "There's always something going around."

"Indeed, there is." Halloran agreed. "Have you called the doctor out?"

"The doctor? Now why would I do that?" Mrs. Walker took a step backward, toward the stairs. "I haven't lived on this earth for forty-six years not to know how to deal with a common cold. Besides, he's almost back to himself. By tomorrow he'll be tearing around the house getting into all sorts of trouble."

"Now that's good to hear. I am sure he will." Father Halloran nodded. "May I see him then?"

"Now?"

"Why yes. I'm sure he would appreciate a visit, given that he's been cooped up for so long. Just a few words, that's all."

"He's sleeping. Poor thing was tired out."

"Well, that's a shame," Halloran said. "And Frank?"

"He's down at the cow barn, checking on the livestock. The joys of the farm."

"A dedicated man if ever there was one." Halloran glanced around the hallway, his eyes settling on the coat rack, and the row of winter garments hanging there. "I can wait for him, if you don't mind."

"He just left. He'll probably be a while. You should get back to town before the blizzard really kicks in."

"I see." Halloran rubbed his chin. "You are probably right."

"You wouldn't want to get stuck up here, now, would you?"

"No indeed. I would not." Father Halloran took a step toward the door.

He reached toward the handle.

Somewhere above, a thud.

Halloran paused, his eyes drifting upward, toward the second floor.

"That would be Thomas." Mrs. Walker turned her head toward the stairs, then back to the priest. "You see, I told you he was fine."

"And wide awake apparently," Father Halloran said, turning to the stairs. "Maybe I will go up and say hello after all."

"No." Mrs. Walker scuttled backward, positioning herself between the priest and the stairs. "I'm not sure that is a good idea. He needs his rest."

"Of course. You know best, I'm sure." Halloran cast a glance past the woman. "Will I see him this Sunday?"

"If he is back to himself, I'm sure you will."

"Good." Halloran turned back toward the door.

Thud.

The sound was louder this time. It echoed in the hallway.

Halloran spun on his heel and fixed the farmer's wife with a questioning stare. "Are you absolutely sure Thomas is alright?"

"Of course, what sort of a question is that?" There was an edge to her voice, a slight tremble. "Everything is just dandy."

Thud.

Halloran's gaze shot upward. "I think I should go up and see him."

"I can't allow that." Mrs. Walker positioned herself at the foot of the stairs.

"It's not a request, Mrs. Walker." Halloran advanced toward the farmer's wife, and taking her firmly by the shoulders, moved her aside and mounted the stairs.

It was dark on the second floor. A subtle musty scent hung in the air, pushing at the priest's nose.

Halloran paused for a moment to allow his eyes to adjust, and then picked his way along the landing toward the furthest door, under which a thin sliver of pale light was visible.

This was surely the boy's room.

Mrs. Walker was climbing the stairs, the old treads creaking with each footfall.

She appeared on the landing; eyes wild.

"Father Halloran, I implore you, let things be."

"I'll just poke my head in and say hello to the boy." Halloran took the doorknob and turned it, his heart quickening as he pushed inward.

Thomas Walker lay on the bed, shirtless. Deep welts crisscrossed his torso, angry and red. His usually combed hair was disheveled and wild. His arms and legs were outstretched to the four corners of the mattress.

For a moment Halloran could see no reason for this unusual repose, but then he noticed the cords wound around the boys wrists and ankles.

The boy lifted his head, arching upward to see who had entered the room, and as he did so, the headboard pulled forward away from the wall. Unable to maintain the pose, he fell back, the headboard slamming into the wall with a resounding thud.

"Sweet Jesus." The priest muttered the words under his breath, barely able to comprehend what he was seeing.

"Father Halloran?" Thomas's voice was reedy, hoarse. "Don't let her hurt me again."

"I won't, son." The priest wondered when the boy had last taken a drink. He thought about fetching him some water, but there were more urgent things to attend to. He moved toward the foot of the bed, intent upon untying the knots that kept Thomas restrained, but then he felt a presence to his rear.

He turned, a cold dread enveloping him.

"I asked you not to come up here." Mrs. Walker filled the doorway. "I didn't want you to see Thomas like this."

"Like what Mrs. Walker?" The priest fought to keep his voice calm and steady. "Lashed to his bed? Scared to death and beaten?"

"You don't understand."

"Then tell me. What possible reason could there be for this insanity?" Halloran asked.

"The devil." The farmer's wife said the words as if that was all the explanation the situation warranted.

"I'm sorry?" Halloran shook his head. "The devil you say?"

"It's inside of him, living with him. Lucifer has claimed his soul. My Thomas is possessed."

"Mrs. Walker, that is preposterous." Father Halloran backed up until his legs hit the bed. "Why would you think something like that?"

"I was told as much."

"Who told you?" The priest glanced toward Thomas. "The boy himself?"

"No. Not the boy."

"Then who?" Halloran pressed. "Did Frank put you up to this?"

"No."

"Then I confess, I am at a loss." Halloran took a handkerchief from his pocket and mopped his brow, feeling warm despite the chill in the air. "Who could have told you such things?"

"The voice in the walls. It speaks to me," Mrs. Walker replied. "It talks at night, when everyone else is sleeping."

"Mrs. Walker, you are not making a lick of sense," The priest said. "What does Frank have to say about all of this?"

"He didn't believe me." Mrs. Walker ran her tongue across her lips. "He said I'm tired, that I'm hearing things."

"Well thank goodness for that. The voice of reason." Halloran motioned toward the bed. "Now why don't we release the boy and wait for Frank to get back from the barn, and then we can have a chat about this, just the three of us."

"Frank isn't coming back from the barn."

"And why is that?" Halloran asked the question even though he feared the answer, and because Mrs. Walker carried something in her hand that he had failed to notice previously. A heavy wrought iron poker.

"Frank didn't think we should help Thomas. He wanted to take him away. But the voice in the walls knew what to do."

"Did it indeed?" Halloran stepped away from the bed, sensing a change of atmosphere in the room. He moved toward the door, praying that the farmer's wife would step aside. He could come back later with the sheriff. "In that case, I think I'll be off if it's all the same with you. I've taken up too much of your time already, and the weather is growing worse."

"You're just like Frank." Mrs. Walker shook her head. "I'm so sorry, may god forgive me, but I need to protect my boy." And with that she shot forward, the poker leading the way.

Halloran stumbled backwards, desperate to escape the charging woman. He bumped into the far wall, his back against the window. And even though there was nowhere else to go, he kept on anyway, because if he didn't, the sharp end of the poker would find him.

The window held firm for a few seconds, enough time for

Halloran to realize what was going to happen, and then gave way with a sharp pop.

As the priest tumbled backwards through the opening, and fell toward the unforgiving, frozen ground below, he saw Mrs. Walker watching from the shattered window, a cruel smile upon her face.

For Sale
DANVERS - ESSEX COUNTY

Colonial Era Farmhouse set on 5+ Acres
Don't miss this unique opportunity.
1690's farmhouse on 5 acres.
Parcel includes pristine woodland and brook.
With a little TLC this historic home can be brought back to its
former glory.
Two dairy barns and several other structures on site.

Chapter 1

Present Day

THERE WAS a steady drizzle the day that Andrew Whelan and his family made the journey from Boston to the dilapidated farmhouse nestled on a swath of land between the Massachusetts towns of Danvers and Salem. Jake was ten years old, and had, so far, been about as good as any boy that age can be when riding in the back of a car. Sarah, now almost three-quarters through her teen years, sat up front with her father. It was better that way. There was less chance of an altercation, which meant there was less chance that Andrew would have to pull over to the side of the road and give them the kind of tongue lashing their mother used to handle.

Sarah was the first to speak, as they left the city and drove north through Saugus, and then Lynn Woods, before cutting across south of I-95 in the direction of Peabody.

"Tell me again why we have to move here?" she asked, staring out of the passenger seat window, watching the New England scenery roll by. "It's not fair."

"You know why." Andrew glanced sideways. If he was hoping to connect with his daughter, he was disappointed.

Her eyes never strayed from the passing fields. "We've been over this a million times."

"That doesn't mean I have to agree to it." She played with the top of her black shirt. It matched the black skirt and black boots, not to mention the hair, which used to be brown. That was before. Now she shunned color like it was some mortal enemy. "I liked our house in Boston."

"So did I, Sarah, but we all need a new start."

"Mom would never have dragged us out into the country like this."

"We're not in the country," Andrew said, not bothering to mention that a move out of Boston was something he and Jennifer had discussed on numerous occasions. It would make no difference. "Salem is only a few miles to the south. There are all sorts of things to do. There's even a mall."

"So?"

"You like malls."

"I don't like drafty old farmhouses." She shifted in her seat, turning from the passing scenery, and glared at him. "I don't like starting a new school in my senior year."

"I'm sorry. I know we decided to make the move after you graduated, but that was before-"

"I know what I did. You don't have to bring it up again," Sarah said. "It was stupid. I get it. I didn't really mean to go through with it. I didn't intend to take that many pills."

"I know."

"So why are you punishing me?" Sarah asked. "It's not like you're any better."

"I never said I was. I've made my mistakes. But this move, it's good for us."

"Good for you."

"All of us. And I'm not punishing you," Andrew said. "This house came up out of the blue, and it was too good a deal to turn down. I don't know why you won't let this go."

"I was just saying, Mom would never-"

"Dammit, Sarah." He felt the anger rise like a black wave, an unfamiliar beast that had lurked inside of him ever since the accident. He did his best to contain it, but sometimes, especially when he was thinking about Jennifer, the monster reared its head. "Your mother's not here. She's gone, okay?"

"I know that." Sarah shrank back, alarmed by the sudden outburst.

"I miss mom." Jake spoke up from the back seat. "I wish she was here."

"I know you do." Andrew said, his voice softer now, the anger ebbing away as quickly as it had come. "We all wish she was here."

"Is mom in heaven?" This was a question Jake had asked on numerous occasions over the past year, yet despite receiving the same answer each time, he still insisted on asking again.

"Of course she is." Andrew wondered if it was a coping mechanism. He had talked about it with a grief counselor a few months back when Jake was struggling to understand what had happened. The counselor didn't think it was anything worth worrying about, so Andrew let it be, and answered with the same calm reassurances each time. "There's no doubt about it."

"For goodness sake, dad." Sarah shot him a withering look. "When are you going to stop with this?"

"Drop it, Sarah." Andrew was in no mood to deal with his daughter's petulance. "Not now."

"Then when, Dad?" Sarah pressed. "When are you going to tell him the truth?"

"What truth?" Jake scooted up and put his head between the front seats, his eyes wide.

"There's no such thing as heaven," Sarah said, glaring at her father when she spoke. "There's no heaven, and there's no hell. It's all made up so that stupid people feel better about death."

"It is?" Jake looked between his sister and father. "So what happens when we die?"

"There's nothing. It's just blackness, for ever and ever."

"Jesus Sarah, do you have to be so mean?" At that moment Andrew felt like slamming on the brakes and leaving his daughter on the side of the road. Instead, he took a deep breath. "This isn't helping."

"I wasn't trying to help." Her gaze returned to the landscape beyond the car. "I'm allowed to have an opinion."

"Yes, you are," Andrew said. "But sometimes it would be nice if you kept it to yourself."

"Whatever." She shrugged and sank back into the seat. "How much further is it anyway?"

"Not far. A few miles." Andrew glanced at Jake, who had retreated to the back seat once more, pulling his legs up and pressing himself into the door. "Hey sport, you want to help your dad out?"

"Sure." He didn't sound convinced.

"There's a tree we need to find, a big old oak with twisted branches. When we see that, we are there. Can you look out for it?"

"How will I know when I see it?"

"Oh, you'll know. It's an ugly old thing. You can't miss it."

"Okay."

"That's my boy. It'll be on the right hand side. Yell when you see it." Andrew's eyes drifted to the rearview mirror. He was pleased to see Jake scoot across to the right side of the car and peer out of the window, craning his neck to see frontward.

A few minutes later, as the car meandered down a narrow road barely wide enough to avoid the foliage on the banks scraping the sides of the vehicle, Jake pointed, an excited tremble in his voice. "I see it. I see it."

"Good job." Andrew had seen it too, a misshapen contorted mass of dead limbs attached to a great swollen trunk that had been split in two, the cleft running almost half way down.

"Can we get that thing taken down?" Sarah asked. "It gives me the creeps."

"I think that chopping trees down will be pretty low on our list of priorities." He slowed the car and turned off the road, past the oak, and onto a dirt trail that ran to a large white farmhouse with a gray slate tile roof. To the left and right were overgrown fields, beyond which stood a line of Hemlock and Maple, marking the edge of the woods. "Wouldn't you rather get the house in shape, so that we can be warm and cozy in our new home?"

"I'd rather be in our old home, which was already warm and cozy," Sarah replied, never missing an opportunity to show her displeasure. At least the hard edge was gone from her voice. She leaned forward, looking through the windshield as they approached the house.

"We're here now, so you might as well make the most of it." Andrew swung the car around in the driveway and came to a stop near a barn that stood several feet distant from the main building. He nodded toward the old wooden structure. "I was thinking we could turn this into a garage. What do you think?"

"I think it will fall down on the car and then we'll be stuck up here when winter comes." Sarah pulled on her door handle and hopped out of the car.

She looked up at the house, grimacing when she saw the fading, chipped paint peeling from the wood siding, and the way the gutters hung, just a little askew. The windows looked like they hadn't been cleaned in years, and one, she noticed, had a crack running from top to bottom.

Andrew climbed out and waited for Jake, who insisted upon collecting his game console and headphones, and then joined his daughter. "Well, what's the verdict on our new digs?"

She looked sideways toward him, narrowing her eyes, but didn't answer.

"Come on. You could try to be a little enthusiastic." Andrew nudged her.

"I'm here, aren't I?" She shrugged. "Isn't that enough?"

"I guess it's the best I'm going to get." Andrew pushed a hand into his pocket and produced a key on a silver heart shaped fob. "Who's ready to go inside?"

Chapter 2

THE INTERIOR of the house was no better than the exterior. Sarah looked around in disappointment. They had closed on the property two months ago, and since then it had undergone some much-needed repairs. The hole in the roof was patched, and the floorboards, those that were too rotten to save, had been replaced with carefully matched modern stand-ins. But the pervasive odor of musty abandon still hung in the air, and the walls were still the same faded cream she remembered from her only previous visit, when they had driven up to view the place for the first time.

"I thought you said things had been fixed?" Sarah said, not bothering to hide her distress.

"I said the major stuff had been taken care of, and it has." Her dad replied. "I know there's still a lot to do, but we couldn't afford to have the workmen do everything."

"Great."

"Hey, at least the house is livable now, which is more than could be said about it the last time you were here."

"I was hoping for a little better than livable." Sarah cast her eyes toward the staircase. The railings were the same dirty brown varnish that she remembered from before, worn in places to reveal the paler wood underneath. A floral runner dropped from stair to stair like a patterned waterfall, the fabric threadbare. Above that, the second-floor landing was a dark mystery. She wondered what new disappointments waited for her up there.

They walked through each room, stopping every so often to inspect some repair or other. Sarah tagged along behind, wrinkling her nose when they came upon a dead mouse laying in the middle of the empty dining room.

"Yuck." She took a step backwards. "You really expect me to live under these conditions?"

"It's just a mouse Sarah."

"It's completely gross."

"This is an old house," her father said. "He probably won't be the last one we see."

"Great. Now I have to deal with rodents on top of everything else?"

"You'll survive." Andrew crossed the room and disappeared into the kitchen, returning with a dustpan and broom. He swept the mouse up and went back to the kitchen. When he rejoined them, there was a smile on his face. "See, all better now."

"Not really." Sarah could feel her throat tightening, and for a moment she thought she would be sick. "I hate mice."

"Hey, I have a surprise for you," her father said, no doubt trying to take her mind off the deceased rodent.

"What is it?" A germ of hope sparked within her. Maybe he was going to say she could stay with her friend, Becca, back in Boston. That way she wouldn't have to start at a new school. It was a suggestion she had made several times over the past few months, not that it had done any good.

"You have to see," Andrew said, and nodded toward the entryway. "It's upstairs."

"Oh." Her heart fell.

"Come on, I guarantee you will like it."

"Fine," She said, less enthusiastic than when she thought there might be a reprieve from living in the moldy old farmhouse.

"You want to join us, champ?" Her father turned his attention to Jake, who was wandering around the entranceway peering through doors.

"Where are you going?"

"Upstairs."

"Nah." He shook his head. "I want to explore down here. Maybe there will be another mouse."

"Ew." Sarah let out a snort of disgust.

"So, can I explore?" Jake looked at his father, an expectant look upon his face.

"Alright." Andrew tousled Jake's hair.

"Stop that." Jake squirmed.

Sarah derived a little satisfaction from the annoyed look on her brother's face.

"Don't go outside, and don't touch anything, especially dead mice. You understand?" Andrew gave Jake his best *I'm serious about this* look.

"I get it." Jake nodded, no doubt pleased to be able to explore on his own. "I won't touch any dead mice."

"Or any other dead things you come across."

"Fine." Jake drew the word out, a mischievous grin plastered across his face.

"It's just the two of us then." Andrew said. "Come on."

He led Sarah from the dining room, back into the hallway, and up the stairs. He flicked a light switch, the single bare bulb ineffective against the gloom.

The second floor did nothing to dispel Sarah's opinion of the old farmhouse. The musty, dank odor from below was worse here, and the weak light made everything look drab and depressing. Five doors led off the short corridor, two on the right, one to their left, and one at the end. The closest door was a bathroom. Sarah could see the claw foot tub through the opening. The others must be bedrooms. She wondered which one would be hers. She hoped it wouldn't stink as bad as the rest of the house. She guessed that it would.

"No one's lived here for a very long time," her father said, reading his daughter's mind. "The smell will go away once we open everything up and get some air through the place."

"I hope so." Sarah lingered near the top of the stairs, unwilling to venture any further than necessary. "So what's this big surprise?"

"Come on." Andrew took off, the barest hint of a smile upon his face. At the end of the hallway he turned left and disappeared from sight. His voice drifted back on the stale air. "What are you waiting for?"

"Hang on." She padded down the corridor toward the spot where her father had vanished, and was surprised to discover that the corridor turned at right angles, leading to a second staircase. This one was narrower than the main stairs, with bare wood treads and smooth plaster walls. It rose steeply to a narrow door at the top, which stood open, spilling light downward. Andrew Whelan stood in the doorframe, waiting.

"Hurry up. We don't have all day."

"Stop nagging me." Sarah said, climbing the stairs as fast as she dared. At the top she stopped, surprised.

In front of her was a huge room spanning the whole width of the house. It had sloping ceilings following the roofline, and two large dormer windows. Unlike the rooms downstairs, this one was bright and wore a coat of fresh paint.

"Well?" Her father was grinning.

"What is this?" She wondered how this space looked so new. Had her father paid the workmen to do all this?

Andrew paused a moment, his eyes sparkling, and then he answered her. "It's your new bedroom of course. What do you think?"

Chapter 3

JAKE WATCHED his sister and father leave the room and head to the stairs. When he heard them climbing toward the second floor, the treads groaning and creaking as they went, he wandered into the kitchen, stopping at the yellow refrigerator that looked like it should be in a museum. It even had chrome on the door handle, now worn and peeling. He pulled on the door, wondering if there would be any old, moldy food to go along with the ancient fridge, but there was nothing inside except a box of bicarbonate of soda, which sat on a shelf, lonely and abandoned. He wondered who had put it there, and why. It seemed a strange thing to put in such a place.

Shrugging, he closed the fridge and carried on through the rest of the kitchen, opening cupboards and drawers, but found little of any interest.

At the other end of the kitchen was a door with four glass panes. He approached it and looked out, pressing his face to the glass, but the panes were so caked in grime he could barely see outside. What he could see, though, was that this door led to the rear of the house, judging by the weak sunlight that filtered through the dirt. He reached down and gripped the doorknob, turning it despite his father's explicit instructions not to venture outside. But a little peek couldn't hurt, and he would make sure not to stray too far. Besides, if he were quick no one would be any the wiser.

He turned the knob and pushed, but the door did not budge. Perplexed, he tried again, but still it remained firmly closed.

Then he noticed the bolt.

It was set high upon the door, and it was drawn across.

Jake reached up, his fingers outstretched, but he could not reach it, even when he stood on tiptoe.

He tried again, pushing himself as tall as he could. The tips of his fingers brushed the bolt, but not enough to get a grip, and in the end he slumped back down, disappointed. Whatever was beyond the door's grimy glass panels would have to wait for another day.

That didn't mean he was done.

There must be plenty more to see in the old house.

He retreated from the kitchen, and across the dining room to the hallway.

He heard voices above, on the next upper floor.

Ignoring them, Jake padded down the hallway toward the back of the house. Surely there was more to discover here.

And then the creak came.

It was soft. Gentle.

Jake stopped, looked around for the source.

And then he found it.

Under the stairs, set into a recess, was a narrow door.

And it was open a crack.

Jake narrowed his eyes, peered at the door. His grandparents house had one just like this, set under the stairs in the same way.

It was the basement.

Jake approached the door and stood there, torn. It didn't seem like the kind of place his father would approve of him going, but who knew what awesome treasures lay in wait, right beneath his feet?

His breathing quickened in excitement.

Who cared if he got caught. It was worth it.

Jake pulled the door wide.

The space beyond was dark, but he could see enough to confirm that it was indeed the basement. Wooden steps fell away into obscurity.

There was a light switch on the wall.

He flicked it on.

Pale light illuminated the room below.

But even so, most of the basement was out of view.

He placed a foot on the top stair, testing it. When nothing happened, when he didn't crash through into the unknown pit below, he tried the next, and the next, until he was halfway down.

Now he could see old boxes, part of a bicycle.

He wondered what was in the boxes. He hurried down a couple more steps, eager to find out.

And then he heard the ringing.

It sounded like the ringtone on his fathers cell phone.

Jake stopped and listened.

It came again, a shrill clanging ring.

Had his dad come back downstairs?

Was he looking for Jake at that very moment?

Boy, would he be in for it, if he was caught snooping down here.

Jake turned and hurried back up to the ground floor, turning off the light and pushing the door closed.

No harm, no foul. **I don't think a boy would know that term or how to use it.**

There was no sign of either his dad or Sarah. He had gotten away with it.

The ring came again, quick and urgent.

It was coming from the living room, the only place on the

ground floor Jake hadn't been yet. He crossed the hallway, following the sound.

The living room was large. Exposed beams ran across the ceiling, and on the far wall, surrounded by built in bookcases, was a wide fireplace, with a stone chimney. The air felt stale and old, and a musty odor pushed at his nostrils.

He paused and waited for the ringing to repeat, but it didn't.

And then he saw the telephone, sitting alone on a shelf next to the fireplace.

It seemed to call out to him.

It urged him to come closer.

He realized that the ringing had come from there. It was not his father's cell phone. It was this phone.

He peered at it, inching closer.

The unit looked old. The plastic was yellowed and dull. Instead of buttons, there was a rotary dial with numbers inside round holes. And the handset was huge, much larger than a modern phone.

He stared at it, fascinated by the strange squat shape and the curly knotted cord that ran from the handset and into the base of the device.

He touched the dial, his finger slipping into the hole above the number one. When he moved his finger the dial spun around clockwise with a clicking sound, and then sprang back when he released it.

He put his finger in the next hole and did the same thing.

Again it rotated back when released.

He reached out to turn the dial a third time, but then paused, remembering his father's words. He was under strict orders not to touch anything.

He glanced over his shoulder, toward the hallway, but there was no sign of his father or sister.

He turned his attention back to the telephone.

He'd only ever seen one other like this, at his grandparent's house in Maine. It was the same shape, but that one had plastic push buttons arranged in a square on the face, rather than the strange wheel.

A sudden memory popped into his head.

It was the previous summer, a few weeks before everything changed.

He was sitting in the back of the blue VW Bug that his mother loved so much. The top was down and it was a glorious summer day. The kind only New England can deliver. They followed the coast from Boston, just the two of them. Sarah was too cool to visit her grandparents, she would rather hang out in Harvard Square with her friends, and dad was always working, tapping away on his laptop, or away on some book tour or other. He supposed it was cool to have a novelist for a father, at least that was what people told him, but to Jake it seemed dull.

They weaved through picturesque seaside towns like Kittery, and Ogunquit, where they stopped to pick up taffy, which he chewed all the way to Portland. It was something they had done every year for as long as he could remember. You couldn't pass through Ogunquit without getting taffy. That was the rule.

When they arrived at Gramps and Granma's house there was blueberry pie, freshly made with berries picked that day in the back yard, and vanilla ice cream.

That was another tradition. Blueberry pie.

Except now it was nothing but a memory.

There would be no more trips up the coast in that Bug, and no more days sitting on the wide back porch with a slice of pie.

It wasn't fair.

His eyes grew puffy and red.

He wiped them with the back of his hand, grateful that Sarah was not around to see his moment of weakness.

Jake sniffed and turned away, no longer interested in the

old telephone, or exploring the rest of the house. That happened sometimes when he thought of his mother.

He slouched back toward the hallway.

The phone rang again.

Jake froze.

The ring repeated, shrill, loud.

He did a one-eighty and stood there, staring.

The ring came a third time.

Jake walked back toward the phone.

Should he answer?

It seemed wrong not too.

The ring came a fourth time, demanding to be heeded.

Jake reached forward, his hand shaking, and gripped the receiver. He lifted it to his ear.

Swirling static hissed from the earpiece.

"Hello?" The word bounced back at him, through the earpiece. "Is anybody there?"

Static buzzed and popped, fading in and out.

"Hello?" He repeated, the word swallowed up in the white noise.

And then, for a brief second, Jake thought he heard a voice. It was low and muted, barely audible above the static, but it was there.

"I can't understand you." He wondered if he should fetch his father. Maybe it was important. Dad was always on the phone with his agent, a small round-faced man who smelled of garlic and called him *the squirt*.

"Jake." The word floated out of the static, still faint, but clear this time.

Jake sucked in a startled gasp.

"Hello?"

"Jake." His name again, the voice scratchy, far away. He almost slammed the receiver down, but the voice didn't sound scary, in fact, it almost sounded familiar. It must be dad's agent, or maybe someone from the school.

"Can I help you?" he asked.
The static roiled and hissed.
The voice stayed silent.
And then, without warning there was a click.
The line went dead.

Continue reading The haunting of Willow House

Paperback available now on Amazon

Printed in Great Britain
by Amazon

63754078R00153